A DIFFICULT ASSIGNMENT

"You are so innocent, Rainey," Thorne whispered. "Any man would want you."

"I don't want just any man. I want Robert. Help me, Thorne," she pleaded. "Help me to learn the things I need to know to make him notice me."

He wanted to cover her mouth with his, to part its softness and enter the moist cavity within. He wanted to feel her body yielding to his, and her arms sliding around his neck. "All right," he said gruffly.

"You'll help me? When will we start the lessons?"

"Now," he murmured. He kissed her, slowly and thoroughly, until she was so weak she could hardly stand upright.

"Lordy, Thorne, if kissing *you* makes me feel so weak, I'll more'n likely pass out from pure pleasure when that teacher man touches me."

A fury such as he'd never known before surged through Thorne. He vowed then that no other man would ever touch her.

"Maybe we'd better practice some more," she whispered, lifting her face eagerly. "You're my best friend, and I like the way it feels when you're kissin' me. Makes me all breathy-like and causes goose bumps to pop out all over me." She smiled up at him. "Are you gonna do it again?"

"Yes, Rainey," he said softly. "I'm going to do it again." He lowered his mouth over hers, more than happy to oblige her. . . .

BOOK YOUR PLACE ON OUR WEBSITE AND MAKE THE READING CONNECTION!

We've created a customized website just for our very special readers, where you can get the inside scoop on everything that's going on with Zebra, Pinnacle and Kensington books.

When you come online, you'll have the exciting opportunity to:

- View covers of upcoming books

- Read sample chapters

- Learn about our future publishing schedule (listed by publication month *and author*)

- Find out when your favorite authors will be visiting a city near you

- Search for and order backlist books from our online catalog

- Check out author bios and background information

- Send e-mail to your favorite authors

- Meet the Kensington staff online

- Join us in weekly chats with authors, readers and other guests

- Get writing guidelines

- AND MUCH MORE!

Visit our website at
http://www.zebrabooks.com

Sweet Words of Love

Betty Brooks

Zebra Books
Kensington Publishing Corp.
http://www.zebrabooks.com

ZEBRA BOOKS are published by

Kensington Publishing Corp.
850 Third Avenue
New York, NY 10022

First Printing: August, 1998
10 9 8 7 6 5 4 3 2 1

Printed in the United States of America

One

"You damned lousy polecat!" Rainey Watson cried. "Turn me loose afore I make you sorry you was ever borned!" She struggled furiously against the strong, masculine hands restraining her.

"Throw 'er down, Zeke!" Willis Johnson urged his cousin. "Stretch 'er out on the ground so's I can get at 'er!"

Although Zeke Brumley was determined to put his captive in that position, Rainey was just as determined to avoid it. She continued to mutter curses through her gritted teeth as she fought desperately to stay on her feet.

But it was a losing fight and she knew it. Willis Johnson knew it. Zeke Brumley knew it. And it was his certainty of victory that was his undoing. He relaxed ever so slightly, just enough for Rainey to jerk her wrist free. Then, drawing back her fist, she punched Zeke on the nose with as much strength as she could muster. The blow landed with a meaty thunk, and blood spurted, spraying the faded-blue homespun shirt she wore with crimson color.

Zeke jerked back immediately, putting several feet of distance between them. Then, wiping his nose, he stared at the blood on his hand.

"Dammit, Rainey," he cursed. "You done bloodied my nose!"

Before she could guess his intentions, he leaped forward. His right fist whipped out and punched her hard on the chin. Her head snapped back and she stumbled backward. She went down like a rock then, striking the ground hard enough to make her ears ring and send the breath whooshing out of her open mouth.

Rainey had no time to recover before Willis joined the fray, throwing his sinewy body across her, using his weight to hold her against the ground while he secured her there by pinning her shoulders with his huge hands. "Give up, Rainey, afore you get hurt!" His lips were pulled back in a snarl, and his eyes glittered with triumph.

Sucking in a huge gasp of air, Rainey tried to throw him off by bucking her body beneath him. "It'll be a cold day in hell afore I give in to the likes of you, Willis Johnson!"

He scowled down at her. "You ain't got no choice, Rainey, 'cause I ain't lettin' you up from here until after you say the words!"

"I ain't never gonna say 'em!" she cried, glaring up at him. "They ain't no way you can make me do it! An' if'n you don't get off me right now you're gonna be sorry you ever laid eyes on me, Willis Johnson!" His body seemed heavier now, almost suffocating, and she bucked beneath him again, desperate to relieve herself of his weight.

Suddenly, as she watched, his expression changed. The mottled color in his face became darker, and something stirred in his pale-blue eyes. His breathing changed, becoming quick and raspy. His lower body bulged, shoving hard against her thighs.

Rainey's eyes widened with sudden understanding. "Get off me, Willis," she choked. Panic stabbed at her stomach like a sliver of glass, and she turned her head aside so she wouldn't have to look at him.

"Not until you say *uncle*, Rainey." His voice was softer, but that fact was not the least bit encouraging.

Rainey forced herself to look at him again and wished she hadn't. His pale eyes glistened with excitement behind his drooping eyelids, and his breath was rapid, uneven. She had to free herself quickly . . . somehow.

Fear warred with fury. The latter won. "You get offa me, Willis Johnson!" she spat.

"Not until you say *uncle*," he said again, pressing his wiry body harder against hers, making her even more aware of the pure maleness of him.

A warning voice whispered in her head that she'd better get him off before things got completely out of hand. The look in his eyes told her of a sudden change in their relationship, but it was a change she couldn't— wouldn't—allow. If she could best him in this fight, then maybe his lust would be forgotten, and the old relationship between them reestablished.

Desperation lent her strength and she wrenched her right arm free and grabbed a handful of hair. She jerked hard, pulling his head back with her effort, and he swore loudly, releasing her long enough to pry her fingers loose. But her efforts had been in vain. The weight of his body kept her pinned to the ground, unable to roll away from him.

"Dammit, Willis! Get offa me!" she cried once more. She raked her nails down the side of his face, hoping the pain would be enough to make him release her. But it wasn't. She was held fast.

Although she'd been wrestling with Willis Johnson and his cousin, Zeke, since they were children, he was heavier and more muscular than the last time they'd pitted their strength against each other. No matter if he was the stronger, though. Her wits and quick reflexes were more than enough to make up the difference. At least she hoped they were.

"Say *uncle!*"

Rainey's chin jutted belligerently, and the heated glare she gave Willis could have started a brush fire. "I ain't gonna say it!"

The fury she'd seen in his pale eyes disappeared almost as quickly as it had come. His voice was husky with emotion as his head dipped lower, his breath hot and moist against her cheek. "Then you sure as hell ain't gettin' up."

Her panic became almost overwhelming, and her stomach roiled with tension. Perhaps she was being foolhardy by allowing her pride to keep her beneath him. She was reconsidering her decision when a voice rang out.

"What in hell is going on here?"

Three pairs of startled eyes jerked toward the newcomer. As her gaze found him, Rainey sucked in a sharp breath while her heart began an erratic dance beneath her rib cage.

Thornton O'Brien Lassiter was a tall, dark-haired man with muscled shoulders that spoke of the strength he carried in his wide frame. He would have been hard to ignore any time, and most certainly could not be when he was wearing such a thunderous expression.

"Get off her, Willis!" Although Thorne's voice was even, it was hard enough to make Willis Johnson scramble to his feet and back away.

"There ain't no call to sound that way, Thorne. We was just funnin'," Willis explained, hunching his shoulders and looking sheepish. "We didn't mean no harm. Did we, Zeke?" He looked toward his cousin, who was holding a bloody kerchief against his nose, trying to stanch the flow of blood.

"Naw," Zeke claimed, shifting uneasily. "We was just wrastlin' like we always do." His gaze flickered between

Thorne, whose stance bore the look of a bear waiting for a reason to charge, and Rainey, who had quickly regained her feet. Then, appearing to find the Winchester rifle held in the crook of Thorne's arm intimidating, Zeke's gaze settled on Rainey. "Tell him, Rainey. Tell Thorne we was just funnin'. "

Thorne turned his silver gaze on her. "That right, Rainey?" His gruff voice slid over her like velvet. "Was it all in fun?"

Licking lips that had suddenly gone dry, she met his eyes and muttered, " 'Course it was." She looked quickly away, brushing at the leaves and grit covering her breeches and shirt, taking her time so she could avoid looking at him again. Even so, she could feel the impact of his probing gaze.

Thorne moved closer and plucked a leaf out of her tangled dark hair, and she shivered at the sudden contact. "Guess I should've gone on my way . . . without bothering the three of you." He plucked another leaf out of her hair and casually tossed it aside. "What do you think?"

What did she think? About what? For some reason her heart was behaving in a most unusual way, and her brain had momentarily taken up residence with the flowers.

What was wrong with her anyway? she wondered. That peculiar glitter in Thorne's eyes couldn't be desire. Not Thorne. Why, he was as familiar as an old boot . . . usually. But today, she sensed something different about him. Like there was about Willis and Zeke.

Tarnation! Was there a fever going around Thunder Mountain that had affected all the menfolk? Or was the fever in her brain causing her to imagine things that weren't there?

As Thorne plucked another leaf out of her hair, she lowered her eyes to hide her thoughts. It *was* there. She had seen it, recognized the glitter beneath the silvery depths and it took her breath away.

But Thorne, devil that he was, continued to pluck leaves out of her hair as though he had nothing better to do. "Hmmmm? What do you think, Rainey?"

Shivering beneath his touch, she forced herself to look at him again, to hold his gaze with her own. "W-what do I think about what?" Despite her attempt at composure, her voice sounded breathy, as though she'd been running uphill as she often did when hot on a bee line.

"What do you think about me going away and leaving the three of you to continue your childish games?" Thorne asked her.

Childish games. His words struck her with the force of a bucket of ice water. There was no passion there, and none in his gaze. No. She'd imagined the whole thing. She hadn't imagined the look in Willis's eyes, though. It had been there. Thorne was right to scold her. The games *were* childish. And she was no child. She was a woman fully growed. She could have been in a lot of trouble if Thorne had not happened along. She knew that now, knew she'd been a fool to indulge in such shenanigans with those two hooligans. But never again, she silently vowed. She'd learned a valuable lesson today. Next time she might not be so lucky.

She looked at Willis Johnson's hopeful expression. It was obvious he wanted her to send Thorne on his way. She looked at Zeke, who had finally stopped the nosebleed, then back at Thorne again. "It don't make no nevermind to me whether you go along or not," she said, watching his gray eyes narrow. Tension vibrated between them. "I ain't gonna be here nohow." She studied the gathering clouds as though they were of extreme interest. "Storm's comin' over the mountain. Gonna rain for sure." She summoned up a smile. "You can come to supper, Thorne, if you've a mind to. It's been a long spell since you was there an' Grandpa would welcome the company."

"I'll walk back with you," he said gruffly, his stance relaxing slightly. "But I'm not so sure about supper, Rainey. The evening chores are yet to be done."

"You got a hired man to tend the chores," she reminded, suddenly eager for him to accept the invitation. "He ain't gonna mind doin' 'em by his lonesome now and then! I got a whole raisin pie just waitin' to be sliced up at home. If'n Grandpa ain't been at it whilst I was arunnin' my bee line."

Thorne's eyes crinkled in a smile. "You would mention raisin pie. You know that's my favorite dessert, Rainey. How could I say no to a slice?"

"How 'bout us, Rainey," Zeke asked plaintively. "Me an' Willis likes raisin pie, too."

Thorne pinned Zeke with a hard gaze. "You two don't have time to stop over."

"How come?" Willis asked with a frown.

"You'll think of a good reason," Thorne assured him.

"Uh, yeah," Zeke responded. He grabbed his cousin's arm. "Come on, Willis. We gotta be goin' now."

Willis stood his ground until Thorne's hard gaze settled on him. "I've been thinking for some time now that I should have a talk with you two boys," Thorne said. "From the looks of it that talk is long overdue. Maybe I'll just drop by the cabin on my way home."

"Whose cabin?" Willis asked quickly.

"Why . . . your pap's cabin, Willis."

"Uh. Whatcha wanta talk about, Thorne?" Zeke queried uneasily.

Thorne smiled at him, but there was no humor in his eyes. They were cold, frosty. "Time enough to learn that . . . later."

Zeke's gaze flickered from Rainey to Thorne and then to Rainey again. "Well . . ." He cleared his throat and began to edge away from them. "Guess I'd best be going now. Uncle Jude will be lookin' out for us." He looked at his cousin. "Come on, Willis. We're gonna be late for supper."

Rainey shared the two young men's uneasiness as she followed Thorne down the trail leading to the little cabin where she lived with her grandfather. She had a good mind to ask him what he intended to talk to them about, yet she quelled the urge to question him, afraid she wouldn't like his answer.

Birdsong accompanied them along the trail, which wound across the ridge, and the wind brushed leafy branches together in soft whispers of sound. Rainey glanced continually at Thorne, wondering at his silence. And at the way he'd looked at her when he'd found her on the ground beneath Willis. When he'd looked at her, with those stone-cold eyes, she'd felt as though she were being chastised, like a child caught in an act of mischief, and she resented that fact. She didn't have to answer to him for her actions.

Rainey had met Thorne shortly after he arrived on Thunder Mountain. That was five years ago, and although she'd only been thirteen years old at the time, she'd seen something in him that told her they were destined to be friends. And they had been, too. She considered Thorne her best friend. The one person she could confide in, who would never let her down no matter what the circumstances.

And yet, today, she'd seen another side of Thorne. A side that she wasn't as comfortable with. And for some reason she felt as though something new had been added to their relationship, something that would make being with him difficult. Uncomfortable with such thoughts, she pushed them aside and looked toward the sky. The dark clouds were rolling in fast. They'd be lucky if they made it home before the storm broke.

It was Thorne who put an end to the silence. "Zeke and Willis are getting too old for you to be wrestling with them, Rainey."

Did he have to keep going on about it? Her irritation showed in her voice when she answered him. "I could take them on, and two others besides," she snapped.

"That's not the point," he said. "Things are different now. You should have sense enough to know what I'm getting at. You didn't look as though you were enjoying the fight back there."

"I was at first," she said quickly. Suddenly she decided to be honest with him. "I feel kinda funny, though. You know . . . when he was holdin' me down thata way and wouldn't move off'n me, my stomach knotted up something fierce and . . ."

"You're a fool, Rainey!" he grated.

Her blue eyes widened and she glared at him. "I ain't, neither!"

"Only a fool would think she could wrestle with men the way you do without suffering the consequences."

"Men?" She gave an unladylike snort. "Tarnation, Thorne! They ain't men! They're just boys!" She looked at him with confusion. "Hell'sfire! I growed up with both of 'em! They ain't never gonna get too big for me to whip." She hitched up her breeches proudly. "I durn near beat 'em, too. Did you see Zeke's bloody nose? And Willis is sure enough gonna have a headache tomorrow."

"Dammit! Didn't you hear what I said?"

She stopped abruptly and stared at him with confusion. "Whatcha gettin' so riled up about anyway?"

"You're not that innocent, Rainey."

His attitude was making her angry. "You ain't got no call to talk to me thata way, Thorne! And you can't tell me what to do!"

"Your grandfather can, though. And I'm sure he

wouldn't approve of you wrestling with those young men."

Her face flushed hotly. "An' I 'spose you're afixin' to tell him about it! Well, tarnation, Thorne! If you're gonna be thata way, then I'm atakin' back the supper invite!"

"I'm still coming with you, you little vixen. You're past the age where you can wrestle with grown men without suffering the consequences. And don't pretend you don't know what I mean, either, because I know you can't be that dumb."

Fury almost choked her. "Don't you go callin' me dumb, Thornton Lassiter, because I ain't! I know what you're goin' on about, but I got more sense than to let some feller put a baby in my belly! And you better keep your nose outta my business if'n you don't want my fist shoved in it!" She waved said fist in his face.

He gripped her shoulders with iron fingers and gave her a hard shake. "Your grandpa is depending on me to keep you out of trouble, Rainey!" he said sharply. "And I aim to do just that!"

"You turn me loose," she snapped furiously. The cabin was in sight now, just a few hundred yards away. And, although she could see her grandfather sitting in the cane-backed rocker on the porch, obviously keeping a watchful eye out for his granddaughter's return, they were still hidden from his view.

Thorne released her abruptly. "You heed my words!" He strode into the clearing, and George Watson raised a hand and waved at him.

"Come on over here, Thorne!" George hollered.

"Don't you dare say nothing to my grandpap!" Rainey spat, glaring at him furiously. "He's got enough on his mind without you adding more trouble."

Although he didn't touch her, his gaze bored into

hers. "Promise me that you're done wrestling with Zeke and Willis."

"It ain't none of your business," she said stubbornly. Although she had no intention of wrestling with them again, it wasn't his place to give her orders.

Suddenly, his anger left him, and his slate-gray eyes softened. He wound his large fingers through hers, and the look in his eyes made her knees feel weak. "I'm not trying to dictate to you, honey. I just worry about you. I know so much more about the ways of men than you do. And I know that you're a babe in the woods about certain things. This is one of them, trust me. I don't want you hurt."

His voice flowed over her, smooth and silky, and something in the sound caused shivers to slide across her arms. At the same time her *goldarned* legs threatened to buckle beneath her weight, making her wonder if she was coming down with the ague or something. She felt a sudden need to placate Thorne. "I ain't gonna wrestle with 'em no more," she said. "But not because you said so. I already decided it afore you come on us like you done."

"You could have said so," he chided, relaxing visibly. A smile twitched at his lips. "Are you going to deprive me of that raisin pie?"

"No. You can have some. And you can stay and visit with Grandpa, too," she said.

She shouldn't have hollered at him, she told herself. Thorne was only trying to help her. He was a dear friend, had been since she'd first met him. From the first moment they'd met, he'd made himself responsible for her, had been there for her whenever she needed someone to get her out of trouble. She couldn't really blame him for butting in when he was so concerned about her welfare.

Grandpa had done his best for her, but there were

some things an old man his age couldn't do. He wasn't as spry as he'd once been—though he'd rather die than admit to it.

It had been more than forty years since George Watson had built the cabin for his bride. Back then, it had only contained one room. Another room had been added when their only son, Caleb, had married the delicate Lily Marsh, who'd come to the hill country to teach in the one-room schoolhouse. But Lily had died in childbirth, and Caleb had lost his will to live. Caleb had succumbed to pneumonia only a few months after his wife was laid to rest, leaving the raising of his child to his father.

"Come on up here, boy!" Grandpa George called from the porch. "It's been nigh onto a month now since I last laid eyes on you. What kinda excuse you gonna give me for stayin' away so long?"

Thorne laid his rifle aside and settled down on the porch rail to talk to the old man. "The farm is taking up most of my time these days," he said gruffly.

Rainey went into the cabin to prepare the evening meal. By the time she dropped spoon dumplings into the broth, which held a simmering squirrel, the storm that had threatened broke with a vengeance.

Lightning flashed and thunder boomed, ripping across the sky. Rain lashed the earth, darkening the world around them.

Reaching for the lamp they kept on a shelf above the table, Rainey lifted the globe and, after setting it aside, she struck a match to light the wick. The resulting flame chased away the nearest shadows and gave her enough light to work by.

When the meal was finally on the table, Rainey called the men to supper. After the last slice of pie had been eaten, and the men were on their third cup of coffee, old George tamped tobacco in his corncob pipe and settled back in his chair.

"Sadie Thompson came over today," he said casually. A smile twitched at Rainey's lips. The whole of Thunder Mountain was aware that Sadie was sweet on Grandpa. "Sadie told me the new schoolteacher would be acomin' to the ridge the day after tomorrow."

"I imagine Miss Henderson was glad to hear that," Thorne said. "She's been holding up her wedding plans until a replacement could be found. I don't think Horace Freely has been very patient about the delay, either."

"Can't say as I really blame him," George said gruffly. "When a man commits his self to marryin' up with his woman, it's usually because he's needin' her mighty bad. And a man with a need like that wouldn't take kindly to delay." He puffed his pipe. "I just hope the new teacher's not so pretty as Miss Henderson, though, 'cause a woman like that don't stay single very long. Too many men an' too few women to go around in these parts. Most of our womenfolk get wedded afore they turn fourteen." He favored Rainey with a hard glare. "But they's some of 'em that's a mite too choosy to find a husband whilst they can. One of these days those choosy ones is likely to wake up and find out they done got too old to marry."

"Too old to marry?" Rainey questioned with wide-eyed innocence. "Why, Grandpa! Does a body ever get that old? Somebody sure oughtta tell Sadie Thompson that 'cause she must not know it. I reckon ever'body aroun' here knows why she hangs around our cabin . . . always casting them cat eyes of hers your way, like she might be sweet on you."

"No such thing!" George snapped, his complexion coloring suddenly. "Sadie just gets lonesome since her man was took away by that wild boar. An' she happens to like your raisin pies."

"She would bake her own self some if'n you wasn't so willin' to cut her a slice of mine ever' time she shows up here," Rainey said mildly. "I noticed they was a goodly sized wedge missin' from this'n tonight."

He raised his eyebrows at her. "We ain't got enough vittles, that we can't share 'em with friends? Since when, Rainey?" He eyed his granddaughter sternly. "I been thinkin' real hard about that school lately. You never had no chance to get much schoolin'. An' it's a cryin' shame, your ma bein' a teacher an' all. Reckon it ain't your fault, though. You been too busy tryin' to keep us in necessaries to think much about such doin's." He drew on his pipe again, then continued. "Sadie's got them three boys of her'n, who don't do much of nothin' these days . . . since they got no man's hand to keep 'em busy. Maybe was the two of us—me an' Sadie—to wed up, you wouldn't haveta work so hard. And they's a mighty lot of things a girl needs to learn that a man can't hardly teach her."

"Don't you go marryin' up with no widder woman an' blame the doin' of it on me!" Rainey snapped. "An' I got ways of learnin' the stuff I need to know without you gettin' a wife to teach me!" She felt embarrassed that her grandfather had brought up her lack of knowledge in front of Thorne.

"You shoulda gone to school longer," George said. "You coulda learned some of those things from a woman teacher."

"I know all I need to know," she said stubbornly. She felt Thorne's probing gaze on her, knew he was listening closely to the conversation, and it made her even more aware of him.

Thorne shifted suddenly, and his thigh brushed against her. A shock wave coursed through her, making her body react in the most curious way. She felt as though her belly had turned upside down, like a possum hanging from a tree. It was such an unusual feeling, so strange . . . and Rainey felt a sudden need to put some distance between herself and Thorne.

Shoving her chair away from the table, she averted her eyes from Thorne, looking at her grandfather instead. "Thorne come a long ways to make his howdys, Grandpa. Not to listen to you complain about my schoolin'! So if you don't want him a leavin', you best talk on somethin' else. Leave me outta it, though. I got chores to tend."

Thorne rose quickly to his feet. "Let me help with the chores, Rainey."

"No!" she said abruptly. "You set a spell and jaw with Grandpa." She looked anxiously at the window. The rain was still pouring down. "Looks like you might have to stay over tonight, unless you've a hankering to get soaked on the way home."

He followed her gaze outside. "The rain should let up before long if it follows its usual pattern."

"Might as well stay the night," George Watson said. "We'd be mighty pleasured by the visit. Wouldn't we, Rainey?"

"You're most welcome to stay," Rainey told Thorne. "We got quilts enough to make you a pallet by the fire."

"I appreciate the invitation," Thorne replied. "But I need to go home. I was planning on plowing that patch of ground bordering Angus Frye's place at early light."

"The ground ain't gonna be dry enough to plow, come morning," George predicted. He stretched his long arm to reach the deck of cards he kept on a shelf high on the wall behind him. "How about a game of poker?"

"Fine with me," Thorne said. "Maybe my losing streak is over."

"Wasn't a losin' streak you was on, son," George Watson said with a grin. "It was pure skill that set me to winnin' the last time we played."

Their voices droned on as Rainey washed the dishes. By the time she'd wiped the last pot and stacked it with the other cooking utensils, the rain had stopped falling. She pushed the door open and stared out at the rain-washed forest, barely illuminated by the soft moonlight. She heard a chair being pushed across the wooden floor and looked around to see Thorne approaching.

"Guess I'd better be going," he said gruffly.

"You're welcome to stay the night," she said, feeling obliged to extend the invitation again. "The ground ain't gonna dry anytime soon, an' you're bound to get wet on the way home since you're afoot. 'Course you could borrow the mule, if you've a mind."

"I'll enjoy the walk home," Thorne said, dealing with both offers at once. He strode away then, leaving Rainey with a peculiar sense of loss as she watched him disappear into the night. She was puzzled by the feeling, wondered about it and about him, as she had so often done in the recent past.

He was so different from the hill folk, the people who had been born and bred in the Ozark Mountains. What made him different? What kind of world had he left behind? Since he rarely spoke of his past, she had no idea what his family was like, knew only that he had a father and sister somewhere.

Knowing she would find no answers to her questions, Rainey pushed them aside as she had done so many times in the past. She knew that, even if she voiced the questions, they would not be answered. But then, she couldn't blame him. He had a right to his privacy. It was a fact that she cherished her own.

But Thorne had interfered in her life today in a way that nobody had ever dared before, and she wasn't happy about his interference. Her life was her own, and she cherished the freedom to do as she pleased.

He'd just darned well better keep his nose out of her affairs, she thought huffily, or she'd give him what-for.

Even as that thought occurred, Rainey knew it was only an unspoken threat. She knew she could never intentionally do Thorne any real hurt. Just as she was certain that he could never do anything to harm her.

But she wasn't about to tell him that.

Two

It was more than five miles from the Watson cabin to Thorne's farm, but the moonlit night held no surprises for him as his long strides carried him home. It was just as well because his thoughts were not on his surroundings. Instead they were occupied by Rainey, as they so often were these days.

What was it about her that disturbed him so much lately? he wondered. And it was a fact that she *did* disturb him. But try as he would, he couldn't pinpoint the reason. He remembered the day he'd met her as though it were only yesterday. It was late afternoon and, as was so often the case on Thunder Mountain, a storm was brewing. He'd been filling a bucket from the spring located near his house when a young girl had burst from the sheltering woods and, with her eyes focused on a spot near the treetops, had rammed straight into him. The resulting blow would have knocked her off her feet if he hadn't steadied her. And although he'd expected she'd be grateful for his efforts, when she recovered her breath enough to speak, she'd yelled at him for being in her way.

As long as he lived, Thorne would never forget the way she'd looked that day, with her black hair tumbling around her waist and shoulders, her intense blue eyes glittering furiously while she lambasted him for making her lose her bee line.

He smiled at the memory. That meeting, stormy though it was, had begun a friendship that was destined to become stronger with each passing day.

From the beginning they had gravitated toward each other. He knew they had been a sight, man and child. She taught him to laugh again, made him feel important. He longed for that again, because something new had been added to his feelings. He now wanted more from her than friendship, something that she could not give. No longer did he find solace in her company. Instead, there was a sense of excitement that kept his nerves alive, his muscles tense, his heart racing, his body hungering, wanting . . . needing . . . Rainey.

God, she tormented him.

Rainey!

With her sky-blue eyes and her ebony hair flowing down to her waist. Hair so fine and silky that he longed to run his fingers through it, to feel its softness against his bare chest.

"Rainey, Rainey, Rainey," his heart cried. *"Will you ever see me as a lover?"* How could he stand being near her, and not being able to touch her?

Rainey, so womanly, yet still so childlike in her innocence. If he wasn't careful she was going to cause trouble for him in the future. He was certain of it, and yet he felt just as certain that he could do nothing to prevent it from happening.

Why hadn't he recognized his feelings sooner? They most certainly hadn't developed overnight, had probably been developing for years, just as her body had been changing. Yet, he had kept those feelings carefully subdued, had even denied their existence. Until he'd come up on her wrestling with Zeke and Willis. That had been the catalyst to bring his feelings to the surface, the reason he was now forced to acknowledge them.

Damnation! It had taken every ounce of control that he possessed to keep from beating Willis into a bloody pulp for daring to lay hands on her, for daring to spread himself over her rounded curves.

Thorne's lower body stirred at the memory. The way her breasts had heaved beneath her homespun shirt while she lay beneath Willis, her face flushed, trying to buck him off. His hands clenched into fists, and his strong fingernails cut into his calloused flesh as he remembered the slumberous passion he'd seen in Willis Johnson's eyes as he whispered in her ear.

He swore at the memory, promising he'd mop the ground with Willis Johnson's clothes—with Johnson still inside them—if that young man ever laid a hand on Rainey again. He ground his teeth together. Both Willis and Zeke had better think twice before they indulged themselves in that manner again.

Thorne realized his jealousy was eating away at him, making him react in anger, and he realized, as well, that he must never allow Rainey to realize how he felt, lest he lose what they had together.

Just the mere thought was more than he could bear. He had no wish to make her uncomfortable around him, because she might try to avoid his company. And the thought of not seeing her would be painful.

Rainey was the epitome of budding womanhood, yet her mind had not yet accepted that fact. But it *was* a fact. And one day soon she would realize it and wreak havoc on the hopeless males who populated the ridge.

That thought disturbed Thorne. When she fell in love he would lose her. He was certain of it. The relationship they had—innocent though it was—would most certainly not be allowed by the man she chose for a husband. Not if he loved her as Thorne did. And, dammit, if he were deprived of her companionship, he would sorely miss it.

Thorne knew his own limitations, knew he was a man who found it hard to make friends. Perhaps his raising had been responsible for that. His mother had died soon after he was born, and his father had blamed him for her death. Although he'd married again, and his second wife had borne him a daughter, Eugene Lassiter had continued to mourn his first wife, continuing to blame his son for his loss. Perhaps that was the reason Charity Lassiter had given up on the marriage. She'd run away, leaving behind her infant daughter. But she hadn't enjoyed her freedom, had succumbed to smallpox barely a year after leaving.

Any kindness Eugene Lassiter had ever had, disappeared completely then. He was a cold, hard man, capable of spreading misery over anyone who chanced to venture close, be it family or the unfortunate beings who found employment at the Lassiter Shipping Lines. And even though Thorne was aware at an early age of his father's disposition, he nevertheless took it personally. He had grown to a man feeling like an extra person in the world, unwanted by everyone except his sister. The lack of love and security in his young life had turned him hard.

There had been a time, though, when Thorne thought he'd found his place in the world. He had been a young man then, a student at Harvard. It was there he'd met Pearl Brewster, and her memory still caused a bitter taste in his mouth.

He'd been so young then, so foolish, so damned ignorant. How could he have been so blind? He had been convinced she loved him, but had soon realized it was his wealth that attracted her. And that attraction quickly faded when she learned Thorne was the black sheep of the family and could expect no inheritance from his father. It hadn't taken her long to find herself another man, one with richer prospects.

But that wasn't the end of it. When the elder Lassiter learned his son had been planning a future with a woman of questionable family, Eugene Lassiter ordered his son to leave the house. His fury had been a sight to behold. Eugene had shouted out his anger for anyone to hear, telling his son that he had bad blood, given to him by his Irish mother.

Stunned at the insult to his mother, Thorne had wasted no time leaving. Without hesitation he had taken the inheritance his mother left him and wandered through the Ozarks until he had found Thunder Mountain. He had bought the farm and made a new life for himself. And he'd found a new family. Rainey's family.

He couldn't bear to lose another family, one that was so dear to him. No, he would proceed carefully, would not allow these new feelings to surface, lest he lose her.

The sun was barely topping the eastern horizon when Rainey looped the handle of a sorghum-syrup bucket over her arm and set off down the trail. There was no syrup in the bucket, however. Instead, it contained honey that she would burn if she couldn't find the bee line she'd been running the day before. The sweet, strong scent of burning honey would attract bees to her when nothing else would.

The trail she followed led down into a deep gorge, dense with trees both large and small, and along a wildly boulder-strewn streambed, where the water roared unseen through its channel.

It was there the lofty silver spruces towered, each so delicate of hue and graceful in outline.

Sunlight filtered through the foliage, and everywhere

Rainey gazed was evidence of this forest's wilderness, in timber and rocks and windfalls, in the huge masses of driftwood, in the precipitous banks of the stream, showing how the flood torrents tore and dug at their confines.

Rainey saw nothing of birds or squirrels, nor did she hear the sound of another living thing. But that was not surprising; the roar of rushing water would have drowned any ordinary sound.

Gradually the trail left the vicinity of the stream and began a slight ascent, winding among beds of giant boulders covered with trailing vines.

She'd always felt a sense of peace there, where the scent of the woodland was almost overpowering. It appeared to be dominated by the fragrance of pine, but there were other scents besides the spicy tang that were not as easily identifiable.

She could see through the woods ahead a glimpse of light and open sky, and knew she was fast approaching the meadow where flowers grew in such abundance beside a narrow creek.

Loping along its bank, Rainey followed the stream to its source; a spring that formed a shallow basin, which bubbled on the bottom, where water surfaced from beneath the ground.

As she drew nearer she heard the almost melodious hum of countless bees at work on the flowers surrounding the spring.

She knelt beside the spring and watched the honeybees, waiting quietly until she saw one separate from the others and light on the water. It was mere moments before the bee rose and flew toward the forest, with Rainey hot on its trail.

The sky would have seemed empty to anyone not as experienced as Rainey, whose gaze never left the bee as it flew in a straight line toward its destination. But she was used to keeping sight of the tiny brown honey-bees, had learned years ago . . . when Grandpa was still nimble enough to run . . . how best to do it. And she didn't worry overmuch about losing sight of her target, either. If that should happen, she had her syrup bucket of honey to draw the bees to her again.

The Watson family depended greatly on the bees. It was honey from their hives that made it possible for Rainey to acquire the funds necessary for their survival. And the last time she'd taken her honey to Elizabeth Crocker, who owned the general store at Lizard Lick—the woman had said she'd buy all the honey Rainey could supply.

That conversation was the reason Rainey spent more time these days running the bee lines. She needed the money her honey would bring.

The going became more difficult as Rainey entered the forest again, but she had known it would. It was impossible to follow a bee line as straight as the bee flew. There were too many obstacles in the dense wood-land that human feet must overcome, too many logs to scramble over, too many windfalls that blocked her way.

Even so, she managed to keep sight of the small light-brown honeybee . . . until a loud whistle distracted her.

Rainey spotted the intruder almost instantly. It was Willis Johnson. He leaned against the trunk of a spreading cottonwood tree as though the tree might need his weight to hold it upright.

"Hey, Rainey!" he called, straightening from his position against the tree. "Whatcha doin' way out here?"

"What do you think I'm adoin'?" she asked waspishly, remembering how he and his cousin had interfered with her bee hunt the day before. "I'm ahuntin' me another honeytree like I was adoin' yesterday when you an' Zeke got in my way."

"You got a bee line?" he asked, tilting his head and peering toward the treetops.

"Why else would I be arunnin' so fast?" she snapped, irritated by the certain knowledge that he had been waiting for her to pass this way. "And you better keep outta my way, Willis. I ain't got time to bother with you today. I gotta stay on that honeybee's trail."

She shifted her gaze back to the high trees. When she found no sign of the honeybee, she inwardly cursed Willis for interfering again.

Then she saw it. It was only a mere flicker of movement among the foliage high above, but it was definitely the bee. That knowledge sent her forward, leaping over a branch that blocked the trail, intent on keeping the flying insect in sight.

Willis wouldn't be so easily dismissed, she realized, when he began to lope along beside her. "You ain't gonna mind if I come along, are you, Rainey?"

"I do mind," she said, her gaze never wavering from its target as she jumped over a fallen log. "You know I can't keep my mind on what I'm doin' if I got company, Willis. Now go away and leave me alone!"

"Now that ain't neighborly," he complained, keeping pace with her.

"I ain't tryin' to be neighborly, Willis. I'm atryin' to find me a beehive."

"I'll just go 'long with you then. Four eyes is better'n two at spottin' bees."

Realizing he was bent on following her, she fell silent, concentrating on the honeybee. When she reached the bank of a wide creek, she plunged down the slope, sliding to the bottom of the forty-foot embankment. Then she waded quickly through the shallow water, which covered the creek bed, barely aware now of her companion as she tried to focus on the bee again.

It was nowhere in sight.

"Tarnation!" she muttered. "Where did it go?" Using the roots against the far bank as a ladder, she scurried to the top and raced into the woods again, following an imaginary line that traced the path of the honeybee.

A flurry of movement high above caught her attention. She narrowed her gaze and spotted the honeybee, flying straight and true as before.

"I was wonderin' about somethin', Rainey," Willis said, puffing slightly as he joined her at the top of the slope.

"Go away, Willis," she gritted, leaping over a fallen log and into the heavy timber beyond.

"Now, Rainey, you ain't bein' polite," he whined, continuing to keep pace beside her.

"I ain't got time to be polite, Willis. Thought you'd already seen that." She hurried on, ignoring the young man who stuck to her side like tree sap to a pine.

It was more than an hour later before she reached the top of a knoll and saw the honeybee dip low into a deep hollow and disappear from sight. But the loss was only momentary. Mere seconds had passed before it rose above the far ridge and flew into the thick woods beyond.

Rainey felt an immediate concern as she scanned the area and realized there was little difference in the trees on that side. That meant there was nothing to mark the honeybee's point of entrance. But at least she had her bucket of honey with her. A good thing, too, because if she had lost the bee, then she would need the honey soon enough.

Knowing there was no time to waste, she plunged over the lip of the ridge, heading down into the hollow, with Willis sliding along beside her. He took advantage of their descent to plague her again.

"I been thinkin', Rainey," he said, his breath hissing through his teeth. "You know . . . about the square dance on Saturday. An' I done some deciding, too. I'm gonna squire you to that dance."

So that's why he was following her! Rainey decided to dissuade him of that notion in a hurry. "I ain't goin'," she said bluntly. "Now go home and leave me be."

"Aw, Rainey, don't be thata way," he whined. "I come all this way just to make the invite. Least you could do is say you'll go!"

She kept her eyes on the slope she was descending, knowing she'd need to stop suddenly since it ended abruptly at the cliff high above Coon Creek.

Realizing she was fast approaching that point, she dug her heels into the shaley ground to slow her descent. Willis took advantage of that moment to grasp her forearm, obviously intent on swaying her decision.

"You'd have fun goin' with me," he coaxed. "I took Mary Lou Gorden last time, and she said she'd never had so much fun with anybody in her life. Ask her! She'll tell you! I'm real good at square dancing and—"

Rainey yanked her arm out of his grasp. "You leave me be, Willis Johnson!" she snapped, turning to glare balefully at him. "I done told you I ain't goin' with you!"

"Aw, Rainey, don't be thata way! We could—" He broke off suddenly, his eyes becoming round as silver dollars. Then, whipping out his hand, he gripped her wrist with hard fingers.

Angered beyond reason, Rainey yanked her arm away and plunged forward again. But she'd only taken two steps before she encountered empty air. As comprehension dawned, horror surged through her. Then she was plunging downward, straight toward the creek thirty feet below.

Rainey had little time to contemplate her fate, but she felt death quickly approaching. Although Coon Creek had several deep holes, the normal flow of water was only a few feet deep, not nearly enough to cushion her fall from such a height.

Splash!

Rainey entered the cold water and waited for oblivion. She sank into its icy depths. And continued to sink. Down, down, down. Then it came. Her feet struck the bottom, digging into the sand, and the impact bent her knees outward, her butt striking sharply against the back of her heels.

The impact knocked the breath from her body. Without thinking, she sucked water into her lungs. As they began to burn, she kicked out frantically, pushing hard against the sandy bottom. She rose swiftly upward, bursting through the water to the surface, and coughed hard, spewing out the water she had sucked in only moments before. She gulped at the fresh air, which meant life.

As the burning in her lungs eased, she swiped at the wet tangles of dark hair that was blocking her vision. Then, blinking the water from her eyelashes, she opened her eyes . . . and realized she wasn't alone in the creek.

Thorne was treading water nearby, a look of complete amazement on his face. "Dammit, Rainey," he exclaimed. "Did you need a bath so bad you had to jump off the cliff instead of climbing down? Don't you realize you could have been killed?"

"I didn't do it on purpose," she sputtered. "That damned Willis Johnson was chasing after me, and I wasn't watchin' what I was doin'."

Thorne tilted his head then, and looked up the rock face of the cliff. He saw Willis Johnson leaning over the edge high above, his fright obvious even from this distance.

"You all right, Rainey?" Willis hollered.

"No thanks to you!" she replied in a loud carrying

voice. "You get outta here an' leave me alone afore I climb up that cliff and give you what-for!"

As though intimidated by her threat, he jerked out of sight, and Rainey breathed a sigh of relief. "Never knew him to be so dadblamed bothersome afore," she said shakily. "That dang fool caused me to lose my bee line again."

"Be thankful it was only a bee line you lost," Thorne said grimly. "You're lucky the creek was full enough so you could make that dive without being killed. I hate to think what would've happened if you'd fallen in where it was shallower." He frowned heavily at her. "You *aren't* hurt, are you? Maybe we should check you over."

She noticed him then. *Really* noticed him. And her lips twitched in a mischievous grin. "Why, Thornton Lassiter," she exclaimed. "I do believe you're buck na-ked!" She arched a dark brow at him. "Are you really wantin' to check me over, or do you just want me to check *you* over?" Her gaze probed the clear water, lingering on the mass of dark curly hair that covered his muscled chest. She studied him with interest. She'd never seen him without his clothing before, and the sight of his nakedness—what she could see of it below the water—made her senses reel.

Thorne felt himself flush beneath Rainey's scrutiny. He knew if she continued to look at him in that same way, he wouldn't be able to control his emotions, nor that part of his anatomy that betrayed his feelings.

"Rainey!" His voice sounded choked, but he wasn't surprised by that fact. His breath seemed to be caught somewhere between his lungs and his throat. "Where's your sense of decency?"

When she jerked her eyes upward, there was a look in them that made him want to snatch her into his arms and feel her against his hard body. And those darn clothes of hers didn't help at all. They clung to her like a second skin, the shirt plastered against her breasts, her nipples taut and erect. More than likely it was the cold water that made them so, but whatever the reason they were damned distracting. And his body was reacting to her presence in a way that would be obvious in a moment if he didn't break the spell that bound him.

He flailed at the water then, putting distance between them. He had chosen the path he would follow last night, when he'd decided to keep his feelings secret, lest they come between them and make it impossible for their relationship to continue. He must remember that. At least until he had a chance to feel her out, to search her innermost heart and learn her secret desires.

No. He couldn't allow his desire to show, lest that desire frighten her so badly that she would never be inclined to accept him for a suitor.

He would bide his time for a while, would try to make her look at him as a man who could be more to her than a friend. And at that time, if she was so inclined, then he would ask permission to court her.

But for that time to arrive, then he must do nothing to make her uneasy in his presence. And with that uppermost in his mind, he leaned lower into the water, and swam swiftly and surely with strokes that carried him to the opposite bank, where he'd left his clothing.

Keeping his back to her so she wouldn't see the evidence of his desire, he waded out of the creek, picked up his clothing, and wound his way through the trees that would hide him from view.

Three

The sun was high overhead when Rainey mounted Samson and guided the mule down the trail that would eventually lead to the schoolhouse. She felt impatient with her errand—to invite the new schoolmarm to dinner on Sunday—because the new beehive still remained undiscovered.

Thanks to Willis Johnson! she thought venomously. She'd have found that beehive for sure if he hadn't pestered her until she'd taken that plunge over the cliff.

Damn his ornery hide!

Their food stores were almost gone, and there was no way she could replace them without first selling another batch of raw honey. The money gleaned from that sale would buy flour, soap, and cornmeal. Grandpa needed new shoes—not that he ever went anywhere—and she could use another pair of trousers, because the ones she wore now had been patched so many times she had begun to apply patches over patches.

She cursed Willis again. She would have had the funds to buy those badly needed items if it hadn't been for him. It was his doing that she'd lost the bee line, and the bucket of honey she'd intended to burn had been lost, as well. It was pure luck the fall over the cliff hadn't killed her. It most certainly would have if she

hadn't fallen into the deepest pool of water in Coon
Creek.

A grin twitched her lips, and her eyes glinted with
humor as she remembered how quickly he'd disappeared from sight when he'd seen Thorne.

Thorne.

He had been occupying too many of her thoughts
lately, ever since she'd dropped into that pool of water
where he was bathing. She felt a curious tingling as she
remembered the way he looked beneath the water, his
naked shoulders and chest rippling with muscles, the
dark hair curling in a huge mat across his chest and
tapering down to his waist and even farther below.

Rainey's lips twitched with amusement. "Ol' Thorne
took off like a scalded cat when he saw me alookin' at
him, Samson!" she told the mule. "Wouldn't of thought
it, neither, him bein' a man of the world an' all. I 'spect
there ain't too much that he ain't seen in his day." She
considered his age, knew he must be over thirty years
old. "Near his middle years," she mused. "But he's a
good man, Thorne is. Been there to help me plenty of
times when the need was there." She couldn't imagine
a world without Thorne in it.

Samson stopped dead still, snorted once, twitched his
tail and looked back at her.

"Get on there, Samson," she said, digging her heels
in his flanks. He plodded forward again. "Hurry up
there, mule." She smacked his rump with her palm,
but his pace stayed the same. Samson had two speeds,
she knew, slow and slower. "We gotta get to the schoolhouse while them kids are let out for dinner," she told
him. "Else we'll set that new schoolmarm's neck outta
joint. She ain't gonna want nobody frettin' her classes,
or causin' a commotion by coming in whilst school is
in session."

Rainey might as well have saved her explanation, be-

cause the mule paid her no heed, merely switched his
tail back and forth as he ambled along at his slowest
pace.

The narrow trail curved and wound through a dense
growth of pines and live oaks, making it impossible to
see more than a few hundred yards up the path. But
that didn't matter. Even if it had been the darkest night,
Rainey could have found her way. The noise from the
school yard would have made it impossible to miss; the
children shrieked and shouted and laughed, obviously
happy at being let out into the sunshine for a while.

As she drew nearer, the noises became more identifiable. The loudest sound of all was the shrill, childish
voice of a young girl. Counting.

". . . seven . . . eight . . . nine . . . ten!" A long
pause, then "Here I come, ready or not!"

Rainey smiled wistfully, remembering her own years
at the schoolhouse—few though they were. She had enjoyed the hide-and-seek game, too. She'd only completed her third year when her grandfather decided she
was old enough to help him run the traplines. His intent had been to use her in the fall and allow her to
go to school during the winter, but it hadn't worked
out that way. A bad fall resulted in a broken leg, leaving
only Rainey to attend him. By the time the leg healed,
Grandpa felt it would be a waste of time for her to attend classes that would soon be over. When fall rolled
around again, the cold weather ached his bones so bad
that he'd needed her help again. He'd never mentioned her schooling anymore. Not until recently.

"I see you, Chubby Caldwell! You're out! You're out!"
The high-pitched voice alerted Rainey just before she
saw the schoolhouse. Samson rounded a thick stand of
pines, and Rainey saw it—a single-room building set in
the middle of a clearing.

"You couldn't see me from there," a young voice

shouted furiously, then Chubby Caldwell slunk from behind a thick plum bush. "You musta peeked while you was counting! Cheater! cheater!" he screamed.

"I ain't, neither!" a young girl about seven or eight years old cried. "I ain't a cheater, and don't you go callin' me one, neither."

"You musta cheated!" Chubby insisted, picking up a small rock and flinging it at her, although it was carefully aimed to strike a few feet away. Chubby was a good three years older than the girl and would surely get a licking with the teacher's strap if the stone struck her. "I hid really good. I—" He broke off as he caught sight of the new arrival. "Hey, Rainey! Whatcha doin' here?" He raced toward her. "Did you come to see Teacher?"

Rainey grinned down at Chubby as she slid off the mule. "Now why else would I be comin' here?" she asked solemnly. "Certainly not to see a bunch of ruffians like you all." Although she enjoyed being around children, there were few chances available to her since most of her time was spent working to supply food and necessities for the cabin.

Ignoring her words, Chubby tugged at her hand. "When're you gonna take me on a bee line, Rainey? You said you was gonna do it an' you ain't kept your word yet."

"I don't break my word when I give it, Chubby Caldwell, but I just ain't had time to take you." She ruffled his brown hair affectionately. "I will, though. Just as soon as I find time. Right now I come to see the new schoolmarm. I guess she's in the schoolhouse."

"Schoolmarm!" he giggled, his blue eyes dancing with some secret joke. "Our new teacher is in the schoolhouse right enough, Rainey. But you're gonna be surprised if'n you're expectin' a schoolmarm."

Her gaze narrowed on the boy's curious expression.

"What's teachin' you then, Chubby, if it ain't a school-marm. You got a hog for a teacher?"

"I've been called a lot of things in my time but no-body has ever called me a hog before," a purely male voice said from behind her. "At least not to my face."

Rainey's head whipped around and her jaw dropped, her stomach doing a double flip as she gaped at the golden-haired man standing in the schoolhouse door.

He stood there trapped in sunlight, while the bright rays made his blond curls gleam as though they were pure gold. He had dimples, which deepened as his smile widened. And his eyes, so intensely blue, rivaled the sky on the clearest day.

Oh, God, Rainey thought. *You done sent one of your angels to teach the young'uns on Thunder Mountain.*

She was convinced of that fact, because the man stand-ing before her could be nothing else except one of God's own. Surely, no earthly creature could look so beauti-ful . . . so dazzlingly, sunshiny, first-rate, eye-appealingly gorgeous.

"Did you come to see me?" The angel asked gently, pretending not to notice that she'd been struck com-pletely dumb by his incredibly handsome countenance.

"I . . . I—" Oh, God! The words wouldn't go past the knot that had suddenly lodged in her throat. She swal-lowed hard and tried again. "Wh—what are—you ain't the new teacher!"

He lowered his voice. "The children seem to think so, and I would appreciate it if you don't tell them any different."

"Then you ain't—" She broke off, flushing, as she realized he was teasing her. She stuck out her hand and gripped his hard. "I c-come to make my howdys," she stuttered. "An'-an' to give you an invite to Sunday din-ner."

"How kind you are," he said, and his incredible smile

spread to his eyes, which made them crinkle at the corners. "Allow me to introduce myself. I'm Robert Golden, newly arrived in these mountains from St. Louis." He lifted her hand and brushed the back of it with his lips, and she thought she would pass out from pure pleasure.

Golden, she thought. *My God! Even his name is Golden.* He *is* one of God's angels. Couldn't be anything else the way he looked. Her heart beat faster, thundering in her eardrums. "It ain't kind at all," she said stupidly, her stomach doing a quick flip-flop. "We'd be mighty pleasured," she heard herself saying. "Me and Grandpa would . . . to have you eat with us and—and to set a spell after dinner. Grandpa don't have near enough company these days." A bold-faced lie, she knew, since Sadie Thompson was there most every day.

"I'm afraid I didn't catch your name," Robert Golden said gently, those intense blue eyes of his never leaving hers.

"It's . . . it's Rainey," she stuttered, reluctantly releasing his hand. She wished her name had been different, something elegant like Rebecca or Katherine or Elizabeth. But it wasn't. Wasn't even a name, neither, just something her pa had called her because it was raining the night she was born. Coulda been worse though, she supposed. If there'd been a tornado that night no telling what he'd of called her.

"Rainey?" Robert Golden queried, casting a quick, confused look toward the cloudless sky.

A high-pitched laugh erupted from the boy at her side, and Rainey frowned at Chubby, who was immediately silenced.

"My name's Rainey," she explained. "Rainey Watson. Ever'body hereabouts knows where the Watson cabin is located." She looked at him anxiously. "You are gonna come, ain'tcha? I was plannin' on fryin' up some chicken and makin' pan gravy and turnip greens and biscuits and bakin' a raisin pie for afters."

"It sounds delicious," he said. "How could I possibly refuse such a meal?"

Rainey was so flustered at his acceptance that she couldn't hold his gaze. She looked away and realized for the first time that the children had all left their play and had gathered around the two adults.

Robert Golden noticed, too. He smiled at the lot of them. "It looks like I won't have to ring the bell today," he remarked solemnly.

The girls, obviously as smitten with their teacher as Rainey, hurried inside while the boys did a slow shuffle behind them.

Robert Golden turned his attention to Rainey. "You're welcome to attend classes while you're here," he said.

One part of Rainey wanted to accept the invitation, while the other part wanted him to know that she was a grown woman, too old to attend school. "I ain't been in school for years," she said.

He smiled wryly and showed those beautiful dimples again. "I beg your pardon for thinking you were only a schoolgirl, Miss Watson."

Oh, Lordy, he had fine manners. Rainey wished she dared to enter that schoolhouse and could slide onto one of the long benches and stay there all day feasting her eyes on him. She so desperately wanted to watch him at work, to listen to his wonderful voice, and yet she could not. Because if she did, he would likely realize the affect he had on her, and it was too soon for that— much too soon.

Nevertheless, Rainey knew her feelings.

Lordy, did she know!

The knowledge had struck her—like a bolt of lightning—the moment she'd laid eyes on him.

Rainey was in love.

For the first time in her life, she was in love. And it had to be with a man who was so far above her in so many ways that he would never think of her that way.

But even though Rainey realized that, she had never been one to give up easily. Not when she wanted something so badly. And she *did* want this man. This beautiful, golden-haired man, who must have dropped straight out of heaven to land amongst the mortals who lived on Thunder Mountain.

Rainey, still awestruck, left the school, bemused and befuddled. It was a good thing Samson knew his way home, for her thoughts were filled with the new teacher. She could recall their every moment together—short though that time had been—and she vowed to remember them eternally, to keep them locked firmly in her memory . . . treasures to be enjoyed for the rest of her life.

She shook herself into awareness. She needed desperately to find the bee line again, and that need was suddenly uppermost in her mind. Without the honey from the beehive she was doomed to wear her breeches and shirt on the day Robert Golden came to dinner, and she was determined that she would not. She would find the new hive and she would rob the bees of their honey. Then she would carry every jar to the store and buy some material, because she had a gown to make, a gown that would be pretty enough to make the teacher sit up and take notice, even if she had to bust a gut doing it.

As that thought occurred, so did another one. There was more to catching a man's eye than pretty dresses.

She needed to know things . . . things other women already knew. Like Mary Belle Carter. Now, there was a girl who fluttered her lashes and managed to blush rosily whenever anything wearing pants looked at her. But Rainey knew those blushes weren't real. The girl hadn't a lick of sense about what was right and proper, but men seemed to like that sort of thing. And the teacher was definitely all male.

Well, Rainey could outdo Mary Belle Carter any old day. She'd learn those things. And she'd practice them until she had it right. And when it was done, she'd be just as turned out as any other woman. That teacher man, Robert Golden, would sit up and take notice of her. And when supper was over, they'd go out into the moonlight and he'd say pretty words to her. Never mind that she'd invited him for the noon meal. It was Rainey's intention to keep him with her all day.

"Tarnation!" she swore softly. "What am I gonna do if'n he wants to kiss me in the dark, Samson? I ain't never been kissed afore. Not even by Grandpa. An' I ain't rightly sure how it's done."

Samson snorted and switched his tail, but otherwise paid no attention to her panic. "I bet Willis Johnson knows how to kiss real good," she muttered, then quickly rejected that thought. Willis would most certainly teach her if she asked him, but he was already making a pure nuisance of himself. If she allowed him such a liberty she'd never be able to get rid of him.

Rainey realized she'd have to consider other choices, but, as none came to mind, decided to shelve the problem and concentrate on more pressing matters. If she didn't find that beehive, learning how to kiss would make no difference. Robert Golden wasn't about to kiss a woman who dressed like a man, and without that honey there'd be no material for a gown.

That thought caused her to jab her heels so hard into Samson's flanks that he decided to run. And that suited Rainey just fine because she had a beehive to find before the day was over.

* * *

It was Saturday when Thorne rode into Lizard Lick to pick up supplies. After he'd bought feed and seen to the loading, he pushed open the door of the general store and stepped inside.

He was surprised at the crowd—mostly female—that he found there. At the center of the crowd stood a tall, blond man who looked vaguely familiar.

"Thorne," exclaimed the short, plump woman who stood behind the counter. Her graying hair had been twisted into a bun at the back of her head. "Didn't expect to see you today," she said. "How have you been?"

"I've been keeping well, Elizabeth," Thorne replied, returning her smile. "And you?"

"I guess I've been doing okay," Elizabeth Crocker said. "Mostly anyway. The rheumatiz never seems to go away, though. Gets in my bones, you know. Makes them ache so bad that I'm afraid one of these mornings I'm gonna wake up and find my limbs all twisted up like Hildy Johnson's was before she up and died from her misery."

Thorne had been hearing about Elizabeth Crocker's rheumatism since the first day he'd walked into her store, and he was sure she'd keep telling him about it until the day she passed on.

"Howdy, Thorne." Charles Crocker joined them. "Good to see you, boy! What can we do for you?"

"I need some rope, Charles," Thorne replied. "What's going on here anyway?" He indicated the cluster of women. All of them seemed to be speaking at once. "Are you hiring your store out to the Women's Sewing Circle now?"

"It looks that way, don't it?" Charles Crocker laughed. "But no. That's not the Women's Sewing Circle. Although most of them ladies are likely here by now. The man over there is responsible for the gathering. He come in for supplies, and word got around town and all them women began showing up."

"Who is he?"

"The new schoolteacher. And he's made quite a stir among the ladies."

Thorne looked at the blond man and was struck again by the feeling that he'd met him somewhere before. But the memory somehow eluded him.

He wasn't really surprised the ladies found him so attractive, but he *was* surprised about the new teacher being a man. "I didn't know the school board hired a man for the job," he said.

"Neither did the rest of us," Charles replied. "The school board left the choosing up to Jude Grant, and he told us—after the teacher showed up—that he was tired of replacing the women every time he turned around. Said he figgered a man would stay single longer . . . or at least stay with the job."

"I don't know about the single part," Thorne said. "From the looks of it, every eligible young lady on Thunder Mountain has come to meet him."

"I expect there ain't too many of 'em that ain't here," the other man said. "It's most certain he won't be eating at Billy Joe's Eatery very much. There'll be plenty of invitations to home-cooked meals coming his way."

Thorne's frown was thoughtful. "I suppose so," he mused. "I know the Watsons planned to extend an invitation to Sunday dinner."

"And so does everybody else know it." Charles Crocker chuckled. "Why, Rainey come in here the other day with more jars of honey than she's ever brought at one time. Twenty-four jars it was. And when she left here she weren't carrying no pants like she usually does. She took some dress goods and ribbons instead. Along with some other womanly folderols."

"Rainey did that?" Thorne lifted a puzzled brow.

"I'm surprised, Charles. She's never been interested in dressing up before. In fact, I don't believe I've ever seen her in anything but pants."

Crocker grinned. "I'd bet money, things are gonna be different now."

"What do you mean?"

"You're an educated man, Thorne. You can add them things up as good as me. The teacher's going to the Watson cabin for Sunday dinner, and Rainey comes in here and buys dress goods and ribbons and lace, and even a chemise. Now I'd be plumb dumb if I couldn't add those things together and come up with the right answer. Rainey is smitten with the new teacher."

A chemise? Just the thought of Rainey in a chemise raised Thorne's blood pressure. "You're on the wrong track," he said gruffly. "Now, how about that rope?"

Charles Crocker took the rope off the wall and handed it to Thorne. "Wanta lay a bet that Rainey ain't already sweet on the man?" he asked with a grin.

Thorne suppressed his anger. "I don't bet," he said abruptly. He dug into his trouser pocket for change. "But if I did, I'd lay odds against it." He slapped the coins on the counter, then strode out of the store, aware that Charles Crocker's gaze had not left him.

Thorne's fury stayed with him as his long strides carried him swiftly to his wagon. He didn't like what he'd heard, and he didn't like the looks of the new teacher. He was too damned good-looking. And such looks just might catch Rainey's eyes. But the fact that he was so good-looking meant that every woman on the mountain would be chasing after him, and with all those women to choose from, Rainey would have a hard time catching his interest.

Not that she wasn't beautiful, because she was. But she was little more than a child. Any man, whether educated or not, would most certainly be aware of her innocence, because she had no affectations whatsoever, was completely without guile. A man of the world—and the teacher was certainly that—would never feel attraction for a child like Rainey.

At least Thorne hoped he wouldn't.

Perhaps, though, it would be in his best interest to attend that dinner. Thorne felt certain it would be easy to wangle an invitation from George Watson. And if he were there to keep an eye on things . . . well . . . if Golden *did* cast his eyes toward Rainey, then Thorne would be there to see it, and could do whatever was necessary to protect his own interests.

Yes, he decided. He *would* attend that dinner. And afterward, if he found it necessary, he would accompany the teacher home and set him straight about Rainey's future.

Because, if Thorne had his way, Rainey's future most certainly did not include the new arrival on Thunder Mountain.

Four

Rainey smoothed a wrinkle from her blue gingham skirt and tugged nervously at the bodice. The rounded neckline scooped so low that her bosoms appeared to swell above it. And, although she wanted to appear feminine, she worried about so much of her bare flesh being put on display.

Drat it! She needed a mirror that would reflect her full length. She looked down at herself and smoothed the skirt over her hips again. Was it too tight? Too loose? She didn't know. She picked up the silver-backed mirror that had belonged to her grandmother and peered into it. Blue eyes, bright with excitement, looked back at her. She examined the oval of her face, looking for blemishes that might have appeared overnight, but there were none.

She frowned at her image, deciding to seek her grandfather's opinion. She found him on the porch. "Grandpa, what do you think?"

The old man, seated in his cane-backed rocker, had been perusing the storm clouds overhead while he puffed on his corncob pipe. Attending to her question, he inspected her carefully, his gaze lingering overlong on the swell of her bosoms. And when his eyes raised to hers, she saw the bewilderment in his gaze.

"Well, Grandpa," she said, shifting impatiently. "How do I look?"

Slowly, he took the corncob pipe from his mouth and waved it in her direction. "When did all that happen?" he asked gruffly.

"What, Grandpa?" She looked down at herself, but could find nothing unusual there.

"Never mind." He stuck his pipe in his mouth again and turned his attention to the sky once more. "Looks like it's gonna rain for sure," he said around the pipe stem.

"Oh, no!" she cried. "It can't!" She'd been aware of the gathering clouds, but had dismissed them from her mind. "The rain will mess up my dinner!"

"I didn't know you was plannin' to serve dinner outside," Grandpa grumbled. "Darn fool idea, if you want my opinion."

"I'm not serving dinner outside," she told him. "But Robert might not come if it rains."

"Might be just as well," he said shortly. "That man has knocked the sense right outta you, girl. I ain't never seen you in such a dither before. You'd think we was havin' the queen of England here to eat with us."

"Robert Golden is more important to me than the queen of England," she said. "I can't wait for you to see him, Grandpa! I ain't never seen a man like him afore. There's not a man in these hills could hold a candle to him."

He removed his pipe and eyed her severely. "Judging a man by his looks is a bad thing, girl. Can't never tell what he's like inside. And if he's so dadblasted comely, every woman in these hills is gonna be pantin' after him like bitches in heat. It ain't fittin' no granddaughter of mine should join the pack."

"No such thing, Grandpa!" she snapped. "And don't you go callin' me no bitch, neither!" She felt hurt that he would speak to her in such a manner. "You oughtta be ashamed of yourself for talking to me thata way!"

"The man ain't even come yet and he's already set the two of us against the other," George growled.

"Don't you go blamin' that on Robert, Grandpa!" she said coldly. "He ain't got nothing to do with what comes outta your mouth."

He studied her for a long moment. "Something bad's happening here, Rainey. You're so smitten by that man you'd set family aside without a second thought if it meant bein' with him. An' you don't even know him." He looked confused. "I'm your grandpa, girl. Don't that count for nothin'."

She sighed and knelt beside him and took his gnarled hand. "Grandpa, you have to understand. I ain't no little girl no more. I'm a woman growed an' I found the man I want to marry up with." She searched for understanding in his gray eyes. "Don't you understand? Has it been so long since you courted Grandma that you can't remember how you felt about her?"

"That was different," he said gruffly.

"How?" she asked.

"Grandma an' me loved each other."

"An' I think I love Robert."

"One meetin' ain't enough to know," he said. "Love is somethin' that grows with time, child. You don't look at a man an' make up your mind like that." He patted her cheek. "You shoulda had a woman to teach you what you needed to know about things like that. If your ma hada lived, she coulda—"

"But she didn't live, Grandpa. And I don't have no woman to give me advice. But I'm gonna get by just fine anyways."

"I hope so, child. I promised your pa I'd look after you an' I'm atryin' my best to do just that."

"I know. But there comes a time when you gotta let

go, Grandpa. And the time's now. I found my man. Now all I gotta do is make him see I'm the woman he's been awaitin' for all these years." She looked at him anxiously. "You won't do anythin' to drive him away. Will you, Grandpa?"

He sighed. "No. I won't do nothin' to make him leave. I hope you ain't settin' yourself up for a fall, young'un. But I'm afraid you are. And I'm afraid it ain't gonna be an easy fall, neither, but a mighty hard one."

As though brought on by his ominous words, a jagged streak of lightning flashed overhead. It was followed by a tremendous boom of thunder, which caused Rainey to flinch and jerk to her feet.

"Rain's comin'," old George growled.

Curling his gnarled fingers around the cane resting beside his chair, he rose stiffly and lumbered painfully toward the door.

Although his arthritis must be paining him, he would utter no word of complaint, Rainey knew, because it wasn't in his nature to grumble about what couldn't be helped.

"Do you want some coffee, Grandpa?" she asked.

"Don't mind if I do, Granddaughter." He lowered himself onto a chair beside the kitchen table and sighed with relief. "You got the dinner cooked up already?" he inquired.

"It's done." She put his coffee on the table within reach of his hand, then went to the open door to peer anxiously outside where rain splashed gently against the hard-packed earth.

"Please, God," she muttered. "Don't let the rain keep him away."

She heard Grandpa muttering behind her, and turned to look at him. "What did you say?" she asked.

"Nothin', girl," he said shortly. "I done said all I'm agonna say on the subject."

"Thank the Lord for that!" she snapped, becoming impatient with him. " 'Cause they ain't nothin' you could say would change my mind. I found the man I been lookin' for an' I aim to have him. I ain't never told you who to keep company with." She set her chin at a stubborn angle and flung a long lock of dark hair across her shoulders. "Ain't nobody, nor nothin' gonna get betwixt Robert an' me. An' you can lay your money on that, if you've a mind to."

"You keep a civil tongue in your head, Rainey."

"I ain't meanin' to be disrespectful, Grandpa. But I ain't lettin' nobody—not even you—keep me from latchin' onto Robert."

Old George frowned heavily and swirled the coffee in his cup. "It takes two to make a match, girl. He may not be willing to go along with what you got planned."

"He may not be of the same mind at first," she admitted. "But afore it's all over, he'll come around to my way of thinkin'."

As though ignited by the tension in the cabin, the storm broke with all its fury. Lightning zigzagged overhead, streaking across the sky. Thunder boomed, seeming to shake the little cabin to its foundation. And the rain that had been falling gently began to pound the earth with such intensity that nothing could be seen more than a few yards away.

Anxiety dimmed her anger, and Rainey hurried to the door, peering out at the deep puddles of water forming in the yard. "He prob'ly won't come now," she said mournfully. "Not when it's raining so hard." She looked back at her grandfather. "Do you think he'd do that, Grandpa? Do you think he'd just stay home when he's expected here?"

"Would if he's not a fool."

"He's not a fool!" she snapped, her irritation surging forth again. "And it wouldn't be polite to stay home after sayin' he'd come. He'll be here right enough. I just know he will."

"Then why do you keep asking me?"

Ignoring him, she peered out into the rain. Suddenly, her eyes widened as she saw a horseman emerging from the forest. "He's here, Grandpa!" she cried, her heart quickening its pace. "Robert's come." Mindful of her appearance, she shook out her skirt and straightened her bodice, pushing the neckline ever so much lower, then waited eagerly to greet the slicker-clad man who was dismounting beside the porch.

It seemed an eternity before their visitor finished wrapping the thin leather reins around the porch rail and turned to face her.

"Hello, Rainey," Thorne said gently. "Are you going to ask me inside?"

Before Rainey could gather her scattered wits, George Watson called out a greeting. "Come on in here, Thorne, boy!" He rose stiffly to his feet to greet the newcomer. "What're you doin' out in that rain?"

"I was looking for a stray when I got caught in the storm," Thorne replied.

Seeming unaware of Rainey's extreme disappointment, Thorne removed the slicker and hat, then hung them on a nail left outside the door for that purpose.

When he turned his attention to Rainey again, his brows lifted in surprise. "Well, now," Thorne drawled slowly. "Don't you look pretty today."

Mumbling her thanks, Rainey peered past his large frame into the pouring rain. "You didn't chance to see nobody else out there, did you, Thorne?" she asked hopefully.

"Sure didn't," he answered cheerfully. "You expecting somebody, Rainey?"

"Robert Golden is comin' to dinner," she mumbled.

"Golden?" Thorne's eyebrows lifted. "That name sounds familiar."

"He's the new teacher."

"Rainey fried up two whole chickens for dinner, Thorne," George Watson said. "There's more'n enough for four people, and we'd be mighty pleasured if you'd break bread with us."

"I wouldn't want to intrude where I haven't been invited," Thorne said, his gaze on Rainey.

She ignored his look and felt guilty for having done so. "Well, hell!" Grandpa growled. "I just invited you, boy!"

Rainey felt like strangling the old man. Any other time she'd have welcomed Thorne, but not now. She wanted Robert to herself, had relied on Grandpa napping after dinner. But there was no chance of that if he had company to visit with.

Thorne sniffed the air appreciatively. "I've yet to meet anyone who can turn out fried chicken like Rainey. Something smells delicious."

"There's raisin pie for afters," George Watson said eagerly.

Their voices faded from Rainey's consciousness as she became aware of another horseman. "He's come," she cried. "Oh, Grandpa, Robert's here! He came, just like I said he would!" She hurried onto the porch, unmindful of the drips that dampened her dress and hair, her gaze locked on the man she'd selected to share her future.

"She's in an all-fired hurry to see him," Thorne said morosely, watching Rainey greet her guest.

George Watson's bushy brows lowered. "She's right taken by the new teacher, Thorne. Been talkin' about nothin' else since the day she asked him over."

"I couldn't help but notice," Thorne said quietly.

He hadn't expected Rainey to look so darned feminine in her gown. He should have known, though. He'd seen the way her breasts had been outlined by her wet shirt the day she'd fallen into the pool where he'd been swimming. He remembered that as he took in the sight of her now, standing on the porch, dressed in her finery, her full breasts pushing against the cloth of her bodice.

That memory caused a tight sensation low in his groin, but there was no sign of the tension that stretched his nerves, as well as his breeches, when he spoke again. "She's going to get wet standing on that leaky porch."

"She don't see them leaks," George muttered. "She ain't got eyes for nothing nor nobody except that teacher. It's a shame, too. A pure-dee shame. She worked mighty hard on her dress and now she don't even know it's gettin' wet." He heaved a sigh. "Rainey never set much store by female doin's afore, but I'm aguessin' things are gonna change around here."

Thorne knew George was right. He was deeply worried by that fact. He watched Rainey enter the cabin followed by Robert Golden. Introductions were made and, although it obviously pained old George, he tried to hide his feelings. "Robert Golden, eh. Never heard of a man wearing a last name like that afore."

Golden smiled. "It's not an unusual name in my part of the country."

"And where is that?" Thorne asked, intent on learning more about the man who might prove to be a contender for Rainey's hand.

"St. Louis," Robert replied. "Do you know the area?"

"I know it."

"You set yourself down there, Robert," Rainey said quickly, pointing out the chair that Thorne usually occupied when he was there. "And you, Thorne, take that chair over there."

Thorne concealed his displeasure at being moved across the table from Rainey. But instead of seating himself as the other men had done, he followed her to the stove. "Let me help you put the meal on the table, Rainey." He wanted to establish his relationship with the Watsons and could think of no better way to do it.

After grace had been said and the food passed around, the men began to talk among themselves about the latest doings on the mountain. Rainey was content to sit and listen to the sound of Robert Golden's voice as he answered questions about his home in the east and his family members that were still there. He spoke of society balls and tennis games and sailing and other things—people and places that she knew nothing about. His way of life was strange, so different from her own life here on the mountain.

"What made you decide to come to Thunder Mountain, Mr. Golden?" Thorne asked politely.

"Call me Robert." The invitation seemed almost a command. "The answer is simple, Thorne. At one time I thought of entering the ministry. My family objected strenuously and I conceded to their wishes." He smiled sadly. "They were right, of course. And in time I realized that. But I never quite gave up my dream. When I heard about this position—working with deprived children— it seemed the answer to a prayer. I applied and was accepted, and here I am."

Thorne glanced quickly at Rainey and spoke with deliberate calculation. "So you consider your work here on Thunder Mountain as an alternative to the ministry."

"Yes. You could say that." Robert's teeth gleamed whitely as he smiled at Thorne. "You appear to be an educated man, Thorne. I take it you're not from these parts?"

Thorne felt irritated at the teacher's assumption that anyone from these parts couldn't possibly be educated. But he curbed his irritation, knowing it was a natural deduction since the man had probably not encountered anyone on the mountain who had been educated beyond the eighth grade. But then, neither had Thorne. "I was raised in St. Louis," he said shortly.

Robert's eyebrows lifted. "You're not Eugene Lassiter's missing son?" he inquired.

"I admit to being his son, but I didn't realize I was missing," Thorne replied, knowing his tone was abrupt.

Robert's eyes crinkled at the corners as his smile widened. "What in the world are you doing here? And on a farm, too. Surely, a son of Eugene Lassiter has no need to work."

Thorne felt Rainey's curious gaze. "You seem to know a lot about my family," he told Robert.

"It's none of my business, of course," Robert Golden said quickly. "I was just curious."

Rainey glared at Thorne, silently accusing him of being rude to her guest. Thorne ignored the look but fell silent, allowing the conversation to wash over him without hearing the content. His mood matched the weather, but by the time the meal was finished, the storm clouds had dissipated but his emotions remained unsettled.

Rainey worked hurriedly, intent on cleaning up as quickly as possible so she could join the men on the porch. She had been tempted to leave the dishes but had resisted the temptation, needing to show Robert how neat and tidy she could keep the cabin. Finally, though, the last plate had been dried and stacked with the others, and she removed her apron and brushed her hair into a silky mass, then hurried outside. Robert Golden was just on the point of leaving.

"You can't leave yet!" she cried, unable to hide her disappointment.

"I'm sorry, but I must," he said, smiling down at her. "I've been invited to Julia Given's home for supper and have papers to grade before I go there." He shook hands with the men, then kissed Rainey's knuckles. "The meal was excellent, Miss Watson. And your company was delightful. You have my undying gratitude for extending the invitation."

Undying gratitude. Her disappointment at his departure was tempered slightly by those words. She would make it her business to invite him for the evening meal next time. "We was real pleasured by your visit," she said, the back of her hand still tingling from the feel of his lips against it. "Don't be no stranger here, Robert. Hear? Come see us again . . . anytime."

Her eyes drank in the sight of his lean body as he mounted his horse and rode into the forest. Then she turned to the men watching her silently. "All right," she said, putting her hands on her hips and glaring angrily at them. "What did the two of you do to make him leave so fast?"

"We didn't do nothing," George Watson said quickly. "He was just ready to leave, Rainey. What's the difference anyway? The man had done filled his belly with fried chicken and taters and good raisin pie an' they was no more reason for him to stay. Can't say as I mind him goin', neither, 'cause he ain't our kind of folk. A body can't rightly feel comfortable with his sort."

"Grandpa! You *did* do something." Her eyes flashed to Thorne's. "Or was it you, Thornton O'Brien Lassiter? It would be just like you to drive away my only beau!"

"Is that what he was, Rainey?" he asked softly. "I'm

afraid I didn't know. He certainly didn't have the look of a man who'd come here to court you. Didn't even offer to help with the dishes when the meal was over."

"He didn't have to!" she snapped. "He was a guest here! Just like you are! And I never saw you offering to wash the dishes, neither."

"Now, that ain't fair, Rainey," George said. "Many's the time Thorne offered to wash the dishes for you. And he's always bringing in wood for the stove. He ain't never come here without askin' was there somethin' that needed doin'."

"None of that matters one whit to me," she snapped. "I didn't ask Robert here to wash dirty dishes. But I *did* expect him to stay and set awhile with me." She looked down at herself, and tears of pity misted her eyes. She thought of the long hours she'd spent gathering the ruffles and sewing them to the long skirt. "I made this here dress just so's I'd look like a woman for Robert and . . . and he d-didn't even notice."

"I'm sure he did," Thorne said gently. "It's a lovely dress, Rainey. The blue in that gingham exactly matches your eyes."

"Them's words I wanted him to say," she said, sniffing. "Just like that, too, all soft-like. But he didn't really see me, did he? Didn't hardly even look my way." She felt a wave of depression settle over her. "I don't know how to be a lady, don't know how to catch a man's attention. I'm no good at things like that."

"You don't have to learn those things, Rainey. You come by them naturally," Thorne said.

"But he didn't hardly look at me," she wailed, allowing her tears free rein. "And after all the trouble I went to." She clutched his shoulders. "What's wrong with me, Thorne?"

Although Thorne felt secretly glad that Robert Golden had left, he found himself sympathizing with her. She had gone to a lot of trouble and, although the teacher had said a polite thank-you, there had been no real appreciation in either his voice or his manner.

But then, to give the devil his due, Robert Golden hadn't the slightest notion of how hard she'd worked to make the dinner a success.

"I have needle holes in my fingers from sewing this dang dress," she cried piteously. "And he didn't say nothing about it, didn't even seem to notice how pretty it was."

"Man didn't notice much of nothin' 'cept for the food on his plate," George Watson muttered, stomping inside the cabin.

Thorne slid a comforting arm around her waist and reveled in the feel of her warmth against him. "I'm sure he noticed," he comforted, even as he wondered why he bothered.

"I tried so hard," she muttered, wallowing in self-pity.

"I know you did," he sympathized. "But maybe you tried too hard, Rainey."

"I *had* to try hard! I don't know nothing about anything! Least ways the things that catch a man's eyes." She looked piteously at him, her eyes glittering with moisture, and, like a man hypnotized, he reached out and touched her cheek. It felt warm, soft, silky. He wanted to take her in his arms, wanted so badly to cradle her head against his shoulder, but he couldn't move. He merely stood there, cupping her cheek as though it were something precious.

She was so childlike in her innocence, and yet so womanly, too. It was all he could do to keep the desire he felt from showing.

"You know what a man like him wants, don't you, Thorne?" she asked.

"I suppose he's used to women who flutter their lashes and practice their feminine wiles," he said.

"What's feminine wiles?" she asked, knuckling the tears away. "Tell me how to practice them."

Feeling a sense of deep frustration, he ran a hand through his dark hair. "It's not something I can tell you about, Rainey. It's something women just learn by themselves."

"Well, I didn't, Thorne." Her tears were gone now, and there was sudden determination in her voice. "And you know it. I don't know nothing about things like that. But it's past time I did! And you could teach 'em to me." Her words startled him, and he wondered if she'd lost her senses.

Him? Teach Rainey how to trap another man into marriage? Not on his life!

As though she had guessed his thoughts, Rainey dug her fingers into his shoulders. "Don't you look at me like that, Thorne! I set my mind that I'm gonna have that man for my own. And you're gonna help me get him! You're gonna teach me what I need to know so's that man will look at me like I'm a woman!"

Five

Thorne's visage went through a series of expressions. Astonishment came first and he looked stunned. But as comprehension dawned, his dark brows came together in a heavy frown. His eyes narrowed and his lips tightened.

"Me?" he questioned roughly. "You really expect *me* to help you snare Robert Golden?"

"Who else would I ask 'ceptin' you?" She smiled up at him. "You're the onliest one I'd trust, Thorne. They ain't nobody else that'd be willin' to help without expectin' somethin' outta the doin' of it." She waited expectantly for his response. He would do it. She felt certain. Thorne had never refused her before. Nor would he now.

"Dammit, Rainey!" he exploded. "I won't do it!"

His reaction stunned her. "You won't do it?" she asked, her blue eyes wide with disbelief. "But why, Thorne?"

His expression was thunderous. "Never mind my reasons," he grated.

"You're mean, Thorne," she said, turning away from him so he wouldn't see the glitter of tears that suddenly dimmed her vision. How could he refuse her request? she wondered. Was it so much she asked of him? She didn't think so. "You might just as well go home," she muttered. "I ain't gonna talk to you no more."

"Rainey . . ." He gripped her forearm and turned her toward him again. "I don't mean to be harsh, but you must understand. I can't—"

"You could but you won't," she interrupted huskily. "Now you let go of me and be on your way. An'-an' don't you come here again without an invite, Thorne. If'n you do, you ain't gonna find no welcome waitin' for you."

He stared hard at her for a long moment. Then his fingers loosened and she was free. "Very well. If that's what you really want." He released her abruptly.

Rainey swallowed hard around the knot that had suddenly formed in her throat. What had she done? she wondered. Thorne had been her only friend and she'd thrown him away as casually as she would have disposed of a wilted flower. There was a peculiar pain in the region of her heart as she watched him walk away and disappear into the cover of the forest.

Three days later she was still trying to accept the breaking off of their friendship. But it was an impossible task. She felt as though her world had fallen apart. Thorne had been her ally since the day they'd met, and now he'd turned against her.

Why had he reacted in such a manner? It was such a simple thing she asked of him. And yet, he'd not only denied her request but had become infuriated by it.

"He coulda just said no," she muttered, scrubbing the plate she was washing furiously. "He didn't need to stomp off in a huff." She'd forgotten her grandfather's presence until he spoke.

"Why don't you go on down to the farm an' make up with him."

"I ain't done nothin' wrong, Grandpa, an' I ain't sayin' sorry for nothin'."

"You musta done somethin' gal, or he wouldn't of gone off thata way." His tone was rough, and she curbed the impulse to cry.

"Ain't no call for you to come down on me, too, Grandpa."

"I ain't comin' down on you." His voice was soft, yet gruff. "I'm just tryin' to make you see the sense of settlin' the squabble betwixt you an' him."

"It ain't a squabble," she said. "I just asked him to do somethin' and he said no. Then he got huffy and left."

"That sure don't sound like Thorne, young'un. What did you ask him to do . . . slit somebody's throat?"

"No. If that needed doin', I'd tend to it myself."

"Guess you would, at that," George grunted. He took out his pipe and lit it. "Why don't you go down to the fishin' hole and ketch up a mess of catfish, Rainey? An' try to settle yourself down whilst you're doin' it. You been nervy as a cat covered with pine sap."

An hour later, Rainey sat beside the creek, fishing pole in hand. She'd chosen the spot not only for the silvery catfish that could be found in the deep hole of water but for the solitude, as well. The latter had been hard enough to come by lately. Since that ill-fated wrestling match Thorne had interrupted, Zeke Brumley and Willis Johnson had been popping up at the most inopportune moments, and she was doing her best to avoid both of them.

Feeling a tug on her line, she yanked it hard to set the hook, then pulled a sizable catfish to the bank. She measured it with her eyes and guessed it would weigh close to five pounds. More than enough for their supper, since there were only two of them.

She wondered if Thorne would ever join them for a meal again and quickly put the thought out of her mind. Surely he would come around, sooner or later. Surely.

Drat it! Why couldn't she stop thinking about Thorne and the way he'd strode stiffly away from her?

Rainey threaded her fish onto her stringer and began the trip home again. She'd only gone a short distance when a tuneless whistle warned her of another presence.

Her lips tightened grimly. Although the whistler remained unseen, she was certain of his identity, had heard that tuneless whistle often enough in the past. It was Zeke Brumley.

Damn and tarnation! she silently swore. Couldn't he leave her alone? She didn't want to see him, had felt a sense of uneasiness whenever he was nearby ever since the day they'd wrestled together. She had seen something in his eyes then that had lingered on.

Her footsteps slowed and she caught her lower lip between her teeth. Maybe she could circle around him. The thought had only occurred when she dismissed the idea. She'd be damned if she'd allow Zeke to control her actions! The trail was the shortest way to her cabin and she'd darn well use it!

Her strides quickened. She would hurry around him, not allow him to halt her progress, yet not allow him to see her uneasiness, either. She narrowed her gaze as she rounded a thick stand of trees, searching the forest for him.

There! Beside the mountain laurel. He ignored her approach, fingering a blossom as though he found the petals especially interesting. As she neared, he looked up and pretended surprise.

"Rainey! What in tarnation are you doin' here?" He sauntered over, hands in his pockets. "Didn't know you was anywheres around."

"I ain't got time to stop," she told him, quickening her steps as she attempted to move past him.

"Don't matter, I'll just walk a spell with you."

Willis had used almost those same words the day he'd interrupted her bee hunt. But Zeke made her nervous in a way that Willis never could. Of the two, he would be the one to watch.

His gaze touched on her stringer of fish, then lifted to her again. "Nice-lookin' catfish you got there, Rainey. You fryin' them up for supper?"

"I wouldn't be taking them home if I wasn't." Her voice was short to the point of abruptness. She hoped it would discourage him.

"You been changing a lot lately, Rainey." His dark eyes swept down the length of her, then stopped at the swell of her bosom. Rainey wished she hadn't left the top three buttons on her shirt undone. "You look more like a woman these days," he went on. "Never noticed that afore." His voice became musing. "Don't know why, neither. Guess I just got used to seein' you as one of the boys."

She stopped abruptly and looked squarely at him. "You got something on your mind, Zeke, then spit it out."

His lips twisted wryly. "You ain't changed much inside, Rainey. Not nearly as much as you done on the outside."

"Is that what you want to talk about? The way I changed so sudden-like?"

"Ever'body's noticed it, Rainey. Folks is talkin' about how you made yourself a fancy dress afore you had the teacher over to Sunday dinner."

"They must be hurtin' for gossip if they don't have nothin' better to noise around," she said sharply. "Did they tell you what I cooked for the teacher?"

"Fried chicken, taters, turnip greens, biscuits and raisin pie," he answered quickly.

Irritated beyond belief, she said, "You forgot the pan gravy."

"Nobody said nothin' about gravy," he replied.

"Where's all this leadin', Zeke," she asked. "Why're you so interested in my doin's?"

"I always been interested in you, Rainey," he said. "I was just kind of hangin' around waitin' for you to grow up. And now it seems you done it."

She pretended ignorance. "Done what?"

"Growed up."

She heaved a sigh. "Zeke, if you got a point I sure wish you'd make it. I got supper to cook, and you're keepin' me from gettin' on with it."

A slow grin spread across his face. "Guess they's no sense beatin' around the bush. Folks say Willis is bent on squiring you to the barn dance on Saturday."

She frowned at him. "You heard right. But that's betwixt the two of us. It don't concern you."

"Heard you turned him down."

"You heard right."

Zeke appeared unfazed by her sharp tone. "Don't you like dancing?"

"You know I don't go to them shindigs, Zeke. An' if I ever decide to go, I don't reckon I need nobody to squire me. I know the way right enough."

"You can't just go to a dance by your ownself, Rainey. It just ain't done. A lady's got to have an escort." He grinned down at her. "You don't want folks getting the wrong idea about you. Do you?"

Her scowl deepened. "And what idea is that?"

"You know." His grin widened. "They'll likely think you ain't got no use for men."

"Maybe it's just *some* men I ain't got no use for, Zeke."

"Whatcha mean by that?"

"You ain't dumb, Zeke Brumley! An' neither am I. I know what you're after! Why you and your cousin, Willis, keep on apesterin' me. But you might as well stop your shenanigans right now, 'cause it ain't gonna do neither one of you no good."

His gaze narrowed suddenly, his expression darkening. "You're gettin' awful high and mighty these days, Rainey. An' I'm wonderin' 'bout it mighty hard. How come me and Willis ain't good enough for you no more when we always was before. What made you change so sudden-like?"

"It ain't me that changed," she said bluntly. "It's you an' that ornery cousin of yours."

"We ain't changed. At least, I ain't."

"You have so. And I don't like it one bit, neither. You look at me an' your face gets all red an' your eyes glitter somethin' fierce, like a wolf that's cornered a rabbit an' is about to rip into its belly."

"Now, that ain't so."

"It is! An' I know what you're after, but I got no use for the likes of you when it comes to things like that. I got me some big plans for the future and they sure as shootin' don't include you."

The temper he'd barely held in check suddenly exploded. His hand whipped out, snaking around her waist and yanking her hard against the length of him. She dropped the stringer of fish and lashed out with her fist, landing a blow smack-dab against his right ear.

"Let go of me!" she snapped, drawing back her foot and kicking him hard on his right leg.

Although he flinched at the blow, he didn't release her. Instead, he bent forward, attempting to cover her mouth with his, but she jerked her head aside, evading his kiss.

"Keep still, damn you!" he snarled.

Her struggles did little to gain her release, but she continued to evade his mouth. "Turn me loose, Zeke!"

she cried, pushing at his head to keep it away from her own.

Suddenly, a horse and rider broke through the dense forest and stopped beside them, and Rainey was released as abruptly as she'd been seized. With her heart racing from her exertions, she turned to see Thorne watching them from his position astride his buckskin stallion.

Her heart leaped with gladness, then slowed to a steady beat. He'd come to her rescue again. Just like before.

Thorne studied her disheveled form for a long moment, a heavy frown creasing his forehead. "Are you two wrestling again?" he inquired gruffly.

"No," she said quickly, pushing her long, tousled dark hair back from her face. "I don't wrestle no more, Thorne. Not less'n I have to."

"Then what's going on?" His voice had changed, had become as cold as the ice on Muskrat Pond in the dead of winter.

Zeke backed up several feet, and his expression took on a wary look. "I was just invitin' her to the barn dance on Saturday."

"An' I told him I don't need no help gettin' there."

Something flickered deep in Thorne's silvery eyes. "You're planning to attend the barn dance, Rainey?"

Rainey felt as though a great weight had been lifted from her shoulders. They were on speaking terms again. She smiled up at him. "I been thinkin' on goin'," she admitted.

"You can't go alone," Thorne said.

"I told her that," Zeke said, smiling smugly at Rainey. "But she don't have to go by her lonesome, Thorne. I'm gonna squire her to the dance."

"You ain't—" Her protestations were quickly interrupted by Thorne.

"No need to put yourself out, Zeke," he said. "If Rainey wants to go to the dance then she'll go with me.

I haven't been to one in years . . . not since I first came to Thunder Mountain."

"But I offered first," Zeke said angrily.

"And you was refused," Rainey reminded. She smiled up at Thorne. Once again he'd come to her rescue. "I'll thank you kindly for taking me, Thorne. I was a mite worried about coming home so late at night. They's too many varmints running around these parts. 'Specially the two-legged kind." The last was aimed at Zeke, who flushed darkly, acknowledging the words had found their target.

"Climb up here, Rainey," he said, reaching toward her. "I'll take you home."

She hurried to accept the invitation. "Thankee kindly," she said. Snatching up her fishing pole and stringer of fish, she curled her hand around his and mounted behind Thorne. He waited until she was settled, then urged the buckskin forward.

When Zeke had been left behind, Thorne said, "I take it he was giving you trouble?"

"He was, for a fact." She sighed heavily. "I don't know what's got into him and Willis. They follow me around all the time now. Ever since—" She broke off quickly, unwilling to remind him of the wrestling match.

"That young man would bear watching," Thorne said gruffly. "Take care not to be alone with him again, Rainey."

"I'm trying," she complained. "But I got my traplines to run and my bee line to follow. And ever' time I go out, I find one of them waiting in the trees for me to pass by. I'm gettin' plumb disgusted with the two of 'em."

He fell silent then, allowing Rainey time for her thoughts.

She envisioned herself at the barn dance, dressed in her new gown. Men were clamoring around her, begging for a dance, each of them wide-eyed at her beauty.

And she would be like all the other women there, she decided. She would be as female as the rest of them, her boyishness a thing of the past.

Closing her eyes, she dreamed of the dance. She would be waiting when Robert arrived. He would enter the room and he would see her there, standing amidst a crowd of masculine admirers. Robert's eyes would meet hers. He would walk straight to her then, across a roomful of people, ignoring those who spoke to him, seeing no one but her. And then they would dance together. Oh, Lordy, how they would dance. And when the dancing was over, and the fiddler had laid aside his bow, Robert would take her into a quiet, moonlit place and ask for her hand.

"Yes," she enthused exultantly.

"What did you say, Rainey?"

Thorne's voice jerked her back to reality, and she realized they had already reached the cabin.

After dismounting, Thorne turned to help her down, curling his hands around her waist and settling her on the ground before him. He fingered a long lock of dark hair, letting it slide slowly through his fingers.

"Maybe I'll just run along and have a talk with both Willis and Zeke," he said. "I should have done it long before now."

"Talkin' ain't gonna do one bit of good," she said. "They'll say whatever they think you wanta hear, and when you're gone they'll do whatever they've a mind to do. You can't follow me around the mountain to keep 'em from bothering me, Thorne. It makes more sense for me to start packin' my pistol whenever I leave the cabin."

"Would you shoot one of them if it became necessary?"

"I can't say for sure. Never had to shoot a man before. I guess it would depend mostly on what he had in mind."

"I think by the time you discovered their intentions it would be too late to stop them," he said harshly. "They would have dispensed with your weapon by then."

"Maybe. And maybe not."

"You may be willing to take the chance, Rainey. But I'm not."

"It ain't you that's being bothered," she said shortly.

"You're wrong there." He cupped her chin and tilted her head slightly, holding her gaze with his own. "We're friends, Rainey," he said softly. "If you're bothered, then I'm bothered."

She smiled up at him. "You been a mighty good friend to me all these years, Thorne. Don't know what I'd of done without you. You was always there when I needed a helpin' hand or just somebody to talk to when I got riled at Grandpa's shenanigans whilst he was still adrinkin' white lightnin' so heavy. If'n it wasn't for you, he'd anever stopped, neither." Her voice softened with remembrance. "I still mind the day you lit into him about his temper. You wasn't the least bit skeered of 'im, an' he was a big man then. It sure made life easier for me after that. Grandpa still gets liquored up some, but not like he done before you skeered the *bejesus* out of him." She lifted her hand to his cheek and stroked it softly. "I felt awful when you was mad at me, Thorne. You ain't never done that before, an' I hope you never do again. I know I ain't one to show my appreciation much . . . it comes kinda hard to me . . . but I'm atellin' you now that you mean a lot to me. An' I'm thankin' you for bein' my friend."

The look in her intense blue eyes, and the feel of her hand against his cheek, was almost his undoing. Thorne wanted to take her in his arms and hold her against him, to feel her breasts pressed against his chest, but he forced himself to stand still beneath her touch, lest he frighten her away.

"I need no thanks, Rainey," he said gently, his gaze roving over her dear face. "From the moment we met I sensed a need in you and I tried to fill that need."

"And you was a stranger, too," she mused. "You saw something in me other folk didn't even know was there. Or maybe they saw and just plain didn't care."

"Of course they cared."

"Us folks on Thunder Mountain spend a lot of time keeping out of other folks' business," she said. "You mighta noticed that."

He smiled. "Yes, I did notice. And I respect that. It's one of the reasons I came here. The people here expect . . . and allow privacy. That's not the way of it back home, though."

"Folks there make a habit of messin' in other folks' business?"

"A lot of them do just that."

"Why's that?"

"I guess it's because in St. Louis society there isn't much to do except wonder about your neighbors."

"Nothing to do? I can't hardly imagine that. It's all a body can do around here to keep food on the table. There's always huntin' and fishin' and runnin' traplines and skinnin' the varmints for their hides and runnin' the bee lines and cookin' and cleanin' and runnin' to town with the hides and honey . . . so much work to do to keep body and soul together."

"It's different there . . . in society anyway."

She frowned up at him. "And this society. Do you think that's where Robert come from?"

"Robert Golden?" Now, what had made her think of that man again? "Yes. His family are society people. They have old money from way back."

"Old money? Well, I guess that's better'n no money at all."

He smiled at her. "Yes. It's a good thing, having old money there."

"You know so much about what interests a man like him, Thorne." Thorne could see the way her mind was working. "You could help me if you would. I know you could. Please, Thorne. I'm abeggin' you to help me. Say you will."

"I can't, Rainey," he said hoarsely. "I don't want you hurt. As you're bound to be."

"I ain't gonna be. I'm gonna get that man for myself."

"To be so determined." He shook his head. "You don't know him really. You only see what's on the outside, not the inner man."

"A man that looks so good on the outside has got to be that way on the inside, too. And I just know if I could learn what he likes, then I could get him for myself."

His eyes fell to her lips, and he wished he dared to lay his own over them. The desire was so strong that he had to force a rigid control to keep himself from grabbing her.

By God, he thought. He wasn't about to allow Robert Golden to have her! Thorne wouldn't have cared if Golden had been a saint. He wasn't about to turn his back and allow the woman he loved to be taken by another man without a fight.

But what in hell was he going to do to convince Rainey that the teacher wasn't the man for her?

Six

On Saturday afternoon, at ten minutes past four, Thorne arrived at the Watson cabin to escort Rainey to the dance.

Having been waiting anxiously for his arrival, Rainey hurried outside when she heard the sound of approaching hoofbeats.

Thorne was just emerging from the forest, and he looked magnificent, dressed in his black suit, atop a black gelding with a white star marking its forehead. Loping along beside him, its lead reins held firmly in his right hand, was a bay mare.

"Oh, Thorne! You brung Lightfoot," she exclaimed. She hurried down the porch steps and stopped beside the bay. Then, reaching out a slim hand, she stroked the mare's velvety nose, then lifted her gaze to Thorne. "Are you gonna let me ride her to town?"

"Of course." He dismounted and took her hand, his gaze traveling the length of her. "You look beautiful, Rainey. I'll be the envy of every man there."

"Sadie come over and helped frill my dress up some more," she said. "This flounce on the front was her idea. See how the lace is sewed along the edges? Sadie done that." She fingered the delicate lace. "Done it real fine, too, with little bitty stitches and all. And she put my hair up in these big curls atop my head and twined the ribbons and flowers through 'em."

He studied her hair for a moment, then met her gaze again. "She did a beautiful job, Rainey. You look quite elegant in your finery."

"You do, too, Thorne," she said. "Real elegant. Right pretty, too, with them fancy britches and shirt and coat and all. But you don't hardly look like yourself. It's gonna take some gettin' used to." She arched a dark brow at him. "Do you 'spose Robert's gonna like me this way?"

"A man would be out of his mind not to like you," he said huskily. His gaze lingered on her mouth for a long moment, and his head lowered slightly, then halted mere inches from hers.

Feeling suddenly nervous, she pulled back slightly. "Do you want to come in and say howdy to Grandpa afore we leave?"

Thorne straightened quickly. "We need to be moving along," he said brusquely. "I was later getting here than I intended."

"Then I'll say a quick goodbye to him," she said. "Sadie's keepin' him company for a while. Her boy, Frank, is comin' after her afore dark."

She'd barely uttered the words when George Watson strode through the door, followed closely by the buxom Sadie Thompson. George spoke to Thorne for several minutes, passing the time of day until Thorne reminded him they would have to be going along.

After helping Rainey onto the bay, Thorne mounted his horse, and they rode down the mountain and took the road leading into town.

They arrived at the Meeks' homestead near the edge of town shortly after dusk. Although the house was lit, they passed it by, knowing the dance was being held at the barn.

Light streamed through the wide doors, which had been left open. And through those doors Rainey could hear the lilting sound of music. Excitement caught at Rainey and she curbed the impulse to leap from the bay and run into the barn. She forced herself to wait quietly instead. Thorne would help her down, and her gown wouldn't be as wrinkled as if she just slid down from the horse.

No sooner had the thought occurred than Thorne's hands circled her waist and he lifted her from her mount. But instead of setting her on her feet, he pulled her close and let her slide down against him. His grip was firm, strong, and his eyes glittered as they locked on hers. For the briefest moment her heart stopped beating. She stared at him, her breath caught, and she felt completely mesmerized by the look in his eyes, while butterflies took wing inside her stomach.

"You're beautiful, Rainey." His breath whispered across her forehead, stirring the fine tendrils of dark hair curling there.

"Hey, Thorne!" The voice was male, and it came from somewhere nearby. "Who you got there with you?"

Rainey's head jerked back as though she'd been struck. She felt a flush creeping up her neck and she stepped away from Thorne quickly. What was the matter with her anyway? She'd been feeling such longing, so darned hungry to feel his arms around her, to feel his body pressed hard against hers that it shocked her. This man was Thorne Lassiter, the man who'd been friend to her for so many years. And inside that barn somewhere was Robert Golden, the man she'd set her mind to have for a husband. Robert would be the man to share her future . . . not Thorne. And she must never lose sight of that fact.

"I wonder if Robert is here yet," she said.

Thorne's gray eyes darkened until they resembled the

storm clouds that so often gathered over the mountain. "I have no idea," he said abruptly. "But I'm sure if he is, then you'll find him soon enough."

A tall, brown-haired man approached them, and Rainey recognized Keith Larson. "I don't believe I've met this young lady before," he said, his admiring eyes traveling the length of her before lifting to her face again. He studied her for a long moment, then his jaw dropped. "Rainey?" he gulped. "Is that you, Rainey Watson?"

She laughed up at him. "Don't look so stupefied, Keith. You don't look much like yourself, neither. That fancy suit you got on makes you look like a drummer. Didn't know you had such fancy riggings. Thought you might be stuck permanent-like to them buckskins of yours."

He grinned down at her. "I may be a trapper, Rainey, but I ain't so ignorant that I'd wear buckskins to a shindig like this. Looks like you had the same notion since you left your britches and shirt at home." His gaze turned to Thorne. "I don't suppose you'd let me squire her inside?"

"Rainey's a free agent," Thorne said shortly. "She can do as she pleases."

"It really don't matter to you?" Rainey asked Thorne. When he shook his head, she curled her fingers around Keith Larson's arm. "Then I'd be mighty pleasured to go inside with you, Keith."

Thorne grunted. "Then I'll see you both later." He strode away from them toward a group of men who were talking among themselves. Oddly enough, Rainey felt hurt that he'd been so willing to turn her over to Keith. She knew she was being unreasonable, though, and turned her attention to the barn.

The moment they entered the brightly lit room they were surrounded by curious people. Many compliments came her way from both men and women. But soon the crowd drifted away to greet other arrivals, leaving Keith and Rainey alone.

Rainey's gaze continually roamed the room as she searched for the man she'd come to see. Keith, having noticed her lack of attention, watched her curiously. "Looking for anyone in particular?"

"Yeah," she replied. "I come here special-like to see Robert Golden, the new teacher." She turned her wide eyes on him. "Have you seen him?"

The grin that curved his lips was slightly caustic. "I should have known. Half the women in the room are waiting for him. Not all of them are single, either. He'll have to watch his step around the married ones, if he don't want that pretty nose of his busted."

Rainey felt horrified. "They wouldn't mess him up! Would they?"

"Damn right they would."

He looked beyond her to the refreshment table. "Do you want some punch, Rainey?"

"That'd be right nice, Keith," she replied, shaking off her feeling of horror. Keith had been fooling. He must have been. "I'll set myself on the long bench over yonder with the other womenfolk and wait for you." She'd chosen that particular spot because it allowed her a clear view of the wide door.

Rainey tried to put Keith's words out of her mind as she hurried to the bench and seated herself beside a woman wearing a purple gown. It was Bessie Howard, the local seamstress. "Hello, Bessie," she said. "That's a mighty pretty gown you're wearing."

"Why, thank you, Rainey," Bessie said. "So is yours. Did you make it yourself?"

"Most of it," Rainey replied. "I made it to wear when Robert Golden, the new teacher, come to dinner last Sunday."

"You've done a wonderful job, Rainey. I never knew you could sew such a fine seam."

"Sadie Thompson come over last night and done the fancywork," Rainey admitted. "So's it would look right for the dance." She fingered the deep flounce decorating the front. "I don't know much about such things," she said slowly. "Not havin' been to parties and such before."

"You look lovely," the woman said. Her velvet-brown eyes crinkled at the corners when she smiled. "Did you come with Keith, dear?"

"No. He only brung me inside. It was Thorne, who brung me to the dance."

"Thorne Lassiter?" The woman's dark eyebrows raised slightly. "I don't know why that surprises me. The two of you have been like glove and hand since he came to the mountains. I remember my man, Silas, sayin' you followed him around everywhere he went. I knew you were good friends, but I guess I never thought of him as a suitor for you."

"Oh, he ain't that!" Rainey felt flustered at the thought. "He just brung me so's I wouldn't have to come by my ownself."

"Oh? Are you sure that was his only reason, my dear?"

Rainey frowned. "Sure enough. Thorne ain't never thought of me thata way. He's been my best friend for years, Bessie. An' this is his way of watchin' out for me. I wanted to come here so he just naturally offered to bring me. They ain't nothing more betwixt us."

"I guess you would know."

Rainey realized the other woman wasn't entirely convinced, but rather than continue to argue the point, she fell silent. Bessie would realize soon enough how wrong her suspicions were.

She watched the fiddler as he tuned up his instrument. As though it were a signal, several more musicians climbed the makeshift stage and plucked at the strings of their instruments. As couples who'd remained outside began to stream through the barn doors, the caller took his place in the center of the platform and raised his hands to quiet the crowd.

"Gather around, folks," he said in his strong carrying voice. "We're about to start off this shindig. Everybody choose your partners."

Rainey anxiously scanned the crowd. Where was Robert? He was late in arriving, and she'd so badly wanted the first dance to be with him.

A wiry form separated from the crowd, and she recognized Willis Johnson. He approached her. "I'm claiming you for the first dance, Rainey."

Rainey shook her head at Willis. "Not now," she said abruptly, continuing to scan the crowd for the one man she'd come to see.

She was aware of Zeke joining his cousin. His eyes glinted as they ran the length of her. "You're mighty pretty tonight, Rainey. You been waitin' for me?"

"No, Zeke," she replied shortly. "I ain't been waitin' for neither of you." Suddenly she saw Thorne, who stood almost a head above the crowd.

Curious about what had caught her attention, both Willis and Zeke followed her gaze to see Thorne approaching. Hurriedly, they merged with the crowd, intent on choosing another partner for the dance.

"I believe the first dance is mine, Rainey," Thorne said huskily, capturing her hand and pulling her to her feet.

"Not now," she said anxiously, tugging at her hand, afraid that if she danced with Thorne, she would miss Robert Golden's entry. She was vaguely aware that Thorne had stiffened, and would have apologized to him if she hadn't suddenly spied Robert entering the room. Her heart picked up speed. "There he is!" she

cried. "He's here, Thorne! Robert has finally come."
She hurried across the room toward him, unmindful of
the fact that she'd left Thorne standing alone in the
middle of the floor. "Hello, Robert," she said, skidding
to a stop in front of him. "I been waiting for you to
come. Now the dancing can commence."

His eyes crinkled at the corners as he smiled down at
her, and she felt her heart skip a beat. He was so *dad-blamed* beautiful that he took her breath away. "Hello,
Rainey," he said casually. "It's good to see you again."

"Come on, Robert," the woman beside him said. She
tugged at his arm. "If we don't hurry, we'll miss the
first dance."

Robert smiled apologetically at Rainey. "Susie's
right," he said. "Save a dance for me, Rainey." And
Robert hurried after the woman.

Rainey felt a surge of anger. Drat it! She'd been waiting especially for him and he'd come with another
woman. She watched as they joined the crowd gathered
in the middle of the floor and imagined herself in the
woman's place. It would have been heaven to swirl
around the room with him. And she would! There was
no way Rainey would allow the woman to keep him to
herself!

Realizing she had no partner for the first dance, she
looked for Thorne. But it was too late. He had partnered up with Clara Whitcomb. She'd have to settle for
Willis or Zeke after all, if she didn't want to sit against
the wall with the old maids. Even as the thought occurred, she saw Willis and Zeke, lined up with the other
dancers.

Dagnabbit! She'd waited too long to get a partner.

"Hello, pretty lady." The voice spun her around. A
stranger—tall and lean, with a long, narrow face, intense green eyes and dark hair—held out his hand.
"Dance with me?"

He had a lupine grace when he moved, and his direct stare seemed almost predatory. He reminded her of a wolf, somehow.

"Do I know you?" Rainey asked, placing her right hand in his.

"Not yet," he admitted, "I'm a stranger to these parts. But we're about to remedy that. The name is Cage Larson."

"And I'm Rainey Watson." Although she wasn't sure she particularly liked him, she didn't want to be left sitting with the women lined against the wall. Robert might get the impression that nobody wanted to dance with her. It was for that reason alone that she smiled up at the stranger and allowed him to lead her to the group lined up on the dance floor.

To her extreme dismay, Cage Larson stopped beside Thorne and his partner. Thorne frowned when he looked at them, then turned his attention to his partner. That nettled Rainey. She studied his partner closely, wondering what she had that Rainey didn't. Granted, she was a pretty girl. And her dress was cut low to show an enormous amount of bosom, but surely Thorne wouldn't care about that. Anyway, most of the dresses were cut embarrassingly low. Except for Rainey's. She looked down at herself. Maybe she should take a pair of scissors to her gown before she came to another dance.

Suddenly the music started. The caller shouted instructions, and the dancers began to dip and bow and swirl, and Rainey had no more time to contemplate the cut of her gown. She whirled this way and that, trying to follow the instructions while keeping her partner from touching her where he wasn't supposed to.

When the dance ended, she looked for Robert but he seemed to have disappeared. Even Willis and Zeke—who were preferable to the stranger—were busy with partners of their own. She saw Thorne and would have gone to him but, catching her eye, he turned away. It was a deliberate snub, and Rainey felt hurt stab through her.

But she had no time to contemplate her feelings. Another dance began and she was whirled around the room so quickly that her head began to swim. When the dance finally ended, she felt so dizzy that she swayed unsteadily. She was hot, breathless, and needed some fresh air.

"It's hot in here," she said, pulling her hand free of her partner's grip.

"My thoughts exactly. We'll go outside and get some fresh air." He took her elbow and began to guide her toward the door. When they passed a woman with a punch glass lifted to her mouth, Rainey realized Keith had never returned with her punch.

What had become of him? she wondered. "I could use some of that punch over yonder," she told Cage Larson.

"I'll get some for you," he said gallantly. "You go on outside and wait for me."

Rainey found it much cooler outside. She climbed the corral poles and seated herself on the top rail. Moments later she heard Cage Larson calling to her. "Where are you, Rainey?"

"I'm settin' on the corral," she replied.

He came to her quickly and handed her a glass of punch. "Here you are," he said, climbing the corral to sit on the rails beside her.

Tilting her glass, she drank deeply, and the punch slid warmly down her throat and struck her stomach with a jolt. She hiccuped and put a hand over her mouth. "What's in that stuff?" she asked, frowning at the empty glass.

"It has a touch of white lightning in it," he admitted. "Not much, though. Just enough to warm you."

"I was plenty warm afore I drank that down," she said.

"Come here." He slid his arm around her shoulders and pulled her close to him. "I've been waiting all night for this." He crushed his lips against hers.

Thorne scowled at the doorway angrily, waiting for Rainey to return. But as time dragged on and she remained conspicuously absent, he began to get anxious. He left his partner and hurried outside, but Rainey was nowhere to be seen. Thorne knew she had to be there, though. He'd seen her leave, then watched her partner depart with a glass in each hand.

Crash! The sound was loud in the night. Thorne hurried toward the noise, then stopped short as he saw Rainey struggling with the stranger who'd partnered her.

"Let her go!" Thorne snapped.

"This ain't none of your business!" the man snarled.

"That's where you're wrong," Thorne said. "Anything to do with Rainey is my business."

"That right, Rainey?" Cage asked. "Does he have a say over you?"

"Yes!" she snapped. "And he's gonna bash your nose in if you don't turn me loose!"

"Get away from her!" Thorne said grimly.

Cage Larson eyed him belligerently for a long moment, then finally shrugged his shoulders. "Hell! Take her then. She ain't worth fighting over."

Rainey looked stunned. Tears glistened in her eyes as Cage Larson strode into the darkness.

Thorne took her in his arms. "You didn't really want to be with him, did you, Rainey?"

"No. But he didn't have to say that." She looked up at him with wounded eyes. "Guess ever'body but Willis and Zeke thinks I ain't worth much," she said shakily. "I was a fool to come down here, was a fool to think I was as good as these other folks."

"Stop that!" He shook her gently. "That man didn't mean what he said. He was angry at being ordered away from you. You really don't care what he thinks anyway, do you?"

"Not him. But I do care what Robert thinks. If Cage thinks I ain't worth much, then I 'spect Robert does, too."

"I'm sure he knows how much you're worth." Thorne hated to help the other man but didn't want to see her so hurt, either. "You are so innocent, Rainey." His thumb traced her lower lip. "Any man would want you."

"I don't want just any man. I want Robert."

His stomach tightened.

"Help me, Thorne," she pleaded. "Help me learn the things I need to know to make Robert notice me. Help me make him see I'm a woman growed."

His eyes slid to the pink perfection of her lips and he saw the faint tremble and knew a hunger so violent and unexpected that it made him tremble.

"Thorne," she whispered pleadingly.

He wanted to cover her mouth with his, to part its softness and enter the moist cavity within. He wanted to feel her body yielding to his, and her arms sliding around his neck, wanted those firm breasts pressed against his bare flesh.

When she looked up at him, the glitter in her eyes made his heart pick up speed. He hadn't known he was capable of such need, such absolute urgency.

"Please," she whispered. "Help me know what to do afore somebody else catches his eyes."

"All right," he said gruffly.

"You'll help me?" she asked eagerly.

"Yes."

"Oh, thank you, Thorne. You don't know how much this means to me. When will we start the lessons?"

"Now," he muttered, lowering his head until his mouth was hovering only inches above hers. "Open your mouth, Rainey. Let me show you how a man kisses the woman he desires."

She opened her mouth without hesitation, and he covered it with his own.

He kissed her then, slowly and thoroughly, until she was so weak that she could hardly stand upright. When he finally released her, she spoke in a breathless voice.

"Lordy, Thorne, if kissing *you* makes me feel so weak, I'll more'n likely pass out from pure pleasure when that teacher man touches me."

A fury such as he'd never known before surged through Thorne. He vowed then that no other man would ever touch her that way. He couldn't bear the thought of another man teaching Rainey the ways of love. And he couldn't believe how weak-kneed he felt from kissing her, either.

"Maybe we'd better practice some more," she whispered, lifting her face eagerly. "I never knowed mashing lips together could be so downright pleasurable or I'da been doin' it a long time ago."

"It's not the same with everyone, Rainey," he said gruffly.

"It's not?"

"No."

"I guess I ain't surprised. The thought of mashing lips with Willis or Zeke gives me the shivers. And they ain't like the shivers I get when you're akissing me, neither. I sure didn't like the way Cage Larson did it." She looked up at him innocently. "What do you reckon makes the difference, Thorne? Do you have to like the

person you're kissing before you get the right kind of
shivers? The kind that makes your belly warm and wob-
bly, and makes you want to squinch closer to the one
that's makin' you feel thata way?"

"I guess that's it," he said.

"Well, it's a fact that I like you well enough. You're
my best friend. And I like the way it feels when you're
kissin' me. Makes me all breathy-like and causes goose
bumps to pop out all over me." She smiled up at him.
"Are you gonna do it again?"

"Yes, Rainey," he said softly. "I'm going to do it
again." He lowered his mouth over hers, more than
happy to oblige her.

Seven

The kiss was so unlike the one that preceded it that Rainey gasped, clinging tightly to Thorne, her half-opened eyes locked on his as she wondered dazedly if she'd been struck by a bolt of lightning.

He lifted his head slightly and whispered, "My God, but you're beautiful."

"What're you doin'?" she whispered.

"Open your mouth," he said gruffly.

She had no thought of refusing, no thought other than compliance. As her lips parted, he crushed her mouth under his, and his tongue darted possessively into her mouth, his body pressing hard against hers.

Rainey moaned softly, hunger eating at her. She was aware of the abrasive softness of his cheek beneath her palm as his mouth moved with expert sureness against hers. His tongue traced the inner softness of her lips, easing past her teeth to move slowly, suggestively, inside her mouth. Another moan escaped her lips before she could stop it.

Thorne's fingers trailed down her throat, reaching toward breasts that were outlined by the fabric of her gown. He traced the low neckline with a caressing touch, which caused her fingernails to bite into him.

With his mouth biting softly at hers, his knuckles

brushed teasingly, skimming maddeningly over the creamy swell of her bosom.

Rainey surged closer, wanting, needing to feel his hands close over her flesh. But he resisted, continuing to brush light caresses across her flesh, teasing and tormenting her until her flesh ached with hunger.

Arching desperately toward him, she uttered another cry, one so faint that the sound was almost muffled beneath his hungry mouth.

Her knees seemed to have no more substance than wet noodles. They threatened to buckle beneath her weight, making her aware that it would be impossible to stand upright if Thorne had not been holding her so firmly.

He lifted her against him and moved backward, into the sheltering shrubs that grew in such abundance on the south side of the barn. Then he pushed the shoulders of her gown down her arms to allow him access to the fullness of her breasts.

Rainey's breath came in short gasps as his fingers tweaked her exposed nipples. Oh, God, she thought. What was he doing to her? What incredible magic was he working that made her feel so helpless to deny him anything. As his lips found the smooth skin of her neck, she threw her head back to allow him more freedom to graze where he would.

"Rainey," he muttered huskily. Then his mouth came back to claim her lips in a driving possession. The raw urgency of his kiss completely overwhelmed her and she gloried in his strength.

Snap! The sound was loud in the night, jerking Rainey back to awareness.

"Thorne?" The voice was obviously female, and it posed a question, as though the speaker were not quite certain of encountering the man she sought. "Are you out here, Thorne?"

As though with great reluctance, Thorne lifted his mouth from Rainey's. She stared at him, wide-eyed, hardly able to believe what had just gone on between them.

"Thorne!" The voice was louder now, as the speaker approached them. "Where are you, Thorne?"

Only then, did Rainey realize they were hidden behind a huge, spreading wisteria. Thorne's eyes were glazed and his face suffused with color. He seemed to shake himself, the way a dog would when leaving the water. Then, Thorne carefully pulled the neckline of her gown up and cleared his throat. "We'd best go," he said hoarsely.

Rainey was speechless, unable to utter a single word. She nodded her head and followed him toward the woman he'd been partnering so recently.

The rest of the dance was a haze of confusion for Rainey. She was aware of laughter and music, but wasn't required to speak. It was a good thing, too, she realized later because she was so caught up in that moment when Thorne had kissed her so hungrily that she wouldn't have been able to think of a reply to save her life.

They left soon afterward, and the ride home was uneventful, accomplished without a single word being exchanged between them. And when it was over, and Rainey had been deposited safely at her door, Thorne brushed his mouth briefly across her forehead, mounted the gelding, and rode away.

Three days later, Thorne entered Crocker's General Store with a list of badly needed supplies. As he strode across the room toward the farm tools hanging from nails on the wall, he was interrupted by a hail from Charles Crocker, who was sorting mail in the sectioned-off area that was used for mail.

"Thorne Lassiter!" Crocker called out. "Glad you came to town. Thought I'd have to send someone out to your farm."

"Why's that, Charles?" Thorne asked, taking note of the letter in the man's hand.

"Got a letter here for you," Charles said. "And it's marked urgent." He handed the letter across the counter and watched with avid interest as Thorne glanced at the return address.

St. Louis. The letter was from home.

Although he gave no outward sign, Thorne felt a great reluctance to open the letter. Yet knowing delay would accomplish nothing, he quickly slit the envelope with his knife and pulled out the single sheet of paper. A quick glance at the signature scrawled at the bottom confirmed the writer's identity. It was from his sister, Eloise.

Thorne felt a momentary alarm as he realized the letter had been written hastily. Was something wrong with Eloise? He read the words she'd written.

> *Dear Thorne,*
> *So much time has passed since we corresponded that I find this letter hard to write. I know you have no wish to return home and yet you must do so. Things have gone from bad to worse here. Father's situation is desperate and I know not how long I can continue to handle the situation alone. Please, please, Thorne. Come home. I implore you. Do not leave me alone with this trouble any longer. As always,*
>
> > *Your loving sister,*
> > *Eloise*

Thorne read the words over and over again, trying to make sense out of them. What could be wrong? he wondered. It was obvious there was trouble of some kind there, but what kind of trouble? He read the words again. *Do not leave me alone with this trouble any longer.* Dammit! What trouble? *Father's situation is desperate.* Desperate? Was Eugene Lassiter ill?

Thorne thought about sending a telegram to his sister asking her to explain in more detail, then realized that would be wasting time. Eloise would not have written if her need was not great. She'd obviously been under great duress when she'd penned the letter. No, he mustn't waste time. He'd book passage on the next train out.

"I couldn't help noticing the postmark, Thorne. Saw the letter came from St. Louis," Charles said, studying Thorne's worried expression.

"Yeah," Thorne said. "It's from my sister. Looks like I'm needed at home."

"Good thing you got a dependable hand to take charge while you're gone."

"Yeah. Good thing," Thorne agreed, tapping the letter against his chin thoughtfully. "But he can't manage alone long. And I'm not sure how long I'll be away."

"You gonna look for help for him?" Charles inquired. "I hear tell, Sadie's boy, Jed, is looking for work. You might check with him."

"I might do just that. Right now I need to book passage on the stage for tomorrow morning." After bidding Charles farewell, he strode out of the store toward the stage office. Mention of Sadie's son, Jed, had brought Rainey to mind. He didn't like the idea of leaving her now. Not when he'd just begun to make her realize her potential as a woman.

No. He couldn't leave her behind. The only thing to do was take her with him.

Rainey bent over the stove and opened the oven, feeling the heat rise immediately in ever increasing waves.

She tested the biscuits, which were nicely browned on top, and found them firm to the touch. After pulling the pan out, she closed the oven door and set the pan of bread on the back of the stove to keep warm. Then she firmly stirred the pot of beans, which were bubbling noisily, with a wooden spoon.

With dinner almost ready, she pulled out a chair and sat down. Propping her elbows on the table, she rested her chin on her clasped hands. In that restful state she allowed her mind to wander back to the night of the dance, as it had so many times in the past few days.

Thorne Lassiter was a puzzle to her, she decided. She'd asked for his help, practically begged for it. Yet, when he'd relented and given her what she'd asked for, she'd been flabbergasted at the results. He'd muddled her thoughts with his kisses, with his incredible tender caresses. Even now, her breasts tingled from the remembrance. Her body began to burn furiously with an inner heat that spread throughout her belly. And her heart picked up speed, causing her breath to quicken, as though she were racing through the forest, following a bee line to its source.

"Hallo the cabin!"

Thorne! It was as though she'd conjured him up by thinking about him.

She hurried to the window, eager to see him, but her heart plummeted when she saw their visitor. It was only Willis Johnson.

Rainey frowned heavily. What in tarnation did he want? He stopped beside Grandpa, who had been rocking on the porch, soaking up the warmth of the noonday sun in hopes that it would help his rheumatism.

Without waiting to be invited, Willis seated himself on the porch and began to speak rapidly to George Watson.

What had brought Willis to their cabin? she wondered.

At that moment Willis shifted his position, and Rainey ducked quickly out of sight. Her wandering gaze stopped on the pan of biscuits, and she crossed the room quickly to slide them in the warming oven. Dinner would just have to wait until Willis's departure.

She peeked out the window again.

Willis was still there, jawing with her grandpa like he had nothing better to do with his time.

Rainey poured a cup of coffee and carried it to the table, where she slipped into a chair. Might just as well be comfortable, she thought, sipping the steaming liquid. It might be a long spell before Willis took himself off.

As though the very thought had conjured him up, the door was suddenly flung open and Willis stood facing her. "Howdy, Rainey," he said with a grin. "You got some more of that coffee? I sure could use a cup."

"Then go home and get it," she snapped. She knew she was being impolite, but she didn't care. She had no wish to see him since he'd become so obnoxious. "I ain't gonna wait on you, Willis Johnson."

He looked momentarily confused. "What's eatin' at you, Rainey? You got no call to talk to me thata way."

"It's the only way you're gonna get talked to around here," she said shortly. "You and that cousin of yours has deviled me plenty lately, and I ain't gonna put up with it no more."

"Rainey!" George Watson's voice thundered across the room, reaching out to his granddaughter. "You got more manners than to talk to company thata way!" he said grimly. "Now, you make your 'pologies to Willis and get him a cup of coffee."

"Sorry," Rainey muttered, tightening her lips as she hurried to pour coffee for Willis. Grandpa was a sight to behold when his dander was up. Anyway, he was right. She *had* been rude to Willis. He was a guest in their

home. And to treat a guest unkindly was an unpardon-
able sin to the hill folk.

"Pour me a cup, too," Grandpa said gruffly. He eyed
the stove with displeasure. "Them beans about done?"

"Yes," she admitted. "And the bread is in the warming oven. I saw you had a visitor and I didn't want the
biscuits to get cold."

"It ain't my intention for 'em to get cold," George
Watson said. "Just set another plate on the table and
Willis can eat with us." He eyed Willis sternly. "You ain't
et yet, have you, boy?"

"No. I ain't." Willis's eyes glittered darkly, like he was
pleased she'd been scolded. "If Rainey don't mind me
eating with you all, I'd be right pleasured to share your
meal. Would you mind real bad, Rainey?"

"Ain't no skin off my nose," she muttered.

"What did you say, girl?" Grandpa asked severely.

"I said he would be welcome to sup with us," she
claimed, hurrying to put food on the table.

During the meal Willis was inclined to conversation.
"That stranger that was sparking you at the barn dance
turned out to be a drummer," he said.

"What stranger was that?" George Watson asked,
peering at Rainey from beneath beetled brows. "You
never mentioned nothing about no stranger to me,
Rainey."

"They wasn't nothing much to mention," she said.
"And he wasn't sparking me, Willis! He just squired me
around the dance floor." She looked at him curiously.
"How do you know he's a drummer?"

" 'Cause he came to our cabin with his satchel," Willis
explained. "Set and talked with Pap for most of the day.
Mam asked him to supper an' he et two plates of turnip
greens and hog jowls. I'm s'prised he could ask all them
questions of his'n around all that food he crammed in
his mouth. Managed, though. Mighty curious feller."

She frowned. "Curious about what?"

He laughed, and the sound grated on her nerves. "Not what? Who. It was you he was curious about. You and your grandpa and Sadie Thompson and Thornton Lassiter—"

"Me an' Sadie? Why would he be curious about us?"

"Don't know." Willis shoveled a forkful of fried potatoes in his mouth. But that didn't stop him from talking. "It's my guess that drummer was just makin' conversation. You know . . . butterin' us up so's we'd buy some of his pistols and knives."

"Is that what he was selling? Pistols and knives?" At Willis's nod, she said, "I hope he stops by here. I could use a new knife. The blade's comin' loose from the handle."

"If I'd knowed that, I'd of bought you one," Willis claimed.

"I can buy my ownself one," she said sharply.

Silence descended and they turned their attention to the meal. When Willis had scraped his plate clean and washed the last bite down with coffee, he said, "That was a real tasty meal, Rainey. You're gettin' to be a mighty good cook these days." His gaze lowered to her shirt, which was stretched tautly across her breasts, and then lifted to meet her eyes with a long look. "Let's go outside and jaw awhile. I reckon it's past time I told you what I come here for."

So there had been a reason other than a free meal! She'd suspected as much. "I got no time to fool around," she said smartly. "If you got somethin' to say, then spit it out."

Willis shrugged his shoulders. "I guess it don't need no fancyin' up. Ol' George knows what I got in mind, Rainey, and he's already give his go-ahead."

Rainey's gaze flickered to her grandfather, who looked away quickly to evade her eyes. Her lips thinned and her eyes narrowed sharply on the old man. What had he given his approval on anyway? "Speak your piece, Willis. I ain't got all day."

He sat up straighter. "I been thinking hard about marryin' me a wife," he said slowly. "And I had in mind that you'd suit me just fine."

Fury surged through Rainey. "Oh, you did, did you!" She scraped back her chair and rose abruptly. "Well, I ain't of such a mind, Willis Johnson! I'd rather marry up with our mule, Samson, than to marry up with the likes of you!"

Rainey stormed out of the cabin and fled into the woods. Although Willis was the main source of her anger, her grandfather was allotted a good share of it, too. How could he have agreed to Willis's proposal? Willis, of all people! The moment her erstwhile suitor departed, Rainey returned to the cabin and faced her grandparent.

"How could you do that, Grandpa?" she fumed, hands planted firmly on her hips. "You know dang well he won't make no kind of husband. He's lazy as an ol' hound dog that's lost its smell."

George Watson sat down in his rocker and pulled a plug of tobacco from his pocket and bit off a chew. "He ain't my first choice, Rainey," he admitted, working the tobacco around in his jaw. "But I ain't heard no other offers comin' your way. You're nigh onto eighteen years old now. The folks hearabouts is already sayin' you're over the hill. Ain't no man gonna want a woman who's been left on the shelf like last year's sour pickles."

"Don't you call me no pickle!" she said, glaring heatedly at her grandfather. "An' I ain't gonna marry up with just anybody. I aim to be a mighty finicky chooser when it comes to pickin' myself a man. It's for sure I ain't takin' no bottom-of-the-barrel man like Willis Johnson!"

"Did I come at a bad time?"

The amused voice turned both their heads. Rainey glared at Thorne, who stood in the doorway. His gaze was penetrating, as though he'd heard every word her grandfather had said, the way he'd compared her to a sour pickle. Did he, like Grandpa, think she was over the hill? Surely not, else he wouldn't have kissed her the way he'd done. Neither would he have agreed to her proposal.

Perhaps Grandpa should be made aware of their agreement.

"You come at the right time," she said. "I don't have to choose somebody like Willis for a husband, Grandpa. They ain't a bit of need for it. Thorne's teaching me how to be a lady. He's gonna help me bait a hook for the teacher man."

Grandpa ceased his rocking, looking stunned.

"That so, Thorne?" Grandpa asked.

Rainey waited a long moment for Thorne's reply. "I said I would teach her," he admitted.

"Did, eh?" George Watson was silent for a long moment, seeming to take fresh measure of the man he'd known for so many years. "You think this Robert Golden suits her, then? That he'll make her a good husband?"

"I didn't say that." His gaze bored into Rainey. "But she seems to think that's what she wants."

"Females her age don't always know what's good for 'em," George remarked mildly. "That why you're here this early? To give Rainey lessons on trapping the teacher?"

"No," Thorne replied. "I came to tell both of you that I'll be leaving for a while." His gaze never wavered from Rainey's.

She was silent for a long, tense moment, feeling as though she'd been struck dumb. Then suddenly she found her tongue. "You can't leave now," she protested. "You promised to teach me, Thorne. I need you here."

"My sister needs me more," he replied firmly. "She's alone with my father and he's apparently very sick."

"But Thorne. . . ." Her voice trailed away. What could she say? She felt completely bereft, as though he'd already gone and left her. She swallowed around a knot that had formed in her throat. "You have to go, don't you?"

"Yes, Rainey," he said gently. "I have to go."

"When are you leaving?" she whispered.

"Tomorrow."

"But your farm?" she reminded him desperately. "The fields need plowing! They can't wait, Thorne! You know that!"

"The fields are the least of my worries."

She swallowed hard and lowered her eyes. But he would not allow her to avoid his gaze. He strode swiftly to her, tilting her chin up with a large, calloused forefinger. "I have to go, Rainey. You must see that."

She nodded, her eyes misting suddenly. "I know," she said huskily. "How long?"

"How long will I be gone?" She nodded her head. "I don't know. I suppose as long as I'm needed. Will you be all right while I'm away?"

"Willis and Zeke are gonna be pestering me around every bush when you're gone. And Willis was just here begging Grandpa for me to marry him, and Grandpa—" She sent him a furious look. "—said it was okay, and now Willis ain't gonna take no for an answer since he's got Grandpa's go-ahead."

Thorne looked at the old man piercingly. "There's a solution for that, you know. You could go with me."

Her eyes widened and she caught her breath. "To St. Louis?" He nodded. "But why?"

"You have so much to learn, Rainey. And I'm not

sure how long I'll be gone." He grinned down at her. "We just started the lessons and if we stop them now, you might forget everything you've already learned."

She started to tell him that she'd never forget those moments in his arms but kept her mouth shut. He might decide to leave her behind. And she had to go. She just had to. She looked at her grandfather, silently seeking his permission, and he nodded his approval.

"Sounds like a mighty good idea to me," he growled.

"You ain't used to doin' for yourself," she reminded him hesitantly.

"They's plenty of folks around to see to my needs. Sadie Thompson, for one. She'd come, was she asked."

Rainey was amused by his self-satisfied smirk. "I imagine she would."

Thorne, who had been waiting tensely, replied, "Then you agree?"

"Guess I'd be a pure fool not to," Rainey replied. "I 'spect it would do me good to see how other folks live. When do we leave?"

"Tomorrow. Early."

She could hardly contain her excitement. "How early? I can be up most anytime. I won't even go to bed if you want to leave in the night."

"I think we can spare enough time to sleep a few hours," he said wryly. His gaze traveled the length of her, taking in her breeches and homespun shirt. "Wear that pretty gown of yours, Rainey. Women in breeches have no place in the city."

After settling on the hour they would leave, Thorne bade them goodbye and left them seated on the porch. George had already turned his attention to tamping tobacco leaves in his corncob pipe, but Rainey was watching him, her eyes wide with excitement.

It was hard to believe that she was really going to St. Louis. But it must be true. Thorne wouldn't fib about a thing like that. He was taking her with him. Oh, Lordy, how she loved that man!

That thought brought a momentary frown, which quickly disappeared.

She would consider it later.

Right now she would think about all the things she would see when she got to St. Louis!

Eight

The sun had barely crested the eastern horizon when Thorne and Rainey rode into Lizard Lick to catch the morning stage. He dismounted and unfastened her worn bag from the saddle and dropped it beside the long bench outside the ticket office. Then he lifted her down from the saddle. "The stagecoach won't leave for another twenty minutes or so," he said. "You'd best wait here with the luggage while I take the horses to the livery."

"All right." She looked down at her long skirt and finding it wrinkled, tried to smooth them away. By the time she'd finished, his luggage had joined her own and he was leading the horses toward the livery down the street.

Deciding she might as well make herself comfortable while she waited, she seated herself on the bench and looked westward. The stage would enter town from that direction. She was squinting into the distance when a movement from her peripheral vision caught her attention. Her gaze swiveled and stopped on Willis Johnson who was just exiting the saloon. That was surprising since the saloon should have been closed.

He spotted her immediately. "Rainey!" he called out, waving to her. He staggered slightly as he crossed the street to the stage office. "What're you doin' here?" he asked, in a slightly slurred voice.

"You been drinkin'," she accused. "Shame on you, Willis Johnson."

"Aw, Rainey," he whined, wavering slightly as he tried to keep his balance. "I just had a few little drinks. Not much. I ain't really a drinkin' man. You know that. An' I'd make you a good husband if you'd just—"

"Forget it, Willis," she said impatiently. "I ain't gonna marry up with the likes of you. If I didn't know it before, I'd darn well know it now. A man that'd stay out liquorin' hisself up the whole dang night sure ain't the kind of man I'm lookin' for."

"You got it all wrong, Rainey. I ain't been liquorin' myself up the whole night. I just kinda fell asleep at the table and they left me where I was." His voice had a complaining whine. "It ain't right, leavin' a man lay like that, neither. I woke up with a crick in my neck." He squinted at the luggage stacked beside her and leaned closer. "You goin' someplace, Rainey?"

His stale whiskey breath almost gagged her, and she leaned away from him. "You dang right I am. I'm goin' to St. Louis."

His gaze narrowed. "By your lonesome? You can't go by your lonesome. Your grandpap wouldn't let you do that."

"I ain't goin'—" She broke off as the sound of clatter wheels caught her attention. "It's comin'. The stage-coach is comin'!!" She strained her eyes to catch the first glimpse as it came around the bend. Excitement gripped her and she was barely aware of Willis's obnoxious presence.

"Heeeaww!" the driver shouted, rounding the stand of cottonwoods that had blocked her view. "Heeaww! Get along there!" The horses raced down the road and entered Lizard Lick at a heart-stopping speed, scattering pebbles and sending up a cloud of dust in its wake.

"Whoa!" The horses were reined in beside the stage office, and the driver barely waited for the stagecoach to stop moving before he leaped down from the high seat. "Howdy, Miss," he said in his loud, booming voice. His narrowed gaze took in the luggage beside her. "Be the two of you all we got in passengers today?"

"They's two of us right enough," she answered. "But this'n," she said, jabbing her thumb at Willis, "he ain't one of 'em."

"Well, where's the second one then? We ain't got all day. I got a schedule to keep, miles to cross, an' Lizard Lick ain't more'n ten miles from my startin' point."

Rainey looked anxiously down the street. "We can't leave without Thorne," she said. "He's just seein' to the horses."

"He better hurry 'cause I can't wait." He lifted her bag and piled it in the luggage rack and began strapping it tightly.

"You're plannin' on goin' someplace with Thorne?" Willis demanded, curling his fingers around her forearm. "What for, Rainey?" His fingers tightened, digging into her flesh. "You ain't got no business runnin' off with him. You're mine. You know you are. I been waitin' a long time for you to grow up."

She jerked at her arm and frowned up at him. "Leave go of me, Willis!" she snapped.

The stage driver frowned at them. "What in hell is going on?"

"She ain't goin'," Willis snapped. "Put her bag back down."

As the driver hesitated, a hard voice spoke. "Leave the bag where it is!"

Rainey breathed a sigh of relief. Thorne was back. He'd settle Willis's hash. As the two men faced off, she climbed aboard the stagecoach and settled herself on the seat. She wasn't going to allow anyone to stop her from enjoying this moment. She was going to St. Louis, and with Thorne.

It was only a moment before Thorne opened the door and entered the stagecoach. Rainey peeked out the window and saw Willis staring at her, and the look in his eyes sent a chill sweeping through her. There was hatred there and she felt the heat of it as the stage gave a lurch and jerked forward.

But moments later they rode out of town and she settled back again. Willis Johnson was only a small fly that had been effectively swatted by Thorne. He had taken care of her problem, just as he'd always done. She could forget about Willis and everything he represented.

Later that day they reached Canton. It was there they would transfer to the train. Rainey's excitement was so great that it colored her cheeks and brightened her eyes, giving her a glow that made passersby stop to look at her. They waited on the platform while the train shuddered to a stop beside it. It was then that the conductor, who had been waiting for that exact moment, jumped down from the train and pulled out the steps.

"Need any help with those cases?" he asked Thorne.

"No. I can manage," Thorne replied. "We might as well go on board, Rainey."

She climbed the steps and looked down the long, narrow car that seemed full of travelers. "Where should we sit?" she asked.

"Wherever you like," he replied. "Providing the seat isn't already occupied."

Rainey hurried down the aisle, her gaze going from one seat to another. Most, she found, were already occupied. And when she found one that was not, the seat next to it had been taken. She was despairing of finding two together when they reached the end of the car, but there, as though waiting for the two of them, were two seats. She scooted quickly into the window seat, while Thorne tossed their cases onto the shelf above and then seated himself beside her.

"All aboard! All aboard!" The conductor's cry came from outside and it was followed by several people hurrying into the train to find seats.

Moments later the train jerked, then chugged out of the station.

The journey lasted most of the day. During that time Rainey watched out the window while Thorne pointed out different things to her, a cow nudging her calf, a horse and rider galloping across a meadow. They traveled over high gorges and deep ravines, crossed rivers and creeks and forests that were so dense it appeared as though nothing could penetrate them. As time passed and Rainey became accustomed to the swaying of the train, she began to relax, leaning back against the seat. The action made her bodice pull closer against her breasts, and she felt Thorne's eyes on them.

Although his gaze made her hot, she gave no sign when she spoke. "You're so good to me, Thorne."

"Why do you say that?" he asked, admiring her with his eyes.

" 'Cause it's true." She lifted her gaze to his. "Ever since you come to the mountain you been lookin' out for me. You always seen a need in me afore I ever knowed it was there." She covered his hand with hers. "You been a true friend. Nobody could ask for a better one."

He took her hand in his and stroked her palm with his thumb. "I want to be more than a friend to you, Rainey. Surely you know that by now."

She lowered her gaze quickly, evading his eyes. "I ain't so sure I know what you're talkin' about, Thorne."

"Yes. You do." He leaned closer and his voice was a husky whisper. "You haven't so easily forgotten how it felt to have my mouth on yours for the first time, Rainey." She blushed rosily. "And neither have I."

"It ain't seemly to talk like that," she muttered.

"Why not." His eyes had become dark, slumberous. "Why is it unseemly to speak of an act that is so pleasing to the senses? Even now I remember how smooth and silky your flesh felt beneath my fingertips, and how your breasts became taut and swollen when I stroked them."

"Thorne!" she protested, her voice barely above a whisper. "Don't."

"Why?" he asked again. "How can I keep silent when I think of it all the time. I even dream of you at night, Rainey, the way you were at the dance. With the swell of your breast pushed above your bodice, so creamy and smooth. And I remember how your hair felt silky when I smoothed it back, how your breath came so quickly, and how the moistness I found between your love-swollen lips almost drove me wild with desire."

She pulled her hand away and covered her face with her hands. "Don't say such things to me," she said, her breath rising and falling unevenly. "Not with all these folks around us. They'll know, Thorne."

"They can't hear me," he said. "But I guess I'd better stop before my body reveals my thoughts to them."

Her gaze flashed quickly to that part of his anatomy that would give away the evidence of his desire. His breeches were strained to the maximum, pulled tightly across his muscled thighs. Her face flushed hotly and she looked quickly away and heard him laugh softly.

"Don't, Thorne," she said.

He pushed his hat forward and leaned his head back against the seat. "I think I'll catch a nap before we get to St. Louis. You should, too, Rainey. There's no telling when we'll have the opportunity again."

Then, without another word, he closed his eyes and began to breathe deeply.

Rainey stared at him, amazed that he could so easily fall asleep when her own emotions were so tightly wound that she was certain she'd never be able to achieve that state.

She looked out the window again and stared outside at the landscape, which was passing by at such a swift pace. But the scenery wasn't enough to hold her attention. Her thoughts were on Thorne, and the words he had spoken to her. She mulled them over and over in her mind. He'd said he wanted to be more than friends. Was that his way of telling her he loved her as a man loved his wife? She wished he'd been more explicit. But he had not, had only raised a lot of questions in her mind that she couldn't answer without his help.

She considered waking him and asking those questions, but quickly dismissed the idea. She couldn't talk about such things on a train that was filled with people. But the minute they had time alone, she wanted answers. And by golly, she would have them.

Rainey thought she was too excited to sleep, and yet, she fell into that state unaware. Several hours later she woke to a loud voice, calling out the next stop, and realized it was the conductor. "Next stop, St. Louis," he shouted. "St. Louis, next stop."

The screech of metal against metal told her the brakes were being applied, and she looked out the window and saw they were pulling into the station.

"Did you sleep well?" Thorne asked.

"I sure did," she replied.

"Stay close to me when we leave the train," he said. "The station is large enough that you'd get lost for sure if we get separated."

Thorne hired a carriage and they rode down the street toward the outskirts of town.

"Is it far to your pa's house?" she asked.

"Not far. In fact, there it is." He pointed to a house that looked more like a mansion, built high above the river to allow the scenery to be enjoyed with no danger to the house or its occupants.

Rainey suddenly felt nervous. Her hands were clammy and her pulse beat rapidly. Had Thorne told his sister he was bringing a visitor? Would she resent Rainey for coming?

Her question was soon answered. Thorne barely had time to lift the knocker when the door was opened by a black-suited man who was obviously the butler. A woman appeared at the bottom of the stairway behind him. She was elegantly dressed in a plain skirt over which she wore a jacket decorated with deep-scroll braid.

"Thorne!" she cried, winding her arms around his waist and pressing her head against his chest. "I can't believe you've really come."

He laughed huskily and swung her around in a flurry of skirts before setting her on her feet again.

"Who is that?" she asked curiously, spying Rainey. Then, "My God, you haven't gone and got married, have you?"

"No. Not married." He pulled Rainey forward. "Yet. This is Rainey Watson. Rainey, meet my sister, Eloise."

Having no knowledge of how society women greeted each other, Rainey gave Eloise's hand a quick shake. "Howdy, ma'am," Rainey said shyly. She stared at the elegant woman with bemusement. Although she was similar in features to Thorne, her appearance was definitely not masculine. Her hair was dark, her eyes brown, and her skin a flawless white. It was obvious that she took great care to protect it from the sun.

Eloise smiled at her. "Rainey. That is a beautiful name. I bet I can guess how you came by it, too."

"It don't need no smarts to know that." Rainey laughed, then blushed rosily covering her mouth quickly. "Oh, golly. I don't mean no offense, ma'am. I wasn't sayin' you ain't right smart. I meant you was right if you was athinkin' I was born on a rainy night."

"I knew what you meant, dear child. You have no need to apologize for anything." Eloise looked at her brother. "She's absolutely precious, Thorne."

Rainey frowned at her, wondering if she should take offense at the other woman's words. She'd never been called precious before. At least, not since she'd passed the toddler stage. But since Thorne ignored his sister's remark, Rainey decided to do the same.

"How is Father?" Thorne asked his sister.

The question seemed to embarrass Eloise because she blushed. Her eyes slid away from her brother's gaze. "Nothing has changed since I wrote you," she said slowly.

His gaze narrowed on his sister's rosy cheeks and he frowned. "He's still lingering on?"

Eloise's gaze flickered to Rainey, then back to Thorne again. "We need to talk," she said. "There's something you should know. but I'm sure Rainey is exhausted. I'll get her settled in one of the guest rooms, then I'll meet you in the library."

Rainey was quick to protest. "No need to bother yourself about me," she said. "I'll just set myself down on these here steps and wait for you and Thorne to finish with your jawing. Thorne will be anxious to take a look-see at his pa."

"Don't be silly," Eloise said. "I wouldn't dream of leaving you on the stairs when there are perfectly good rooms upstairs that have been made ready for visitors. Go on in the library, Thorne. I'll be back momentarily."

Eloise gripped Rainey's arm and hurried her up the stairs.

They entered the first room on the right and Rainey's astonished gaze traveled around the elegant room. "Are you sure nobody will object to me stayin' here?" she asked, her gaze lingering on the magnificent four-poster bed.

"Of course they won't." Eloise looked around as though she were looking for something, then shrugged her shoulders. "I think you'll be comfortable enough here," she said. "I'll send Bertha to draw you a bath."

Rainey felt affronted. "I had a bath afore I left home," she said indignantly.

"I wasn't implying that you were dirty, dear," Eloise said quickly. "I just thought a hot bath might relax you. The evenings here can be long and drawn out if you're overly tired. I'm sure you would benefit greatly from a nap."

"A nap?" Rainey stared at the woman as though she'd taken leave of her senses. "I don't need a nap. I'm a woman fully growed."

Eloise looked momentarily confused. "Oh, dear," she said. "I seem to be making things worse."

The woman looked so concerned that Rainey felt sorry for her. Her rising temper immediately cooled. "I guess we both been barking up the wrong tree. Prob'ly 'cause you're city folk and I come from the hill country. I can see I got me a heap of learning to do afore I lay my trap for the teacher man."

"Lay your trap? For the teacher man?" Eloise looked even more confused. "Oh, dear. I don't think I quite understand."

"Maybe Thorne better explain," Rainey said. "I ain't right sure we're up to understanding each other."

Eloise summoned up a quick smile. "You're probably

right. Anyway, I must hurry back to Thorne before someone else reveals my duplicity."

Rainey watched the woman leave the room, wondering what on earth she'd meant by her final words.

Thorne stood before the open liquor cabinet and poured a shot of brandy in a glass. He tossed it back and swallowed quickly. Why had Eloise been so insistent about him waiting in the library instead of going to see his father? he wondered. Perhaps, he thought, it was because his father had already passed on.

But no. That couldn't be the reason. She'd told him there'd been no change in the elder Lassiter's condition.

Thorne had mingled feelings about his father. Uppermost was sadness that the two of them could not be reconciled before it was too late. Beneath that, though, was anger that his father had spent most of his life hating his only son and trying to make his life miserable.

Picking up the liquor bottle, Thorne poured another drink just as the door opened and Eloise entered the room.

"It's so good to have you home again, Thorne," she said, sliding her arms around his shoulders and giving him a quick hug. "I was so afraid you wouldn't come."

He returned her hug, then put her away from him. "I wouldn't have if not for the circumstances," he said bluntly. "Now tell me about Father's illness. Just how serious is it?"

Instead of answering his question, she posed one of her own. "You are still bitter, aren't you?"

"Why should I feel any differently now than on the day he threw me out?" Thorne asked. "Even though he's at the end of his life I'm almost positive his attitude toward me is the same."

"Oh, Thorne. He has changed. He is sorry about the estrangement between you."

"I find that hard to believe." He turned away from her, and stared unseeingly out the window, feeling suddenly plagued by old wounds.

"But it's true," she protested.

"Then why didn't he send for me? He knew where I was."

"He's a proud man, Thorne. You know that. He's never admitted to a mistake in his life, and you are very much like him."

"No! I am not like him," he said sharply. "I would never deliberately hurt a child of mine." He stared reproachfully at her. "Do you know how I felt, Eloise, living in this cold house? Being constantly told how worthless I was? He said that I had bad blood in me . . . the O'Brien blood of my mother."

"I know. We both know how opinionated father has always been—"

"That is no excuse," he said coldly. "If he considered the O'Briens so far below him, then why in hell did he marry my mother?"

"Because he loved her," she said simply. "He loved Mary O'Brien more than life itself. My mother knew that when she married him."

"And still she married him."

"Yes. She thought her love would change him."

"And in the end she ran away."

"Yes. She was strong enough to fight for his love with a ghost but not strong enough to fight a memory."

"A memory? I'm afraid I fail to see the difference in a ghost and a memory. Aren't they one and the same?"

Her eyelids lowered, hiding her expression. "There are things about Father that you don't know. And I'm not certain you can understand."

"And you do?" He arched a dark brow. "You always

were more sympathetic to his moods. But I'm afraid
nothing will change my opinion of him."

"Don't be that way, Thorne," she replied. "It's time
to put old hurts behind us. Time to get on with our
lives."

"Like that old man has done?"

"Thorne, please." She gripped his forearm tightly,
and her eyes were bright with unshed tears. "Just listen,
please. Listen to what I have to say."

"I'll listen." He slumped down in a stuffed leather
chair. "But it will make no difference to my way of thinking. I'll make you a promise, though, Eloise. I won't
utter a word of recrimination to him when I go see him.
I'll let him leave this world without more bitter words
being spoken between us" He eyed her grimly. "I take
it he *is* still alive. That I came before it was too late."

She lowered her lashes again and looked discomfited.
"Yes. It's not yet too late."

He straightened his length and set his empty glass
down on a nearby table. "Then perhaps I'd better see
him now."

He strode across the room, but she hurried to stop
him. "No, wait!" She took a deep breath. "Somebody
is blackmailing Father, Thorne. We're in danger of losing the shipping lines."

His gaze narrowed. "What do you mean by that?
Who's blackmailing him? And what for? And why
should the shipping lines be in danger." He rapped the
words out with the rapidity of bullets fired from a repeating rifle.

"I don't know who's blackmailing him. Father refused to say. As to why he's being blackmailed? I'm not
sure. He told me it was an early indiscretion of his,
something that happened twenty years ago. But that, if
the events ever came to light, he would be so disgraced

that his shipping lines would go under. He said if that happened he would end his life."

"Well, hell!" Thorne exclaimed. "His life is over anyway, isn't it?"

Her eyelashes lowered, covering her expression. When she spoke again, her voice was low. "No. Not yet anyway."

A muscle worked in his jaw. "Then he's better?"

Her hesitation was barely perceptible. Then her eyelids swept up and she met his gaze with a long look. "You wouldn't have come if I hadn't sent the letter," she said quickly. "I only did what I had to do, Thorne. You must understand that."

Something flickered in his gray eyes. "What are you talking about, Eloise?"

"Father is not anywhere near death," she admitted slowly. "He's in his office at the shipping lines."

The heat in the bedroom was oppressive, almost stifling in intensity. It increased the discomfort Rainey felt at having been left in the room by herself. But she could understand Eloise's determination to be alone with her brother. It had been years since they'd last seen each other, and they must be busy catching up on lost time, as well as discussing family matters.

Nevertheless, Rainey continued to feel uncomfortable. She was a stranger here, unused to their ways.

She frowned. Hadn't Eloise promised to send someone to her? A maid, perhaps? Had she forgotten?

Suddenly Rainey realized how thirsty she was. Her mouth was dry as cotton. She needed a drink of water, and there had been plenty of folks standing around the entry hall, gawking at them, as though they had nothing better to do with their time. One of them could have shown her around.

Finding the room suddenly stifling, she wiped beads of sweat from her brow, then crossed to the window and attempted to lift it. But her efforts proved useless. The window was either stuck or had been nailed shut.

Determined to get some fresh air, she opened the door to the upper hallway, and went straight to the nearest window and tugged at it. To no avail, though. It, too, refused to open.

Further examination told Rainey a latch kept it in place. She pushed it aside and the window slid smoothly up, allowing cooler air to flow through. She was leaning out the window, breathing in the fresh air when she heard footsteps coming up the stairs.

Spinning on her heels, she saw a tall, elegant man with silver hair approaching. His austere black suit revealed his position in the household, that of a butler, obviously sent to attend her needs.

Her lips twitched, preparing for a smile that died when she saw the coldness of his silver-gray eyes.

They slid over her.

"What in hell are you doing here?"

Her back stiffened immediately, and she glared at the offending butler, who appeared to think himself above other folks. "Certainly not waiting for the likes of you!" she snapped.

His gaze slid past her to the open window. "Came in the window, eh?" His glare was thunderous as he scanned her person, making her painfully aware of her shabby attire. "What are you trying to steal, girl? Answer me!"

She didn't like the way he spoke to her, nor the tone of his voice. It was downright rude. "You got no right to accuse me of stealin'," she said sharply. "It would serve you right if I told Thorne how you talked to me."

He looked taken aback by her outburst. "I was let into this house by Thorne's own sister," she continued.

"And I ain't so sure you got a right to be, or you woulda knowed that already."

"Thorne?" he questioned, narrowing his cold eyes on her face. "What do you know of Thorne?"

"More'n you're ever gonna know," she said waspishly. "An' he ain't gonna take it kindly that somebody like you—a man who's been hired to do a day's work for his folks—is atalkin' to me like I was no better'n a two-legged low-down polecat."

"Young woman! You keep a civil tongue in your head before I call the constable and have you jailed for break-ing and entering. And whatever else I can think of." His cold gray eyes measured her and seemed to find her lacking in every respect.

How could someone who appeared so stately be so vicious and unfriendly? she wondered.

He started toward her and she backed up, snatching a vase from a nearby table and hefting it over her head. He stopped abruptly, his gaze on the vase.

"Put that vase down," he ordered crisply.

"Make me," she said, her lips pulling back into a cold smile. She raised it higher, preparing to fling it at his head if he moved closer.

"I'm not beyond doing exactly that!" he snapped. "Now put it down before I take it away from you."

"You an' who else?" she spat, her fury almost over-coming her. "It's agonna take more'n some mean ol' man like you to wrestle it away from me."

"I have no intention of wrestling with you, young woman, but I will not allow you to break my priceless Ming vase." His voice rose until it was loud enough to carry all over the house. "Now put it down! If you break it, I'll take its value out of your worthless hide."

A scurrying on the stairway caught his attention. He turned momentarily to look at the servants who seemed frozen in a huddle, their mouths open as though they couldn't quite believe what they were seeing.

"George!" The man who faced Rainey snapped. "Come here immediately. Take this woman out of my house before I lose my temper and teach her some manners."

"You come one step closer, George," Rainey threatened, "and this here vase ain't gonna be so priceless no more."

"Uh, s-sir," the man called George stuttered. "I th-think there's s-something you should know."

"Do as I said!" the other man snapped.

"Uh, y-yes s-sir." George took another step upward.

"You come anywheres near me, George, and I'm gonna lay your head open with this here fancy jar!" Rainey threatened.

Suddenly a stern voice rang out. "What in hell is going on here?"

Nine

A guilty flush swept over Rainey as she met Thorne's eyes. "It weren't my fault, Thorne," she said quickly. "It was his. He started bad-mouthing me the minute he laid eyes on me. An' you know how quick my temper is." She looked beyond Thorne to Eloise. "I'm sorry, ma'am. I get riled real quick-like, especially at folks who act like they're better than other folks. But I shouldn't of started a ruckus in your house. It was plumb unmannerly of me and I—"

She broke off, realizing suddenly that nobody was listening to her apology. Instead, they were all staring at Thorne and the hateful butler who'd been shouting at her and calling her names.

"Thorne." The man Rainey believed to be a butler spoke, his voice and expression expressing his surprise. "You've come home, Son."

Rainey's jaw dropped. The man she'd thought to be a butler was Thorne's father. Even as she realized that fact she wondered at his swift recovery. She'd been led to believe he was on his deathbed. But the man who stood before them was surprisingly healthy.

The elder Lassiter held his hand out to Thorne, who appeared not to notice. "I'm only here because I thought you were dying," Thorne said coldy. "Since you're obviously not—judging by the way you were shouting at Rainey—then I'll leave."

The elder Lassiter's hand dropped to his side. "So you thought I was dying, did you?" he asked coldly. "I suppose you came back for the pickings."

"You have nothing that interests me," Thorne said shortly. "I came because of Eloise." He held out his hand toward Rainey. "Come, Rainey. We have no more business here."

The elder Lassiter looked at Rainey with some confusion, then his gaze returned to his son. "The young woman came with you?"

Rainey set the vase carefully on the table. The room was thick with tension and she had no intention of breaking the vase and making things worse than they already were.

"She came with me and she's leaving with me," Thorne said in reply to his father's question.

"I-I, but you can't blame me for what happened, Thorne?" His voice was loud, blustering. "What in hell was I supposed to think? After all, the window was open and she was standing beside it, and I naturally assumed that—"

"It matters little to me what you assumed." Thorne gripped Rainey's forearm and urged her down the stairway. "We'll be at the Hotel Carmichael tonight, Eloise. If you want to see me, then you'd best come this evening because I intend to leave for home on the first available train."

"Thorne," Eloise said, "please wait. Just talk to Father. Listen to what he has to say. You could work past your differences if both of you tried."

"I have no wish to work anything out with him. He sent me away and it hurt at the time, but not now. I'm convinced it was the best thing that ever happened to me."

Thorne stopped in the doorway. "I'd appreciate it if you'd send our baggage to the hotel."

"At least wait until the carriage is brought around," she cried. "You can't walk back!"

"We're used to walking." He strode swiftly from the house, pulling Rainey along beside him. The heels of her shoes beat a rapid tattoo against the brick walk as they began the long walk back to town.

Under different circumstances Rainey would have enjoyed the fresh air. But she felt the tension that vibrated through Thorne like a banjo string that had been wound too tightly. She knew he was under a strain, knew as well that it was caused by seeing his father again. What had happened between them to cause such enmity between father and son?

"I know it's none of my business," she finally said. "But don't you think you should of talked to your pa?"

"No! I don't!" he said shortly.

His strides lengthened so that she had to run to keep up with him. She tripped over her long skirt and cried out sharply. "Wait, Thorne! Don't go so fast. I ain't used to runnin' in a skirt." When his footsteps slowed, she continued her argument. "Think about your sister. She prob'ly sent for you because she hates the bad feelings betwixt you an' your pa. He ain't gonna live forever, you know. Think about that, Thorne, an' how you'll feel when he's dead and buried. It'll be too late to make amends then."

"You don't know anything about it, Rainey." His voice was gruff, hard. "I'm sorry you had to bear the brunt of his anger. It wasn't personal, though. And don't take it like that. It's just his way. He's like that . . . with most people."

"Then, he didn't mean what he said about throwin' me in jail?"

"Oh, he meant what he said," he replied. "He would

have done it and had no qualms about it. I just meant his harshness . . . the way he spoke to you . . . wasn't personal. He's like that with everyone . . . mean and hateful."

Rainey realized Thorne must have had a miserable childhood with a father like Eugene Lassiter. She wondered if he was still tormented by the past. "You don't like him, do you? Your own pa." She hated to see this side of Thorne. He'd always appeared so strong, able to overcome any odds. But seeing his father again had opened up old wounds which he'd tried to keep hidden. "It wasn't all his fault, Thorne. My temper is somethin' terrible. You know that. And he reckoned I was a thief, makin' ready to steal his valuables." She looked down at her gingham gown. "I reckon I ain't dressed fine like your sister. Even the maids in that house back yonder looked finer dressed than me. I guess I never put much stock in things like that before. Guess I should expect city folk to look at me like I ain't much better'n ol' catfish bait."

He stopped abruptly and gripped her shoulders firmly. "You stop that, Rainey," he said harshly, giving her a hard shake. Then, before she could recover, he tilted her face upward and pinned her with a hard gaze. "You always look beautiful, Rainey. Even when you're wearing your breeches and shirt. And in that gingham dress you're wearing, you outshine the sun itself. You'd be as good as anyone—even if you were buck naked."

She flushed at the heat in his eyes. "You're a nice man, Thorne Lassiter."

"No, Rainey, I'm not. If I were so nice, you wouldn't be forced to walk to the hotel."

"You like walking, Thorne. And so do I. You got plenty of reason to know that."

He uttered a harsh laugh, then squeezed her shoulders lightly. "Are you sorry I brought you here?"

"Of course not! I'm havin' lots o' fun," she protested. "An' you would, too, if—" She broke off, hearing the sound of carriage wheels rattling along the gravel road behind them. A quick look told her it was the same carriage that had taken them to the Lassiter home.

Following her gaze, Thorne swore under his breath. "If that old devil has followed us, thinking to sway me, he can go to hell!" The carriage stopped beside them, and Eloise stuck her head out the window.

"Oh, Thorne, I'm so glad I found you!" She sounded near tears. "Please let me take you to the hotel."

Grudgingly, Thorne relented. He helped Rainey into the carriage, then settled back against the seat.

"I'm sorry I caused a ruckus in your house, Eloise," Rainey said softly. "I never meant to. And if I'da knowed that old man was Thorne's pa, I woulda let him call me whatever he wanted without answering back." Her lips thinned. "I ain't sayin' I woulda liked it, though. Just that I'da kept my mouth shut."

Eloise flushed deeply and wrung her hands, obviously distraught. "I'm so sorry, Rainey. He shouldn't have spoken that way, but—no!" Her eyes flashed as though with fury. "I won't apologize for him. He's an old devil. Nobody should be spoken to that way!"

Rainey's anger drained away. "He thought I was a thief," she said. "I 'spose he can't be blamed for treating me like that."

"Don't make excuses for him, Rainey," Thorne said tightly. "He always says what he thinks, no matter the consequences."

Deciding the subject needed to be changed, Rainey pointed out the window. "Would you just look at that, Thorne. Ain't that the most beautiful house you ever seen? And the people . . ." She pointed toward a man and woman who were dressed in the latest fashion. He, wearing nankeen trousers and a brown woolen sack coat, she, in an ankle-length walking dress of navy-blue cloth. "Those two are dressed up real fine, just like the folks who was ridin' on the train." She frowned across at Eloise. "Come to think of it, that lady's dress is like yours, Eloise, and the man's outfit is sorta like Thorne's." She didn't realize Thorne's attire had been stylish six years before when he'd left St. Louis for the mountains. But then, men's fashions didn't change as quickly as did feminine attire.

Rainey looked down at her own gingham dress, the only one she possessed, and was again discomfited. It was no wonder the elder Lassiter had looked at her as though she were a lowlife bent on stealing his possessions. He would have thought the same if he'd seen her come through his front door.

Feeling embarrassed that she'd been too birdbrained to notice how ill-kempt she appeared to others, she sank back against her seat and clasped her hands together.

As though guessing her thoughts, Thorne covered her hands with his own. "Those who judge people by their outward appearance are usually lacking themselves, Rainey. There's not another woman in St. Louis as courageous as you are."

Her lower lip trembled at his tender words, but they did little to soothe her embarrassment. He hadn't said she was dressed well, only that she had courage. Well, she didn't want that to be the only thing about her that he noticed. And, somehow, she felt betrayed by his words.

As though guessing the state of her thoughts, Eloise said, "People won't be judging her by her appearance and finding her wanting, Thorne. Not after tomorrow."

"Tomorrow?" he queried.

"Yes. Tomorrow morning we're going shopping."

He gave her a sharp look. "You're wrong there,

Eloise. Tomorrow morning Rainey and I are going home."

"Pshaw!" she exclaimed. "You're staying here long enough for Rainey to see St. Louis. And if I have my way she'll be wearing new gowns while she's doing it."

"Oh, can we, Thorne?" Rainey pleaded, wide-eyed at the thought. "The gowns don't matter. I'll just pretend folks don't notice me . . . no matter how hard and mean they look. But I would sure enough like to see St. Louis whilst we're here. I ain't likely to ever come again. Especially if Robert's gonna stay in the mountains for good. An' I need to know somethin' about St. Louis, an' the way folks here live, so's we can jaw about it on long winter nights."

"Robert?" Eloise looked confused. "Who is Robert?"

Rainey smiled at her. "He's my intended. Only he don't know it yet."

"He doesn't?" Eloise looked at Thorne, whose expression had become grim.

"No," Rainey replied. "And it's kinda funny in a way 'cause I plumb forgot all about him since we left the hills behind."

"You forgot him?" Eloise smiled widely. "That's quite unusual, Rainey. One doesn't usually forget about one's fiancé."

"It ain't really my fault, you know. Thorne drove him right out of my head."

"How did he do that?" Eloise asked.

"It's always been that way," Rainey explained. "Ever since he come to the hills. When I'm with Thorne I don't never think of nobody else. Guess it's a good thing, too, or I'd sure enough be having the miseries right now from bein' so long without Robert. You sure enough oughtta see him, Eloise. He's a right sprightly-looking man . . . looks so fine it makes my stomach all hot and trembly when I'm lookin' at him."

Eloise laughed out loud. "That's quite a speech, Rainey. You have such a quaint way of speaking I could listen to you forever."

"You best get an earful now then," Rainey said. " 'Cause I already decided I gotta change my way of jawin', or he'll never cast his eyes towards me."

"Your jawin'?"

"Yeah. My speech-makin'. Robert don't jaw like us hill folks. Thorne don't, neither. I figure that's the reason Robert ain't been paying me no heed. But that's afixin' to change. Thorne's gonna help me learn feminine wiles." She leaned closer to Eloise. "That's kissin' and such, in case you didn't know." She slanted her eyes toward Thorne. "He's a mighty good teacher, too."

"I think I'm beginning to understand the situation." Eloise sent a sideways look toward her brother. "I'm quite surprised that you're willing to help Rainey in this endeavor, Thorne."

His face had darkened slightly, as though flushed with color. But when he spoke, his voice was cool. "Why should you be surprised, Eloise? Rainey knows she can count on me for whatever she needs."

She chuckled lightly. "Especially if it happens to be exactly what you need, as well," she said with amusement.

Rainey's gaze flickered between brother and sister. They seemed to have a secret from which she was excluded. But never mind, she thought. It was only natural. They were family . . . blood related. And they were entitled to their family secrets.

A shout from outside caught her attention and she stuck her head out the window and saw a boy playing amidst a field of green. And there, just a little farther on, she saw a ribbon of silver and realized it was the river.

Perhaps she'd be allowed to explore the park later,

she thought. After they had filled their bellies. That thought made her realize how hungry she was.

She pulled her head back into the carriage and stared accusingly at Thorne. "I'm starved enough to eat a buzzard, Thorne. When're we gonna eat?"

Ten

The next few days were a whirlwind of confusion for Rainey. Most of her time was spent in the hotel room, where she was poked and prodded and measured for new gowns, and laced into a corset that was so tight that she could hardly bend in the middle, let alone take a deep breath. Several hours of each day were filled by the tutor Thorne had hired to teach her what a lady of society should know. Although Rainey saw some sense in the elocution lessons, since hill-folk and city-folk speech were worlds apart, she didn't understand why they wanted to teach her how to walk and eat.

Rainey had little time to spare for Thorne during those hectic days. But, since they rarely saw each other except for the evening meal—she guessed he was tending to family affairs.

It was on the fourth day that he entered their suite late one evening and, with hardly a glance at her, strode across the room to the window. She could tell by his expression that something was bothering him. "Is something wrong?" she asked.

He looked at her and sighed. "Not really. I just don't like being here again. Nothing has changed. I doubt if I ever will. I don't know why I expected Father to—" He broke off and struck his forehead with his palm.

"Dammit! Will I never learn? He almost convinced me he'd changed."

"We can go back now if you've a mind to leave, Thorne," she said. "I already learned—shucks! I mean . . . I have already learned so much." She enunciated the words slowly as she had been taught, then said quickly, "Heck, I'd haveta be plumb stupid to mislearn anything that ornery tutor you hired for me teaches. He makes me so *dadblamed* mad! But he says the quicker I learn, the faster I'll get rid of him, so I just purely take in every word he says whilst he's there and—"

"Promptly forget it when he's gone," he concluded with a chuckle.

She ducked her head, then looked up at him with impudent mischief. "Well, it takes too dadblamed long to think about what I'm agonna say afore I say it, that I just purely forget what I had in mind by the time the whole things done thought out."

"Never mind," he said, squeezing her shoulder gently. "I wouldn't have you any other way, kitten."

"You wouldn't?" She heaved a long sigh. "It's just too bad I ain't smitten with you 'stead of the teacher back on Thunder Mountain. Then I wouldn't have all these lessons crammed down my throat."

"Yes. It *is* too bad." His eyes were doing funny things to her, she realized, making her feel that upside-down possumlike feeling that she'd experienced before, and he wasn't even touching her.

Having been reminded of the only lesson she'd ever had in kissing, she said, "When are we gonna—going to—start the other lessons again, Thorne?"

"The other lessons?" His eyes twinkled. "What other lessons, Rainey?"

"You know," she mumbled, lowering her eyelids to hide her expression. "The kissin' lessons, Thorne."

"We could practice now if you'd like?"

"I guess we should," she said, trying to hide her eagerness. "Since that's a mighty big part of courtin'. It is, ain't—isn't it?" When he nodded, she lifted her face, pursed her lips and closed her eyes, readying herself for his kiss.

"Look at me, Rainey." His voice was gruff yet incredibly gentle.

Opening her eyes, she stared at him with a mixture of confusion and disappointment. "You ain't gonna kiss me, Thorne?"

"I *am* going to kiss you, Rainey," he said gruffly. "But I want your eyes open when I do." He tilted her head back farther, then gently ran his thumb over her lower lip in a sweetly caressing gesture. "Open your mouth, Rainey." His breath whispered across her forehead.

Wordlessly, unable to speak if her life had depended on it, Rainey opened her mouth. And when his lips parted, then lowered to cover hers, she swallowed his breath.

Thorne's tongue slid smoothly inside the moist cavern of her mouth, and her eyes widened as she felt a tingling sensation that traveled from the pit of her stomach to the tips of her toes. The kiss was even more intense than the last one had been, and the feeling of weakness even more pronounced. His tongue searched out every nook and cranny in her mouth, even sliding over her teeth and gums, and the look in his eyes as they held hers was so heated that her senses reeled and her legs threatened to buckle.

Rainey wanted to lean against him, needed his strength to hold her upright but resisted the temptation since he seemed to deliberately hold his body away from her own. Although she'd always thought kissing meant touching bodies as well as mouths, she had obviously been mistaken. Thorne was the expert on such things.

By the time Thorne released her, Rainey was shaking like a leaf. Only then, did he take her in his arms. And surprising as she found it—even though he ran his hands soothingly over her back and shoulders, he managed to keep their lower bodies apart. When she looked down, she realized why. His maleness was apparent, as was his urgent need. And Rainey felt intrigued by that fact. She supposed he would have reacted in the same manner if he'd kissed any other woman.

Somehow, the thought of Thorne kissing anyone else was hateful to her. She had always considered Thorne her own special friend, and she had never seen him pay attention to another female. Except, she corrected herself, at that *dadburned* square dance.

Even as heat spread through her body from his warmth, she remembered how angry she had been at the woman he'd been dancing with. That in itself was peculiar since there hadn't been that same degree of feeling about the woman that had occupied Robert Golden's time.

Was it really love she felt for Robert? she wondered. Had it only been his outward appearance that she'd been smitten with. She had no way of knowing what he was like beneath the surface, could only judge him by appearances, by the face that he showed to those around him.

Would Robert be as gentle, as caring of her feelings as Thorne always was? He'd have to be, she decided, if he was going to marry her. She decided right then and there—with Thorne's body pressed so close to hers— that she wouldn't take less than someone like Thorne . . . or Thorne himself.

She looked at Thorne with new eyes then. The woman he chose would indeed be a lucky one. Rainey suddenly wished that woman could be herself. But he was so far above her that he'd never look at her that way . . . would he?

Rainey lifted her eyes and studied him closely, and realized there were new lines in his face, lines that hadn't been there when they'd first arrived in St. Louis.

Why hadn't she noticed them before?

Suddenly Rainey felt ashamed. She was so selfish. She hadn't once thought about what he must be going through, living so close to the man who'd treated him so badly.

"Thorne . . . I'm sorry. I've been selfish, thinkin' only of myself. I never noticed you were so bothered. What's makin' you feel so bad?"

Thorne couldn't find a way to answer her. He didn't want to trouble her with his own particular demons. It was enough that he must bear them himself. He thought about how it would be to have her always beside him and knew that it would be heaven on earth. Rainey was a caring woman who would never think of holding back any emotion that she felt. She would love and laugh as easily as she burst out in anger. And she wasn't one to hold a grudge, either—quite unlike himself.

He pretended nothing was wrong and smiled down at her. "I was just wondering if you'd like to practice kissing again," he prevaricated. "I certainly like teaching you."

"Kissing weren't . . . wasn't any part of your thoughts," she said shortly. "Something's going on here that you're not talking about. You're hurting and not wanting me to know. But I'm gonna know, Thorne Lassiter! Even if I have to nag it outta . . . out of Eloise. Now you tell me what's worryin' you!"

He sighed and sat down in a stuffed chair, pulled her onto his lap and tucked her head against his shoulder. He trailed one finger along her shoulder blade, leaving a trail of fire in its wake. Her breast firmed, and began to tingle with desire.

"My father has himself in some kind of mess," he said gruffly, seeming not to notice how she was reacting to his touch. "I wouldn't worry about it if he were the only one who would suffer the consequences. But he's not. Eloise is in danger of losing her inheritance and I can't just go away and forget about it."

"No," she said softly. "You couldn't, Thorne. You care too much about her, even if you don't care about your pa. An' I ain't so sure you don't care about him, too, but you just won't admit to the feeling."

"I care nothing for him," he said shortly. "But I do care about my sister and her future."

"Then what're you going to do about her troubles?"

"Solve them if I can."

She grinned up with twinkling eyes. "Then what're we waiting for?"

"You are not to get involved in this," he said grimly. "There is no way of knowing how far these people will go to get what they want, and if things go bad I don't want you around."

"How am I going to keep out of all this danger if I don't have no notion what the whole thing's about?" she complained.

"I suppose you're right." He settled her more firmly on his lap, a fact that pleased her no end; she liked being snuggled so close against him. "Well, it appears my father is paying hush money to some blackguard. Has been doing so for several years."

"Hush money?" she questioned. "What's that?"

"He's being forced to pay for someone's silence about his past indiscretions," he explained. "But now the scoundrel wants even more. He wants the shipping lines itself."

"That's the way of varmints like that."

He cocked a dark eyebrow. "What do you know about such things?"

"I know plenty. We got folks like that in the Ozarks, too. Not many, but some. They was a time before you come, that the Widder Simmons was squeezed outta ever'thing she owned." Rainey barely noticed she had dropped back into her old speech patterns. "First he took her plowin' mule, then he come back a few days later and wanted the milk cow. And the more she give him, the bolder he got. Finally he wanted to put her outta her home. But she balked at that. Decided if she was gonna lose her home, then she might as well sell it and move on. She went to the sheriff and he took Smoky Callahan to jail, and ever'body in the county went to the trial to find out what it was the widder was tryin' to hide."

"And did you go, Rainey?"

"'Course not!" she snapped. "I mind my own business and expect others to do the same."

"Well, Father imagines the people of St. Louis will do like most of those folks in the Ozarks. He believes if his secret is revealed his reputation will suffer so badly that the shipping lines will go under. And, strange as it may seem, Rainey, his reputation probably means more to him than the shipping lines do."

"So he's just gonna turn his business over to the lowlifes?"

"Apparently so," he replied. "If they persist in their demands."

"Well hellsfire, Thorne. He ain't got much guts. Or else that thing you was talkin' about—that indiscretion thing—was a lynching thing." She looked curiously at him. "Is that it? Do you think he killed somebody a long time ago?"

"No. I don't know the circumstances. He refuses to tell me. But he claims he took no man's life. All he will say, is that the incident happened more than twenty years ago, said he'd thought it was over, that nobody would ever know." He sighed deeply. "It seems his past has finally caught up with him."

"I feel kinda sorry for him," she murmured.

"I don't see how you could do that after the things he said to you." His voice was gruff, angry. "He ordered you out of his house, Rainey, threatened to have you thrown in jail."

"I don't hold no grudge against him, Thorne," she said. "He's your pa."

"That was merely an accident of birth," he said bitterly.

They both fell silent then, and after a moment Thorne resumed his soothing movements, stroking his palm down her hair, and she shivered beneath his touch. "I like that," she said softly.

"What?"

"You touching me thata way."

His lips curled in a slight smile. "You give me strength, Rainey."

"How do I do that?"

"Just by being here."

His hand moved down her back and he shifted her closer against him. She liked the feel of his hard, muscled chest against her taut breasts and wished the fabric of their clothing wasn't between them. Immediately she was shocked at the thought. He tilted her face toward him and bent closer, his gaze locked on hers. "Don't you think we should resume the lessons, Rainey?"

"Oh, yes, I can't think of anything that I'd rather do right now," she said, opening her mouth to make it ready for his.

His mouth was lowering to hers when a knock sounded on the door.

Eleven

With a muttered oath, Thorne set her on her feet and crossed to the door. He jerked it open and stared with consternation at his sister. "Eloise!" he exclaimed. "What are you doing here?"

Eloise looked flushed, as though she'd run a long distance. "It's Father, Thorne. He wants to see you."

Thorne uttered a sharp oath. "He can just go to blue blazes, Eloise. I have no intention of running when he calls. He can damned well wait until tomorrow."

"Please, Thorne." She twisted her hands in agitation. "We've been talking together most of the afternoon and he's ready to explain the past . . . what that black-guard is holding over his head."

"He told you that?" he asked darkly. "If he's so ready to disclose his secrets, then why didn't he tell you?"

"I don't know. But I think it's because whatever it is, he believes to be too delicate for my ears." Her lips twisted wryly. "I believe he's on the verge of giving up the shipping lines, Thorne, just to keep his past hidden. You must come!"

"Damnation!" Thorne snarled. "It seems he's leaving me no choice except to go."

Rainey spoke up then. "You never had another choice, Thorne. You know that. It's just not in your nature to turn aside when there's trouble."

"It seems you know me well, don't you, kitten," he said tenderly.

"I reckon so."

He turned his attention to his sister again. "Do you want to keep Rainey company while I'm gone, Eloise, or will you be coming home with me?"

"I'd rather stay here," she said quickly. She looked at Rainey. "If you don't mind." Without waiting for a reply, she turned to Thorne again. "Please don't say anything that will stop Father from explaining. We must know what they're holding over him before we can put a stop to their efforts. I don't intend to lose my inheritance without a fight."

"I promise I won't lose my temper."

It was a promise he was unable to keep after hearing what his father had to say.

The elder Lassiter told the story of a young man who had an affair with a Cajun woman, believing he was doing harm to nobody, even though he was married. After all, he reasoned, New Orleans was a long way from St. Louis, and his family need never know of his indiscretions. But a child had come of the union . . . a girl who was now a young woman. She had sent her cousin to St. Louis to claim, not only her own inheritance, but everything Eugene Lassiter owned. His wealth, his business, and the shipping lines.

Thorne looked with revulsion on his father as he tried to deal with what he'd been told. "So I have another sister," he said slowly.

"Not a sister!" the elder Lassiter spat. "Didn't you hear a word of what I'm saying, boy? She's half Cajun! She's white trash! Nothing to be bothered with."

A wry smile crossed Thorne's face. "Perhaps that's the reason behind all this, Father. Maybe she's tired of being ignored and is determined to create enough impact to be noticed."

Eugene Lassiter's eyes were stormy. "The gal is greedy. What are we going to do about all this?"

"What we are not going to do is hand over Eloise's portion of the shipping lines," Thorne said grimly. He strode across the room and looked out the window, his hands stuck in his trouser pockets, his mind worrying at the problem. Finally he looked back at his father, his gaze was razor-sharp. "There's really only one solution," he said. "The girl is your daughter and she's due a portion of the estate. Sign that part over to her. It's her right. Give her her inheritance now."

"Give it to her! *Her* inheritance! Why, dammit, boy, she has no inheritance! Didn't you hear me say she's a Cajun? What do you think people would say if they knew? Dammit! We have to keep this quiet. The Lassiter reputation is at stake."

"The Lassiter reputation? You're a fool, old man," Thorne said coldly. "You're so damned bigoted that you'd deny your own flesh and blood. But then, I should have expected you'd react this way. You've looked down on me for the Irish blood that flows through my veins since the day I was born." He watched the old man look away. "What about her mother?" Thorne asked. "The Cajun wench you consorted with. What does she say about all this?"

"She died a long time ago, Thorne. But she would have had no part in such underhanded dealings." There was certainty in Eugene Lassiter's voice.

"Did you love her?"

"Love a Cajun? God, no. How could you believe such a thing, Thorne? I loved your mother. But, Grace . . . she was the most beautiful woman I'd ever met. Black hair and dark eyes. I was captivated from the first moment I laid eyes on her."

Thorne's fury surged forth, almost overwhelming him. "You bastard. Did my mother know? Is that what killed her? The knowledge of your illicit affair?"

"Her death wasn't my fault!" His father was shocked. "Your mother died of a lung ailment."

"I heard different," Thorne said. "I heard she died of a broken heart."

"Then you heard wrong. It was a lung ailment that took her."

Thorne was silent for a long moment. "Did she know about her, the woman you were involved with?"

"Yes." Eugene Lassiter sighed heavily. "She found out. And confronted me with it. I promised her I would never see Grace again."

"Did you keep your word?"

"I couldn't," Eugene whispered. "I tried so hard to stay away from her, but I couldn't get her out of my mind. Grace was so beautiful, so gentle, that she became an obsession. I traveled a lot on business then, spent a lot of time in New Orleans. And she was there . . . so close that—" He broke off, as though suddenly remembering to whom he was talking. When he spoke again, his voice was cold. "This is all the fault of that girl. She's no good. Not like her mother. Grace was so like her name. Beautiful of face and of heart. There wasn't an ounce of meanness in her body. She would never deliberately cause anyone hurt."

"Like you did?"

"Dammit, Thorne! Can't you leave our relationship out of this? It has nothing to do with this business. I only revealed the past to you because I thought you might be able to do something to stop her so the shipping lines would stay in the family. Maybe the girl would listen to reason if you talked to her."

"Why do you think I can get anywhere with her if you haven't been able to?"

"Because you always know the right thing to say," his father replied. "Except when you're talking to me. Besides, I haven't spoken with the girl."

"Then who have you spoken to?"

"A man who claims to be her cousin."

"Claims to be?"

"I suppose he is her cousin."

"Are you sure Grace had a daughter?" Thorne asked. "And that you sired her?"

"Yes. I had the records checked. She was Grace's daughter and Grace was a virgin before we met." His expression became hurt. "I don't know why she didn't send word about her pregnancy. I would have provided for the child."

"Perhaps Grace thought you'd done enough by siring the child."

"Don't be cruel, Thorne."

"Why not? I learned it from a master."

Eugene Lassiter's eyes slid away from those of his son. "You're not going to make any attempt to help in this matter, are you?"

"I'll do whatever I can," Thorne replied. "Not because of you, though. My sister—Eloise—is my only concern." His eyes were cold as they met his father's. "Where do I find this elusive sister of mine?"

"I don't really know," Eugene Lassiter said. "I suppose you'll find her where I found Grace. In the bayous of Louisiana."

"And her name?"

"Eulalie," he said softly. "Eulalie Grace Lassiter."

"She uses the family name?"

"Yes. But without any right."

"She should have had the right, Father. No child should be denied its father's name."

"She's a bastard, Thorne. And a Cajun. I would never

give my name to a child like that. Why, I'd be the laughingstock of St. Louis."

Thorne turned away in disgust. Although his father obviously held tender feelings for Grace, he had none to spare for her child . . . his own flesh and blood.

When Thorne returned to the hotel, Rainey knew by his expression that things had not gone well between the Lassiter men.

Eloise, who had been waiting anxiously for his return, hurried toward her brother. "Did he tell you what it was all about, Thorne?" she asked.

"Yes. He told me," Thorne replied shortly. "It seems, dear sister, that you are not my only sister."

"What?"

"It seems our father sired two girls, Eloise. The other one's been kept secret for the last twenty years. Her name is Eulalie."

"But Mother—"

"Didn't have a thing to do with her, Ellie," he interrupted. "She is the offspring of our father's alliance with another woman."

"Someone we know?"

"No. He met her in New Orleans."

"Oh, God!" She sank onto a chair. "How could he do that?" she cried.

He squatted on his heels before her and took her hand in his. "Don't let it concern you, Ellie," he said. "I'm going to see her . . . talk to her, try to straighten things out. Father says it would ruin his good name if her identity was discovered . . . because of her bad blood."

"She's Irish?"

Thorne laughed loudly. "No. Her mother was a Cajun. But her blood, of course, must be bad, since it didn't come from the Lassiter line. He called her trash. I've often thought it was too bad he couldn't duplicate himself and come up with a female that he could mate with. It's the only damn way he'll ever find anyone he considers pure enough for himself."

"Horsefeathers!" Rainey spat. "What's wrong with the man anyway? Seems to me he oughtta be down on his knees thankin' the good Lord for giving him another child to love."

"Father?" Thorne's eyebrows lifted. "Why should he love Eulalie when he doesn't love us . . . the children he raised?"

"Eulalie," Eloise said softly. "I have a sister." She smiled at Thorne. "When can we meet her? Where has he been hiding her all this time?"

"He hasn't seen her, nor even talked to her. It's the girl's cousin that he's dealing with. A man."

"A cousin? Is he related to us?"

"No," Thorne replied. "He comes from Eulalie's mother's side of the family."

"I want to see her," Eloise said softly.

"So do I," Thorne said. "And I intend to do just that."

"You're not going to dispute her claim, are you, Thorne? She's entitled to an equal portion of the shipping lines . . . when Father is no longer in charge."

"I know. And she'll get her share. I'll see to that. But she can't have everything. Anyway, the scheme has failed since the old man disclosed the secret."

"Not really," she said. "He won't want anyone else to know. Which means the secret must be kept."

"We'll see," Thorne said. "Eulalie may be reasonable when she realizes we're not intent on depriving her."

"We'll be going to Louisiana then," Rainey said.

"We?" He arched a dark brow.

"I'm going with you, of course."

"Are you now?"

"You can't expect me to stay here in this hotel while you're gone, an' I sure as hell ain't gonna stay at your pa's house."

"Rainey!" He pretended to be shocked. "Hasn't that tutor taught you anything? Ladies do not swear."

"This'un does when she's good and mad, and that's what I'm agonna be if'n you run out on me, Thorne Lassiter."

His laughter was loud. "When you get angry you forget everything you learned these last few days. But you need not fret, kitten. I have no intention of leaving you behind. I haven't finished with the lessons yet."

She grinned at him. "I was hoping you'd say that," she said.

Eloise's gaze flickered between the two of them. She looked confused, like she might have missed something, but wasn't entirely sure what it was.

"I suppose I should go home now," she said quietly, gathering up her shawl. "You won't leave without saying goodbye?"

"No. I'll get tickets for tomorrow but we'll come to the house before we leave," Thorne said.

"You'll bring Eulalie home with you?" she inquired.

"I'm going to try, Eloise."

"You think she won't come?" she asked.

"I don't know. It depends, I guess, on her circumstances."

Eloise's look became almost angry then. "I could shoot Father when I think of that poor child being raised apart from us. I just hope she doesn't blame us for his shortcomings."

"She is probably bitter about it. Why else would she be blackmailing him for the shipping lines?"

"We don't know for certain she is doing any such thing," Eloise reminded him. "There's only that man's word about that. Perhaps he devised the plan on his own."

"The whole thing certainly bears looking into before we know the truth of the situation," Thorne said grimly.

Eloise left then and Thorne turned to Rainey. The thunderous look slowly evaporated and his tense body began to relax. "Now where did we leave off?" he asked gently, reaching for her.

"I think your hand was about here," she said, pulling it around her waist and leaning toward him. "And your mouth was just a little above mine." She stood on tiptoe so that he could see where she meant. And when he resumed the position, she opened her eyes wide, then likewise her mouth and pressed her lips against his.

She heard a muttered word just before his tongue darted into her mouth and literally stole her breath away. She thought the word was "minx" but couldn't be sure. Anyway, it suddenly didn't matter anymore.

The only thing that mattered was the way he made her feel as he taught her the many ways to feel a perfect kiss. And that was good enough for her.

Twelve

The next morning Rainey donned one of her new gowns—a suit of black cashmere trimmed with bows on the sleeves and front—and descended the stairway to the lobby. It was her intention to surprise Thorne with a breakfast tray when he woke.

Crossing the lobby to the restaurant, she paused at the entrance and stared with surprise at the man who brushed past her.

"Cage?" she said questioningly.

"Why, Rainey Watson!" He appeared as surprised as she was. "I didn't expect to see you here."

She sensed an uneasiness about him and it colored her words. "What in tarnation are you doing here, Cage?" she asked. "Followin' me around?"

His face flushed crimson, but he recovered quickly and extended his hand to grasp hers. "If I followed anybody, you'd be my choice, Rainey," he said with a grin. "But the fact is, my sales company is based in St. Louis, and I had to pick up more samples." He gestured toward the restaurant. "Could I buy your breakfast?"

"No." She grinned at him. "I was bent on atakin'—" She broke off and grimaced ruefully. "Dadgummit! I keep forgetting!"

"Forgetting what?" He looked around quickly as

though wondering if the something she'd forgotten might be in the lobby.

"Forgetting to watch my words . . . diction, they call it here." She dropped her voice so it wouldn't carry beyond them. "They're trying to make a lady out of me, Cage. But they're finding it mighty hard going."

"You were already a lady," he said gallantly, squeezing her hand lightly, making her aware that he hadn't yet released it. "So whoever *they* are, they're wasting time that could be put to better use."

She pulled her hand free. "*They* are Thorne—Thornton Lassiter. You met him at the barn dance—and his sister, Eloise," she replied. "And they ain't awastin' their time, neither—shoot! I mean either. Dagnabbit! This speechin' thing is mighty hard to get used to. I can't hardly say a word without first thinking on it."

"Don't worry about it," he advised. "I find you perfectly enchanting the way you are."

"Thorne's sister said those very same words, called me precious, too, but I ain't so sure. I mean, I would rather not stand out when it comes to speechin', and I do here in the city. Folks is—are—treating me mighty fine, though."

"As they should be," he replied. His gaze left her and traveled the stairway that led to the upper floor. "Is Thorne joining you for breakfast?"

"No. That's what I was gonna tell you before. We got us a suite that has two rooms for sleeping in and one for just living in. I never imagined folks needed so much room indoors, not 'til I come here. I come after breakfast for the two of us." When Cage's eyes narrowed slightly, she hurried to apprise him of the situation. "We ain't sharing a bedroom, Cage Larson, so don't you go thinkin' that."

"Of course you aren't," he said. "I never thought you were." He smiled widely at her. "Since you won't allow me to buy your meal, I'd better run along. I only have a short time to conclude my business here before I move on."

"You're selling your pistols and such to the people who run the hotel?"

He laughed abruptly. "No. I just had an appointment with a man who's interested in them." He looked around the lobby again. "We were supposed to meet in the restaurant an hour ago, but he never arrived. I suppose I'll have to catch him at his office."

"Maybe you should ask the hotel clerk. He mighta left a message," she suggested. "If he's just runnin' late you could set on one of those pretty little velvet seats over yonder. That's what they put 'em there for." She pointed at the velvet settees, which were placed at strategic points along the walls.

"No. The man—my prospective customer—was emphatic about the meeting place. Said if he wasn't in the lobby at the appointed time, then he would be at his office." He smiled at her again. "You better hurry and order breakfast, Rainey. The restaurant is already getting crowded."

"I guess I better, then," she said.

Muttering a hasty goodbye, Cage hurried across the lobby and out of the hotel, leaving Rainey to complete her task.

She entered the restaurant, expecting it to be crowded to capacity, and discovered that Cage had been wrong. Only a few people occupied the room, and those had already been served.

After seating herself, Rainey ordered coffee and some of the little French pastries that Thorne had been having for breakfast each morning since they'd arrived in St. Louis. When the items had been delivered to her, she signed the tab as she'd seen Thorne do and scribbled their room number on the paper, then hurried back to their suite.

She frowned heavily when she found the sitting room still empty. Thorne was usually up and about before now, and she had counted on him being awake to drink his coffee while it was still hot.

Setting the tray down on a small table, she sipped from her own cup and found the amber liquid had already started cooling down. She felt impatient with Thorne. She'd taken the trouble to fetch his breakfast and he wasn't up to appreciate that fact.

She hefted the tray, crossed the room and rapped softly on his bedroom door. When there was no sound from within, Rainey pushed open the door and strode to his bedside.

The covers were drawn to his chin and he breathed deeply, obviously sound asleep. She felt tempted to lean over and kiss him awake but managed to resist the temptation.

Placing the loaded tray on the nightstand, she allowed her eyes to devour his masculine face and she wondered momentarily why her heart always beat faster when she gazed upon him.

She shook him gently. "Thorne, wake up."

He opened sleep-dazed eyes and saw her. His lips curled into a lazy smile. "I was dreaming about you, kitten," he said gruffly. "And now you're here."

His smile sent her pulses skittering. "I brung—brought—you some coffee," she said, exerting extreme control to keep herself from climbing into bed with him and pressing her lips hard against his. Just the thought of doing so brought warmth to her cheeks. "And . . . and I brought something sweet for you . . . something special. The very thing you dream about waking up to every morning. It's right here waiting for you. All you got to do is reach out and take it."

He blinked up at her as though she'd lost her mind. Then, incredibly, his face flushed with color. His gray eyes darkened, became brighter, as though he had developed a sudden fever. "What did you say?" he asked huskily.

"I said I brought your breakfast," she said, enunciating each word clearly and slowly.

"Damn!" he swore softly. "I should have known." He pulled the covers higher until only his eyes were exposed to her view. "Go away, Rainey. Get out of here."

"No! I ain't goin' to." She glared down at him. "I took the trouble of fetching your breakfast and now you can damn well eat it!"

He grunted something unintelligible.

"Was that a thank-you, or a 'go away, I want to sleep' grunt?" she asked. When he didn't answer, she reached out and yanked the covers away from his upper body, exposing it to the cool morning air. "Why, Thornton O'Brien Lassiter!" she exclaimed. "You sleep in the raw!"

"Get out of here, Rainey!" he said in a raw, husky voice. "Get out while you can."

"I won't do no such thing," she said in a teasing voice. She had him just where she wanted him now. He was much too dignified to get out of the bed while she was in the room, so she could sit there at his bedside and drink in the sight of him while pretending to tease.

As her gaze dwelt on his wide, muscled chest, her mischievous grin slowly faded. Heat spread through her lower body, moving to her most secret parts and making her feel weak.

Oh, God, but he was beautiful. He was enough to turn a poor girl's head . . . unless she'd already met her true love . . . she quickly added. And she *had* met hers. Hadn't she? Yes, of course she had. But it was funny how she had to work so hard these days to recall Robert

Golden's face. Her memory of him seemed overshadowed somehow by the face before her, by the man whose eyes were so hot and slumberous, whose lips were so finely chiseled; the man whose muscles rippled as he reached out and cupped the side of her face with his right hand.

She couldn't have stopped herself from responding to his touch if she'd tried. And she didn't. She leaned into his palm, loving the feel of his flesh against hers, feeling captured by that moment in time, wishing it would never end.

Rainey knew she should look away from him, knew she should break loose from his hypnotic stare, but she could not. She was caught by his gaze, too helpless to look away from it.

She felt intoxicated with his nearness, as though she'd drunk a whole quart of Grandpa's special white lightning. Her nostrils twitched at the musky scent of his body, and she felt the heat flowing from him, could see the hot glitter of his eyes just before his hand slipped behind her head and pulled her down until her mouth hovered only inches above his.

Rainey shivered with longing. Nothing had prepared her for this. Not the kisses that had gone before—even though they'd set her heart to racing and her body to burning.

Nothing.

Oh, God, she hungered for him so, the way a baby hungered for its mother's milk. And all the while she remained suspended above him, wanting, hungering, voraciously waiting for his next move, aching desperately for it.

"Rainey," he whispered huskily.

And then his mouth covered hers, demanding, insistent. His tongue probed for entrance, and she opened her lips eagerly, feeling the moist, thick intrusion and shivering as electric tingles spread outward from the center of her desire.

He pulled her onto the bed then, spreading her length over his, and she clutched at his shoulders, straining urgently against him as she uttered a low moan of desperation.

That sound—her moan—was the catalyst that caused his lower body to swell dramatically. His manhood pulsed, throbbing with desire, a fact that she could not ignore since there was nothing between them except a thin sheet and her own clothing, which somehow seemed to be coming apart at the seams.

Somewhere in the back of her mind, Rainey realized she should do something, should try to stop what was happening while there was still time. But when she felt Thorne's hand close over her bare breast, she couldn't force the words past the tightness in her throat. Not with his tongue working its magic on her, not when she was filled with such longing for closer physical contact with him. But she must, she realized. While there was still time.

Struggling to get her emotions under control, Rainey pulled away. "We gotta stop this," she said. "Else we're gonna find ourselves in trouble."

"It's too late, Rainey," he said. "We can't stop now. Just feel what you're doing to me." He pressed her lower body harder against his, and she could feel the throbbing of his masculinity. His eyes were glazed with passion. "You don't know how beautiful you are this way. With your soft, silky hair falling against my skin; with your eyes, glittering brighter than the brightest stars at night. And your lips . . . God, your lips, so soft and moist, like early-morning dew against the petals of a perfect rose. And your breasts—" His fingers caressed her taut nipples, tormenting her. "How can you ask me to stop now, Rainey," he whispered hoarsely. "It's too late to go back now." His mouth closed over hers again, and she realized he was right. It was far, far too late. There was no turning back. She was in his arms, being held, being touched in a way that set her body on fire, and she didn't want to stop him, even though she realized she should. Yet she could not. There was no way she could disguise her pleasure from his touch or her need for it.

When Thorne released her mouth, and fumbled with her remaining garments, Rainey moaned and tried to pull his mouth to hers again. "Thorne," she pleaded, "don't stop now. I need it, need you to make this hurtin' go away."

"I will," he muttered, kissing her deeply once again. She knew he was watching her face closely, and realized he wanted to see the rapt, anguished need in her expression.

Suddenly he rolled her over, until he was above her and she strained toward him, her mouth opened for his possession. "Do it, Thorne," she cried in anguish. "Hurry, please hurry."

He lifted her slightly and lowered his mouth to cover her breast. She cried out and arched toward him, deriving such pleasure that she thought she would surely burst from it. He suckled her breast for a moment, then moved his mouth to hers again. "Are you sure you want this," he whispered.

"Oh, yes!" she cried. "God, yes, Thorne!"

And then her clothing disappeared, stripped away as though by magic, and his body was against hers with nothing to separate flesh from flesh. His hands rested on either side of her head as he pushed her legs apart slightly and leaned into her hips.

She whimpered helplessly, shaking all over from mindless need. As she tried to pull his head to hers again, he resisted, but only momentarily. Just a mere pause and he was kissing her again.

Rainey clung to him desperately, her body throbbing and aching, completely out of control, with no thought of hiding her feelings from him.

His mouth was on hers, his tongue thrusting inward, demanding; its very roughness making the pressure build wildly within her. She loved the feel of it, loved the feel of his aroused body leaning heavily into hers. It made her body rigid, tense with desire, and she pushed her hips helplessly upward. Helplessly, convulsively, she felt the tremors of his body as he sought to make his possession complete.

Suddenly, a sharp pain pierced through her. She gasped and stiffened. But it was gone almost immediately, and her body began to relax, allowing him to thrust deeper inside.

Oh, God! she cried inwardly. It was fantastic! More than she'd ever imagined. And all the while he drove deeper and deeper, thrusting farther with each movement. Faster . . . faster . . . faster, building toward some unknown height that dangled somewhere just out of her reach.

Rainey's heart fluttered wildly, leaping like a jackrabbit that was trying to escape from a hungry wolf. Frantically, she sought for that elusive something that would bring her to completion.

Uttering a low-pitched growl, Thorne arched his upper body, remaining that way for a long, shuddering moment. Rainey watched him, wondering at the expression on his face. He appeared to be experiencing some shattering emotion. Then, suddenly he collapsed on her.

Rainey's breathing slowed as she stared helplessly at the ceiling. What happened? she wondered. Where had he lost her? Why was she left with such an empty feeling? Wasn't lovemaking supposed to be a wonderful experience between a man and a woman? She'd always heard it was. She had always envied the newly married couples, whose happiness could be read in their expressions when they looked at each other.

Married. Thorne never spoke of marriage. That thought sent a shock racing through her. Yet it shouldn't have. She'd known all along that Thorne had been teaching her how to attract another man. Robert Golden. But somehow, in the learning, she had become entrapped by Thorne. Oh, God, she cried inwardly. She had fallen in love with him. And he didn't want her! Tears filled her eyes and slowly brimmed over.

Thorne rolled off Rainey and pulled her against him, feeling amazed that he'd been in the grip of such a strong emotion. Never before, in all his years, had he ever experienced anything like that. He stroked her silky hair, feeling the tension in her body, and silently cursed himself. He'd left her wanting and he hadn't meant to. But he'd wanted her for so long, so damned long, that when he found her wanting him, too, he couldn't hold back. But he would make sure she was satisfied, too, he told himself. In a moment he would be ready again, would take her slowly, give her time to climb those same heights that he'd climbed before giving her release.

He felt her move against him, felt the wetness of her tears against his naked chest, and he frowned. "Don't cry," he said softly. "I know you were left unsatisfied and I'm sorry for that. But I'll do better. Just as soon as I've had time to gather my strength I'll—"

Fury surged through her. She rolled quickly away, glaring up at him. "Don't bother yourself!" she snapped. "I don't need you to satisfy nothing!" She scrambled off the bed, snatched up her blouse and held it in front of her. "You polecat!" she cried. "You did that a purpose. You softened me up with sweet words, talkin' about my hair, all soft and silky and my-my eyes that was prettier than the stars at night. And . . . and my lips, all soft and d-dewy like rose petals. And all the time you was—was—" She broke off, unable to continue the tirade.

He frowned heavily. "You weren't trying to resist, Rainey. In fact, you were begging me for more."

"Kisses, you lowlife! Nothing else. You was—were— supposed to be teaching me how to catch Robert's eye. But you had more in mind. You—"

"Don't be a fool!" he snarled, sliding his feet over the edge of the bed. "You came to me, not the other way around."

"My grandpa would kill you if he knew what you done," she said. "He trusted you! And so did I!"

"Well, you shouldn't have!" he snapped.

Her mouth hung open for a moment, then snapped shut again. "You're even proud of what you done!"

"Not proud," he said wearily. "But if there's any consequences you have no need to worry. I'll take care of you."

"What are you talking about? What do you mean conse—" She broke off as realization set in. "You're atalkin' about a baby, ain't you, Thorne? You're a-thinkin' I'm gonna have a baby." She turned away from him, apparently overwhelmed by the notion.

He stood and took a step forward, sliding his arm around her shoulder, but she jerked away from him. "Let me alone," she snapped. "I don't want you to touch me. Not ever again."

"Don't be stupid," he said. "This isn't all my fault. You shouldn't have come into my room like that."

"I've been here before. And don't you call me stupid, neither."

"Don't you know that a man is most vulnerable when he wakes up, Rainey," he said in a more gentle voice. "No," he sighed. "I guess you wouldn't know. Oh, damn!" He raked a hand through his hair. "This is a mess."

"I didn't make the mess, Thorne, it was you. You had me all hot and bothered from your kisses and your mouth on me like you done—did—and you made me ache with the wanting. But then you took me like that, when you knew I didn't know nothing at all about loving, and—and—" She broke off, sniffling, trying to control her trembling lips.

"Rainey," he groaned. "If I could take it back, then I would, but I can't." He took her in his arms, but she jerked away from him.

"Don't do that!" she gasped. "It ain't—isn't—decent, Thorne. You ain't—you're not—wearing anything."

"I know." He dropped his arm. "I'm buck naked. Well, if you're so shocked, then run away. Like the little coward that you are. But we're going to have to face what happened, Rainey, and the consequences of our foolishness."

"There won't be any consequences," she said, lifting her chin and staring haughtily at him. "Nothing much has changed."

"Oh, it has, little mouse. Everything has changed. And you're going to realize it soon enough."

She turned and ran from the room, and this time he allowed it.

Thirteen

Rainey stood at the rail of the *Voyager* and watched the sun rise on the eastern horizon. The wind ruffled her hair, stirring the dark curls at the nape of her neck, as the boat plowed through the water at a swift pace on its way downriver toward New Orleans.

Having never been on such a large boat before, Rainey could have been quite happy, had the circumstances between herself and Thorne been different. But her angry words, hurled at him like stones after they'd shared the ultimate intimacy, had set the tone for their mood these past few days.

Many were the times she'd wished those angry words unsaid, but wishing wouldn't make them go away. She'd even considered returning to the mountains rather than going to New Orleans with Thorne—even though she greatly desired to see that city—but he had refused that notion the moment he'd been approached with it. The reason he'd given was the danger of a woman traveling alone.

She hadn't protested that decision, though. She didn't really want to go home. Things had changed there, almost the moment she'd left. The news-bearing telegram had reached the Lassiter home as she and Thorne were saying goodbye to Eloise. The contents hadn't been a shock, but why hadn't Grandpa waited for her return before he married Sadie?

Was it because he thought she might object? That she might even try to stop the marriage? Surely, he knew her better than that.

Footsteps thumping against the plank deck interrupted her thoughts, and she turned to see Thorne approaching. He halted abruptly as though he'd only just become aware of her presence. His eyes narrowed sharply on her face.

"What's wrong?" he asked gruffly. "You look like you've just lost your best friend."

"Maybe I have." The words were out before she could stop them, spoken without thought.

"No," he said gruffly, "you haven't, Rainey. The friend is still here, just waiting until you accept what happened as something that can't be changed."

She blushed rosily. "I wasn't thinkin' on—about—that, Thorne. I was thinkin' about Grandpa and Sadie. And them waitin' until I was gone before they tied the knot. Why do you suppose they did that?" Her eyes misted and she swallowed hard. "I f-feel like I was in the w-way and d-didn't even know it."

He slung a long arm around her shoulder and gave her a comforting squeeze. "You weren't in the way, kitten," he said gruffly. "But your grandpa has been thinking about marrying Sadie for the past year or more. I saw it coming and I thought you did too."

"I didn't, though," she admitted. "I thought Grandpa was satisfied with his life just the way it was. I didn't make no—any—demands on him, didn't make him help with the chores or nothing like that. I've been doing for us—earning our living—for the last few years." Her chin lifted slightly. "I ain't—am not—gonna do for Sadie and those lazy boys of hers. They're gonna have to make their own living."

"I imagine George plans on putting them to work. He'll provide the heavy hand needed for the job."

She looked out over the churning water again. "Grandpa don't like to do nothing but sit in his chair on the porch. He's not likely to stir himself to keep Sadie's boys busy. He's used to having things done for him."

"Maybe you did too much, Rainey," he said gently. "Did you ever think of that? A man needs to feel needed. And George has been feeling useless for a long time now."

"Useless? Why would he feel that way?" she asked.

The wind blew a lock of dark hair across her eyes, and he reached out and brushed it aside. "I would feel that way in the same circumstances."

She thought about his words. "If Grandpa felt useless he could have done something about it . . . could have told me . . . or something. Or stirred himself and chopped some wood or fetched the water from the spring." A sudden thought struck her. "Do you think he does those things for Sadie?"

"I doubt it. He'd be more likely to make those boys of hers do those chores."

"Yes. He would." She thought about her grandfather, the way she'd last seen him, sitting on the porch and rocking back and forth. He watched them leave without saying a word about what he intended, and she felt deeply hurt.

She looked at Thorne and realized he read that emotion in her eyes. "Thank you, Thorne."

"For what?"

"For being my friend."

"Haven't I always been?"

"Yes. But I was afraid you would be different now, since that—that night at the hotel."

"Forget about that, Rainey," he said, releasing her

abruptly. "What happened was a mistake and we can't allow one mistake to come between us."

"A mistake?" she asked doubtfully.

"Yes. It was. Now forget about it." He looked toward the horizon. "Beautiful sunrise this morning," he said solemnly. "But those clouds to the north are moving fast. More'n likely it'll rain before the day's gone."

He was wrong. The storm clouds stayed north of them. And the *Voyager* moved along at a brisk pace. Rainey spent most of the day on the deck, going below only when the darkness of night was upon them.

After taking a sponge bath and donning her nightgown, Rainey was on the point of climbing onto the narrow bunk bed, when a loud scraping sound was followed by a violent lurch that threw her off balance.

Throwing out her hands, she clutched desperately at the bed, trying to find something to hold onto as the *Voyager* lurched again, but the mattress offered no stability. It slid steadily toward the floor, taking her with it.

Scrape!

Oh, God, what's happening? Rainey barely had time for the thought. The boat lurched again, more violently than ever. She was thrown hard against the farthest wall. Thrown there as though tossed by a giant hand. She landed with a hard thud and was aware of a brief pain before an all-consuming blackness claimed her.

Thorne was on the deck when the boat struck the sandbar. He'd been aboard ships enough to know immediately what had happened and headed for the steering wheel as fast as he could run, which wasn't very fast, considering the angle of the boat.

The captain saw him coming and leaned out of the small window, both hands tugging hard on the wheel.

"Dammit, man!" Thorne shouted. "Turn this boat aside!" He was already beside the captain before he finished his words.

"Can't do that," the captain said. "Looks like we're stuck good." He swore roundly. "That damn sandbar wasn't there the last time I was through here."

"Well, it's there now." Thorne knew the man was a good navigator. He couldn't be blamed for the mishap. The Missouri was a treacherous river, and there was not a man alive who could predict the change in currents. The bottom was sandy and moved at will, waiting beneath the muddy water to trap the unwary traveler.

"Better call out the crew," the captain said. "We'll need the lot of 'em to estimate damages and get us off this shoal."

Thorne didn't have to call the crew. They were already assembling to assess the damage.

More than an hour had passed before Thorne thought about Rainey. And when he went to her cabin, he found it dark except for the moonlight streaming through the porthole.

"Rainey," he called.

No answer. Only silence. He scanned the room and sucked in a sharp breath of alarm. She lay on the floor, crumpled and unconscious.

Hurrying across the room, he knelt beside her supine form. A quick scrutiny found the blood from the cut on her head. He felt along her limbs, but nothing seemed to be broken. "Rainey?" he whispered, cupping her pale cheek. "Rainey!"

She groaned and her eyelids fluttered.

"Rainey," he said again.

Her lids lifted and she stared up at him, her eyes dazed and confused. "Thorne?"

"Where are you hurt?" he asked.

"Hurt? I don't know." Her gaze went past him to the

bunk, and the dazed expression cleared. "What happened?" she asked.

"We struck a sandbar."

She became suddenly aware of the absence of movement. "Are we stuck?"

"Yes." He scooped her into his arms.

"What are you doing?"

"Carrying you to bed." He looked down at her scantily clad form. "We need to get you under the covers."

He laid her down on the bed and pulled the quilt up to her neck. His fingers moved to her cheek, tracing lightly across her jawline. His thumb moved across her mouth in a movement that she found arousing.

Although Rainey felt weak, she became aware of heat seeping through her lower extremities, caused by his caressing touch. She knew she should pull away, yet she could not. Not when the heat of desire was spreading through her lower body so rapidly.

"Thorne," she said hesitantly. "I don't think—"

"Hush," he said. "I want nothing more than a kiss from you. Don't deny me that, Rainey."

He lowered his mouth and captured hers in a long, arousing kiss. She tasted the saltiness of his flesh and found that, too, was arousing. Her breathing became faster, and her fingers bit into his broad shoulders. She could feel the hard tautness of muscles and sinew as his tongue probed for entrance.

"No," she said, but she might just as well have remained silent. He used the word to gain entrance to the moist cavern of her mouth, and she shuddered at the quick penetration.

When he lifted his head, his eyes were bright with arousal. "Thorne," she whispered, "we can't do this."

He seemed to shake himself. "You're right," he muttered. "I had better go."

Even though she'd made him stop, she hadn't wanted

him to do so. And it was with a deep sadness, and an ache in her heart and body, that she watched him leave her cabin.

The *Voyager* was stuck on the shoal for two days. And during that time, another ship came by, saw their distress, and dropped anchor to offer them help. But their efforts proved useless, the *Voyager* remained firmly wedged on the shoal.

Finally, the captain decided to lighten the boat by ferrying its passengers to shore. Rainey was disappointed when Thorne decided to stay behind to help, but she kept that emotion firmly hidden from the others . . . especially from Thorne.

There were only a few children on the trip, but they screamed and laughed and chased each other frantically in their delight at having been put ashore. Rainey watched them at their games and was almost tempted to join them. But she remembered in time that she was supposed to be a lady of sophistication now. And if Thorne should come ashore she didn't want him to catch her involved in such foolishness. Not when she'd been trying so hard to convince him that she was a grown woman.

And there were many times that he did remember, but at those times they seemed to get in over their head. Like the time only a few days ago when he'd found her on the floor. If only she'd kept her mouth shut. He would have made love to her then, she knew. But would he have regretted it? Would she?

"There's no need to worry so much, pretty lady," a voice suddenly said. "The captain knows what he's about. We'll be on our way soon enough."

Rainey smiled at the young man who'd spoken. His was a familiar face—she'd probably seen him many times in the past week on board the boat—but they'd never been introduced. "I'm not really worried," she said.

"Then something else must have put that frown on your face." When she didn't answer, he smiled at her. "I know. I'm prying. But it's my nature to be inquisitive. Or perhaps you just don't want to converse with someone you haven't been introduced to." He looked over her head and made a beckoning motion with his hand. "We'll remedy that right now."

Before Rainey could reply they were joined by a young woman with bright-red hair. "What are you up to now, Sammy?" the girl asked with amusement.

"I need an introduction to this young woman, Charlotte," the man called Sammy said. "And since you appear to be a respectable young woman yourself, I decided you would do the honors."

Charlotte laughed. "I'm Charlotte Cross," she told Rainey. "And this is my irrepressible cousin, Samuel Eugene Cross."

Rainey smiled at both of them. "I'm Rainey Watson," she said.

"Rainey?" Sammy questioned. "It doesn't suit you. If your parents were going to name you for the weather, then Sunny would have described you better."

Rainey laughed and explained the circumstances around her name. Just then, lunch was announced and the three of them went toward the makeshift table where a meal had been set out. They continued to banter back and forth while they ate, and time passed swiftly without the three of them realizing.

When she learned the Cross cousins were stopping in New Orleans only long enough to board another ship, Rainey felt a mild disappointment. She had enjoyed their company immensely. The two of them had kept her from being bored while they were stuck on shore. "Where are you bound for?" she asked Charlotte.

"We're going to Europe," Charlotte said. "To Italy. I'm going to study painting there, and Sammy is going along to keep an eye on me."

"I'd rather keep an eye on Rainey," he said, with an irrepressible grin. "But, alas, you will soon be left far behind us." His eyes took on a dark glint suddenly. "A thought just occurred to me, Rainey. Why don't you come with us to Italy?"

"To Italy?" she questioned, wide-eyed. "My goodness, no! I don't have money for anything like that. I'm just hill folk."

"Hill folk?" he questioned.

"I come from the Ozark Mountains," she explained.

"The mountains?" He eyed her expensive clothing, making her aware of the reason he'd misunderstood her circumstances.

"I don't usually wear such finery," she explained. "Back in the hills I wore men's clothes. Couldn't have worn anything else while I was following my bee lines. There's too much brush a body has to run through. But I couldn't wear those things here. Thorne wouldn't have allowed it even if I'd had a mind to."

"Thorne?" Sammy questioned, raising an eyebrow. "Who is Thorne, Rainey?"

"His pa owns the shipping lines. He's the reason I left the mountains. I came with him."

"This Thorne you speak of," Sammy said. "He wouldn't be Thorne Lassiter, would he?"

"Yes. That's his name." She smiled at him. "You know him?"

"Not personally. But I've heard about him."

"I take it you're not married since you said your name was Watson," Charlotte said, and the warmth that had been there before was somehow missing now. "Are you engaged to Thorne Lassiter?"

"No," Rainey replied slowly. "But they ain't nothin' about the two of us to raise folks' eyebrows." She realized how she sounded as soon as the words left her mouth, but she couldn't recall those words that branded her as an uneducated hillbilly. Oh, why did she have to revert to that state when she became uncomfortable! And she *was* uncomfortable. These two, who had befriended her so quickly, had just as quickly abandoned her. She was certain of that. Knew it for a fact when she saw the look on Sam Cross's face as he carefully avoided her eyes.

It was Charlotte who finally broke the silence that had fallen between them. "Well, glory be," she exclaimed in an unusually high voice. "I see a dinghy leaving the *Voyager*. And there's another one. It looks as though they're coming after us. I guess that means the *Voyager* is finally afloat again." She clutched at Sammy's arm, curling her fingers around it, and blinked up at him in a seemingly deliberate attempt to ignore Rainey. "Come, Sammy. It's time to gather our things together."

Heartsick, Rainey watched the two of them leave her. She wanted to protest, to cry out that she was innocent of any wrongdoing, but she could not. Even as she'd claimed there was nothing about her and Thorne's relationship to raise eyebrows, she realized she was wrong. There was plenty to raise eyebrows. Nobody would approve of what they'd done . . . without the benefit of marriage papers.

Oh, God, she thought. She was a wanton woman, and if those two reported their conversation to the other passengers, then she would be branded as such, most likely shunned by everyone.

She carried that thought with her, walking apart from

the others as they headed toward the water where the boats would soon dock. She tried to keep her face expressionless, tried to keep others from seeing the deep hurt she felt, inflicted by the man and woman she'd thought were her friends. But the hurt was so deep, the wound so fresh, that she was afraid it would show despite her attempt to keep it hidden.

The dinghies drew closer, and Rainey could identify the tall, dark man seated near the front. It was Thorne. He had come for her. The cousins were waiting beside the water, and Rainey, unwilling to be near them, hung back slightly. The boat scraped against sand and tipped slightly as Thorne jumped out and dragged it nearer the shore. Then he was coming toward her.

Schooling her features into a calm mask, Rainey watched him stride swiftly toward her. "Are you ready to go?" he asked quickly. "Do you have every—" He broke off abruptly, his gaze narrowing on hers. "What's wrong, Rainey?"

"Wrong?" she prevaricated. "Why, nothing is wrong. Why would you think otherwise?"

He took her arm. "I know you, Rainey. Something has you upset. What happened?"

"Nothing."

His grip tightened. "Don't lie to me."

She swallowed hard. There was no use protesting. She was upset and he knew it. She jerked her arm away from him. "I ain't gonna—am not going to—discuss it," she said, her eyes bright with tears. "So you better just leave me alone, Thorne Lassiter. Just leave me alone!"

His lips thinned slightly but he remained silent for a long moment. Then, "Very well, Rainey. We'll leave it for now. Where's your knapsack?"

Realizing she'd forgotten it, she pointed toward the tree where she'd left it. He strode away from her, picked up the knapsack, then returned. "Let's go," he said, taking her arm again.

A quick glance told her the cousins had taken the first dinghy, which was already making its way toward the big boat. Since there was no chance of her being forced into close quarters with them, she hurried toward the remaining dinghy, which was already loaded with the remaining passengers.

The hefty oarsmen made short work of the journey to the boat, and shortly thereafter they boarded the *Voyager*. The Cross cousins were nowhere in sight. And Rainey was grateful for that fact. If she'd encountered them, Thorne would have noticed her doing her best to avoid them. And if that happened, he would be sure to question Sammy, and she didn't want him to know the shameful thoughts they had about her.

It was a week later when they arrived in New Orleans, and during that time Rainey had managed to avoid encountering the Cross cousins. Mostly, she supposed, because she rose at daybreak and walked the deck before they were up and about. By midmorning, when the other passengers began to put in an appearance, Rainey returned to her cabin and stayed there throughout the day, reading one of the many books she found in the riverboat's library.

Finally, they reached their destination. And when the riverboat docked in New Orleans, Rainey felt awed by the many ships that were anchored there.

"There are so many!" she exclaimed, standing at the rail and gazing greedily. "I never knew there could be so many boats in the world, Thorne!"

"It's the cotton," he explained. "An enormous amount—tons and tons of it—leaves the port each day. That and the other exports are what cause it to be so crowded."

The dock was a beehive of activity, and the noise level was severe.

After disembarking, they left the boat behind and made their way to a hotel. Thorne signed in for them and asked for a suite. When he'd finished, he handed the register back to the clerk. The clerk read it and then said, "We're mighty happy you decided to stay in our hotel." He looked at Rainey then. "Our suites are the finest in town, Mrs. Lassiter. I know you'll be comfortable in them, but if there's anything I can do to make your stay more pleasurable, don't hesitate to let me know."

Rainey flushed and said, "Thank you. I'll do that." Why had Thorne signed them in as man and wife? she wondered.

"Come along, Rainey." Thorne took her arm and led her toward the stairs. When they were alone in the suite, he turned to her. "Sharing a suite troubles you, doesn't it, Rainey?" he said. "Why? We shared one in St. Louis. It didn't bother you then. Why now?"

"I guess I know how the world feels about it now."

"The world? Or just two particular people. The Cross cousins, for instance?"

She looked at him, startled.

"Yes." His eyes were suddenly cold. "I know about that. I heard them talking together."

"They're going to start gossip."

"No, they won't."

"You can't know."

"I know."

"You spoke to them!" she accused.

"It was a short conversation. They won't be spreading loose talk again. Why didn't you tell me what happened?"

She shook her head. "I couldn't. I felt shamed."

He tried to pull her into his arms, and she moved

quickly to avoid his embrace. She couldn't trust herself where he was concerned. She looked beyond him, toward the window. "This is a mighty pretty room," she said.

"Don't change the subject. We need to talk about this."

"There's no need to discuss it," she said.

"Yes, there is. But we'll leave it for now." He studied her flushed face. "Do you want me to get you a separate room?" he asked quietly.

"No. That would be a waste of money."

"It's not a waste if it will make you feel better. But I don't like the idea of you being in another room in this city. You'd be completely unprotected."

"I'm just being silly," she said. "Don't pay me no mind."

"If you say so."

She forced herself to relax. "Which room do you want?" she asked, crossing the room to peer into one of the bedrooms.

"Either one. You choose."

"I guess I'll take this one, then," she said, her gaze on the flowered wallpaper. "The yellow flowers make it the next thing to sleeping outdoors. Don't you think so?"

"It's pretty enough," he said gruffly. "You might as well unpack your bags while I begin the search for Eulalie." She nodded her head and picked up her valise.

"I'll take it," Thorne said, reaching out to take it from her. "Where do you want it?"

"On the bed where it's easy to reach," she replied. "Do you want me to unpack yours for you?"

"No. I'll take care of it when I return." His gaze was thoughtful as he took in her disheveled state. "I'll have the clerk send someone up to draw you a bath. A good soak in a hot tub will do you a world of good. Perhaps you'll be able to sleep afterward."

"You're spoilin' me, Thorne," she said quietly. "I never took naps before I left the mountains."

"You never stayed up after dark, either," he said. "But that's all changing now. It was past time you broadened your interests. Just as soon as we find Eulalie I'm going to show you the city. There never was a more beautiful sight than New Orleans at night."

She smiled at him. "That sounds like fun, Thorne."

He touched her cheek gently, a light caress. "It will be, Rainey. I promise." He opened the door and with a quick smile, he stepped into the hallway and closed the door behind him, leaving her alone in the room.

Fourteen

It was still early enough for mist to be rising off the water when Thorne left the stronger current of the Red River and entered the sluggish water of the swamp. He paused there, laying aside the pole he'd been using to push them along to consult the rough map.

"According to the map this should be the channel that leads to the old man's house," he muttered.

"How can you tell?" Rainey asked. "This channel looks just like all the others we've passed." She scanned the channel opening for something that might set it apart from the others, but saw nothing different. Everywhere she looked were those strange protuberances they called cypress knees, which reached up from the watery depths. She leaned forward, trying to look at the map he held. "Why do you think this is the right channel?"

"Because, according to the map, the old man lives on the fifth channel. Since we've already passed four, this has to be the one we're looking for."

A loud screech startled Rainey, and she jerked, then settled back into the pirogue. "A screech owl," she muttered nervously. "Only a screech owl." She looked at the knife and rifle that Thorne had placed beside him in the pirogue and wished she'd brought a weapon of her own.

As though sensing her unease, Thorne spoke words of reassurance. "Relax, Rainey. We're safe enough as long as we stay in the pirogue."

"You don't have to worry none about me gettin' out," she said quickly. "I don't figger—intend—to allow an alligator to make a meal out of me." She leaned closer to one side of the boat and it swayed unsteadily.

"Keep still," he said shortly.

She glared at him, made angry by his tone, but he ignored her.

Rainey realized he was still angry at her decision to accompany him. He'd wanted her to stay at the hotel. But she'd refused to be left behind. Although they'd argued about it, Thorne had finally been made to see that leaving her behind might put her in more danger than she'd find in the swamp, because she'd refused to stay inside their rooms while he was away. She'd had enough of being confined while they'd been on the boat.

Even though he'd relented and allowed her to come, he'd made certain she was aware of his displeasure. He'd ignored her most of the time, speaking only when he considered it necessary to do so.

Rainey's lips tightened grimly. She could be just as unpleasant as he could. If he wanted open war, then he'd damned well have it. Even though she'd made that decision she was mindful of her need to keep a watchful eye out for danger. And, as they approached a submerged log, she broke the silence to warn him. "Log on the right."

The log moved then and opened its mouth and slid smoothly toward them. "It's a gator," she said quickly, leaning sideways to take a closer look.

"For God's sake, Rainey," Thorne snarled. "Can't you be still? Or is it your plan to offer yourself for his next meal?"

She glared at him. "Maybe I'd prefer the gator's company to yours," she replied shortly.

His expression darkened, and his mouth thinned, and she was prepared for a blast of thunder. But amazingly, his frown disappeared and he uttered a heavy sigh. "We can't continue this way, Rainey," he said gruffly. "If we do, both of us will be miserable. We've got a long way to go before we get to the old man's house. And neither of us will find any enjoyment if we keep snapping at each other. Why don't we try to put aside our differences? At least until we get back to the hotel?"

Her eyes misted with tears and she struggled to keep them at bay. "You snapped at me first," she said, forcing the words past the thick knot, which had suddenly formed in her throat.

"Does it really matter who snapped first?" His look was dark and intense. When she looked away from him, he said, "Never mind, kitten. I concede. And I sincerely apologize for quarreling with you." He reached out and took her hand. "Is that enough? Will you accept my apology?"

She nodded her head.

"Good." He sighed and squeezed her hand lightly. "I'm glad that's over. It's been hell ever since that morning when you crawled into my bed. I never imagined I would care so much that—"

"I crawled into your bed!" She stared at him, her tongue finally loosened by her indignation. "I never done no such thing, Thornton Lassiter! You drug me into that bed and then you—you—done what you done." The last words were spoken in a low voice, not much more than a whisper.

"What I done, my love," he said, imitating her own way of speaking, "was to make wild, glorious, passionate love to you."

"You can call it what you want to," she said smartly. "But they wasn't no glory in it for me." Although Rainey had fallen into her old speech pattern, she made no effort to correct it.

Thorne was silent for a long moment as he took in her words. He appeared to consider them carefully. "Can we discuss what happened that night calmly, Rainey? Like rational human beings instead of children, each blaming the other?"

"Prob'ly not," she said sulkily. "I don't feel very rational when we're discussing it. You messed up my life, Thorne. And it was all for nothing."

"What do you mean, nothing?" he asked with sharply raised brows. "You call what happened that night— nothing?"

"It *was* nothing. You got me all hot and bothered, wanting something real bad . . . and then you was done with me like I was an old, wet dishrag that was all used up and ready for the trash pile. And all that time I was— was—" She ducked her head to hide her expression from him. "I was all hot and bothered, still burning up with my need." She glared at him. "I never knew it would be like that. I thought it would be like—like a thunderstorm at night, with lightning flashing and thunder booming and . . . or something like that."

He laughed out loud. "A thunderstorm at night? What made you think such a thing? Who led you to believe such hogwash?"

"Suzy Belle. She said on her wedding night that she nearly exploded and—"

"Suzy Belle was probably not a virgin."

"What's that got to do with it?"

"Everything. Making love *is* sometimes like a storm, Rainey. It's supposed to be shared though. A mutual release, but apparently it went all wrong that night." His face was flushed and he struck the water hard with the flat of the paddle, then turned his attention to his rowing. His muscles rippled in his chest and arms as he dug the paddle into the water and propelled the pirogue forward.

Rainey was left with a feeling of confusion. Thorne had admitted there should have been something different for her that night, and yet he hadn't gone on to explain what had happened. He appeared to have put the matter behind him already. Well, she wasn't going to allow him off the hook so easily.

"Why wasn't it, then?" she asked, meeting his eyes with a long look. "If I wasn't supposed to be left hanging like that, then what went wrong?"

"Can we discuss this another time?" he asked shortly.

"No. You started this. Now you can just finish it. What happened, Thorne? Did I do something I wasn't supposed to do?"

"Of course not," he said shortly. "It was me. I just couldn't hold on."

"Couldn't hold on? To what?"

"I lost control of the situation, Rainey. Does that satisfy you? I wanted you so much, for so many years, that I couldn't hold out long enough."

Her blue eyes widened. He'd wanted her for years? What did he mean? Did she dare ask? No, not while they were on the water, with alligators surrounding them. But when they returned to the hotel, she would have her answer.

She looked out across the swamp. "Gonna be a nice sunny day," she commented.

He made a disgusted sound. "Don't try to change the subject now," he said gruffly. "You made me admit to some things that I've kept hidden, and now you're ready to forget what's been said. Well, I won't let you. We need to talk things out."

"I'm done with talking," she said. "At least about those things."

"Why?"

"Because this is not the time . . . or the place for it."

"Will there be a time and place?" When she hesitated, he said, "We've got some serious talking to do, Rainey. I won't allow you to forget what happened between us."

"Why?" She stared hard at him. "Why do you want me to remember?"

"Because I can't forget."

The feeling he put behind those words brought her up short. What did he mean by them? she wondered. What couldn't he forget? The loving itself, or that there might be consequences from the act? Would he believe that he must marry her? That he was bound to do so? No. She couldn't allow him to feel beholden to give her his name. She'd have to find a way to make him understand he need not do that. They could never marry if he didn't love her. Such a marriage would be doomed from the start.

"If you're thinking of marriage, Thorne, then you'd best know that I'll never marry without love."

Her words seemed to have angered him because his lips tightened and he dipped the oar savagely into the water and pulled hard on it.

They continued up the channel for a while then he pulled over and took out his map and studied it again. When he had his bearings, he folded the map again and put it into his pocket, then began to pole the pirogue forward, going deeper and deeper into the swamp.

Rainey began to realize why they hadn't used horses as a mode of transportation. The pirogue was faster than trying to guide a horse through the mire and swamp of tangled underbrush of trackless forests. It glided over withered grass and brown leaves like a light bark canoe over water, while the yellow-circled eyes of a marsh hawk, perched on a graying limb, followed their every move.

Rainey was uneasy in the swamp. It had a ghostly look to it that gave her a creepy feeling as though she were wandering through the land of the dead. The bleached skeletons of long-dead trees did nothing to dispel that notion, either. Instead, the limbs appeared to have a ghostly light this early in the morning, and the wispy strands of moss reached down from the overhanging limbs like long skeleton fingers.

Although it made her uneasy, Rainey was not so fearful that she was unable to see the incredible beauty of the swamp. A sense of magic, not found in any other place, resided there. And the farther they went into it, the more magical it appeared. Her eyes went from side to side as she tried to see everything, for she imagined that once she left, she would never again enter the swamp.

On her right a bed of floating lilies and wild orchids grew near the base of tree trunks.

Water bubbled against the side of the pirogue as Thorne poled them deeper and deeper into the swamp.

Suddenly, Rainey spotted a beautiful white bird ahead and, forgetting her anger at Thorne, pointed to the bird. When she spoke, her voice was filled with excitement. "Look, Thorne. What kind of bird is that?"

"An egret," he replied. And wonder of wonders, he was smiling across at her.

She returned his smile, eager to put the bad feelings behind them. Her uneasiness had disappeared and she felt the incredible beauty of the swamp wash over her. She was so glad Thorne was enchanted by the swamp, too. That fact made her feel closer to him.

She saw a screech owl sitting on a bleached limb,

blinking lazily at her, and she pointed it out to Thorne. He pointed out another egret.

Soon they were entering a shady tunnel of sweet gums, where wisteria grew along the edges of the channel along with water elms and cypress, each adding their own special beauty to that of thick groves of feathery bamboo.

They continued to travel down the channel, deeper and deeper, while all around them the swamp came alive with strange, almost unearthly sounds. There were screeches—but she'd already identified those as a screech owl—hoots, and howls, and so many bird sounds that she'd never heard before. And always beneath those sounds was the constant lapping of the water against the side of the pirogue.

Where they traveled, the sun was only a memory, unable to reach beneath the dense foliage. But when the house they were searching for appeared ahead, Rainey judged it to be almost noon.

"Is that the old man's house?" she asked.

"It must be," he replied. "According to the man who drew the map, he's the only one who lives down this channel." He poled the pirogue closer to the tangled underbrush, until he found a clearing closer to the house, which was fashioned from mud and reeds.

The pirogue bumped against the bank, and Thorne swung his leg over the side, gingerly testing the ground with his weight before lifting the other foot from the safety of the boat.

Moments later, Thorne curled his hand into a fist and rapped on the door. "Gustave," he called. There was no answer, no sound of stirring inside.

Knowing they couldn't leave without seeing the old man, Thorne pushed open the door and stepped inside.

The room was bare of furnishings except for a woodstove and a bed and table. Shelves had been built along the wall to hold supplies, but they were almost bare. Not so the room, though. On the bed, lay an old man, his breath raspy and harsh.

"Are you Gustave Larson?" Thorne asked, bending over the old man. The old man nodded. "Do you need help?"

"Too late," the old man whispered. "I been—been bit by a . . . cottonmouth."

"How long ago?" Thorne asked, knowing the reptile's bite could be fatal if not treated right away.

"Two days now," the old man said. "I been laying here waiting for somebody to find me so's I could send word to my granddaughter."

"I will carry word to her," Thorne said gently, knowing there was nothing he could do. The old man was too far gone. "Tell me where to find her."

"Her name . . . is Eulalie," the old man replied. "She's in New Orleans. Got herself a maid's job in a big house. Visits me whenever she can. About every two weeks. Don't—don't want her to find me like . . . like this." He gripped Thorne's wrist with surprisingly strong fingers. "You gotta see to things when I'm gone. Don't let her find me dead here. It would be too cruel."

"Don't worry," Thorne said. "I came to take care of her."

"You? Who are you?" the old man queried.

"Her brother."

Suspicion darkened the old man's eyes. "She don't have no brother."

"According to my father, she does. His name is Eugene Lassiter."

The old man's expression became bitter. "Where you been all these years, boy? My girl's been needin' folks for a long time now."

"I've only just learned of her existence," Thorne replied. "And I came straightaway. You can rest easy about your granddaughter, old man. Eulalie is my responsibility now."

"I'm gonna believe you, boy," the old man said. " 'Cause I ain't got no choice. But don't you let that girl down, or I'll come back from my grave and haunt you."

"I won't let her down," Thorne promised. "You can count on that."

The old man relaxed, and his hand released Thorne's wrist. He looked over at Rainey. "Don't know who you be, girl, but I'm hankering for the sound of a woman's voice. Come over here and talk to me."

She went to his side. "Would you like me to sing you a song?" she asked, leaning over him. "Some folks say I have a good voice."

"Yes," he said. "Sing to me. I like music. Do you know 'Amazing Grace'?"

"Yes. I know it." She began to sing the old hymn. "Amazing Grace, how sweet the sound . . ." The high trill of her pure voice rang out in the small cabin, and the old man seemed to take comfort from it. ". . . that saved a wretch like me. I once was lost, but now I'm found, was blind but now can see."

She began the second stanza, watching his face closely for signs that would mean he was tired of listening to her, but they didn't come. And by the time she'd finished singing the last stanza of the song, there was a definite relaxing of his body, and peace had drifted over his face. When she'd finished singing, she leaned over and met his eyes. "Would you like me to sing another hymn," she asked quietly.

"Come away, Rainey," Thorne said gently, taking her hand and pulling her away from the bed.

"But he may want another song, Thorne," she whispered. "It seemed to comfort him."

"It did, Rainey, but there's nothing more you can do now. He's beyond hearing us."

"Beyond . . ." She looked at the old man and realized Thorne was right. The old man was gone.

Tears dimmed her eyes then, brimming over and flowing down her cheeks. She hadn't known the old man but it didn't seem right that he'd ended his life this way. Without kith or kin to keep him company.

Recognizing her distress, Thorne pulled her into his arms and comforted her. She allowed his embrace until she felt more able to handle her emotions, then she pulled away from him.

"Take care of him, Thorne. He didn't want his granddaughter to see him this way."

"I know. And I intend to do just that." He closed the old man's eyes gently and pulled the cover over his face. "I have to dig a grave. Do you want to stay with him until then?"

"You don't think we should take him back to New Orleans?"

"He lived here in the swamp, Rainey. I imagine he loved it. And I think it would be most suitable and more to his liking to be buried here. There may even be graves here already, where other family members are buried."

"Do you think he would mind if I go with you?"

"I'm sure he wouldn't mind."

Behind the house they found a well-trodden path leading through thick foliage, which made a tunnel overhead. It was obvious that someone had been careful to keep the vines and underbrush trimmed away to make traveling easier. The trail wound and curved through mimosa and cane until it reached a small clearing where sunlight streamed through. In that clearing were wooden crosses that marked the site of two graves,

which had been carefully tended to keep the weeds out
and help the flowers grow.

When they were close enough to read the markers,
Rainey realized Gustave had buried his loved ones
there.

"Natalie Grace Larson, beloved daughter and
mother," Thorne said softly, and Rainey knew he must
be reading the marker.

"She didn't use your father's last name," Rainey said.
"But he said his granddaughter's name was Eulalie Lassiter."

"I know. And as far as I'm concerned, she's entitled
to the name, just as her mother was."

Rainey moved to the other grave and silently read
the words: *Colette Lacy Larson—beloved wife and mother—
you take my heart with you.*

Tears blurred Rainey's vision as she read the words.
To be so loved was a wonderful thing.

"What is it, Rainey?" Thorne asked, noticing the
tears.

She swallowed but emotion clogged her throat making it impossible to speak. He came to her and read
the marker, then looked at her with the dawn of understanding.

"Their love was obviously the most important thing
in their lives. He would have felt a great sadness when
she died. But he's no longer alone, Rainey. They are
together at last."

She couldn't hold back the hot tears then. He took
her in his arms and held her while she cried. Although
she knew he didn't understand her great sadness—for
she had barely had moments with the old man before
he died—he was sympathetic to her tears.

When she finally got herself under control, Thorne
said, "I'll get this grave dug and then take care of the
old man—"

"Gustave," she said.

He looked at her, not understanding.

"His name is Gustave, Thorne. He had a name. We should use it when we speak of him."

"Of course. I didn't mean to be disrespectful." He raked a hand through his dark hair as he was apt to do when he was tired. "He was my sister's grandfather, not some stranger. And he'll be laid to rest with the greatest respect."

Rainey made a marker while Thorne dug the grave, cleaving the earth beside Colette's grave. Rainey was almost finished by the time Thorne considered the grave deep enough. And then the old man—covered with the quilt from his bed—was laid to rest beside his wife.

Thorne surprised Rainey by saying a prayer over Gustave and then the two of them left him with his family, knowing the old man had found his peace at last.

Fifteen

Rainey thought the trip out of the bayou went twice as fast as had the journey into it. But that wasn't the least bit surprising. When they'd gone into the swamp they'd been traversing strange waters. Now those same waters were familiar, each twist and turn expected, and the map need be consulted no longer.

Thorne had been silent since he'd taken up the pole to propel the pirogue forward, and she sensed an air of sadness about him. Was it the knowledge of the old man's death that caused him to be so? she wondered.

"Are you thinking about the old man?" she asked quietly.

"Yes," he confessed. "It's a damn shame Eulalie wasn't with him at the end."

"Yes," she agreed. "It is sad. I hope she doesn't blame herself too much for being away."

His lips twisted wryly. "I suspect she won't overburden herself with guilt."

"What makes you say that?" she asked.

"A woman who would stoop to blackmail probably has no trouble with her conscience."

"Don't judge her too harshly, Thorne. It must have been hard on her, knowing that she was forced to clean houses for a living when her father was a rich man."

"Yes. I imagine it was hard on her. Although I found no problem with earning my own living."

"You're a man," she quickly rebuked. "Society has a place for a working man. But it's harder for a woman to find work."

"You've supported yourself for years, Rainey. And your grandfather, as well."

"I was in the mountains then. Things are different there. You know that. And earning our bread wasn't all that easy there, either. We had next to nothing. You know that as well as I do."

"You were happy enough, though."

"Yes. I was happy." *After you came,* she could have added, but didn't. Instead, she looked out across the water. "Perhaps education is not such a good thing for some people, Thorne. I had no idea what the world was like then. But now I know there's more to life than following a bee line. Sometimes knowledge isn't such a good thing."

"Do you think you'll be unhappy when you return to the mountains," he asked gently. "Can you go back to the simple things in life without a feeling of regret for what you never had?"

If that life was with you, she thought. *I would be happy anywhere, whatever the circumstances, if we were together.* But she didn't speak the words aloud, did not dare, lest he feel obliged to make her promises he couldn't keep.

Realizing he was still waiting for her answer, she said, "I've grown up since leaving the mountains, Thorne. I was a child then, eagerly reaching out for what I couldn't have. Now I see how wrong I was."

And she had been wrong. And selfish. Her head had been turned by Robert Golden's outward appearance and she'd been determined to have him whatever the cost. And all the while there had been Thorne, a man who'd proven his worth many times over in the years past. How could she not see him for what he was? she wondered.

Thorne.

Oh, God, how she loved him.

Rainey tried to envision her life without Thorne, and tears misted her eyes. He looked at her then, saw her expression and said, "Does the thought of returning to that existence make you so sad, Rainey?"

She gave him a weak smile. "No. I'm just being silly."

"You're still worrying about the old man, aren't you? You don't have to, you know. He's at peace now."

"I know." She was glad he hadn't guessed her thoughts. "Gustave's with his wife and daughter. It's Eulalie we need to worry about now." She felt a sense of frustration at not being able to locate Eulalie and knew that Thorne must feel it, too.

"We're bound to find her soon," Thorne said. "Her grandfather said she was working for one of the wealthy families in New Orleans. All we have to do is check with each one of them until we locate her."

"That could be time consuming," she replied. "We've been in New Orleans for several days now, and there is still so much of it that we haven't seen."

"Even so, we'll find her. It might take longer than we originally thought, but someone is bound to know where she is. And we'll find that someone, eventually."

"I hope we find her before she returns to the bayou to visit her grandfather," Rainey said. "I hate to think of her going there and worrying about him not being there." She gave him a speaking look. "We don't know exactly when she'll be going there, Thorne. We might miss her." She frowned worriedly. "Do you think she's in the habit of visiting the graveyard? It would be awful for her if she found out that way . . . by seeing a new grave in that little glade."

"She would have no way of knowing the new grave

belonged to her grandfather. There is no name on the marker."

"I know that. But Eulalie would have to be a half-wit not to guess the truth about that grave. She'll take one look at the freshly dug earth and know immediately who is buried in it."

"Then we'll just have to make sure she doesn't stumble over the grave," he said. "If we don't find her within the next few days, then we'll hire the pirogue again and make the trip into the bayou. We could wait in the cabin for her to show up."

They fell silent then, each busy with private thoughts, and that silence lasted throughout the return journey to New Orleans. As they drew up beside the dock, Sam Sheppard, owner and operator of the Riverside General Store, left his store and tied the pirogue to one of the poles that supported the floating platform.

"Did you find the old man?" he asked.

"Yes," Thorne replied. "We found him."

"Thought you would." Sam grinned. "I draw a good map, even if I do say so myself. Of course if you'd been going to the Devon place it woulda been harder to make a map. There's too many turns and twists to remember every one of them. And too many canals branching off from the main one . . . not like the straight shot you had to old man Larson's place. That was a straight course mostly, except for that one turn from the main channel and—" He broke off when Thorne handed him his money, obviously realizing for the first time that neither of them had much to say. "Hope everything was all right with the old man," he said, taking the money and stuffing it in his trouser pocket. "He's a nice old coot, not squirrely like some of them Cajuns that live back in the bayous."

He was counting out change when Thorne stopped

him with a wave of the hand. "Keep it," he said. "It was kind of you to watch the carriage while we were gone."

"Didn't mind that one bit," the man said, tilting his hat farther back on his head. "Good luck to you folks. And if I can be of any more help, be sure and come around."

"There is one thing," Thorne said, turning back to him. "About Gustave's granddaughter . . . Eulalie . . . the old man told us she was working in one of the big houses here, but he didn't seem to know which one. You wouldn't know, would you?"

"No." Sam Sheppard frowned at Thorne. "She's a mighty nice girl, that one. Real quiet, though. Not snooty, mind you. Just quiet, as though she don't have nothing to say. Keeps herself to herself. Know what I mean? Don't think she's ever said more'n two words to me that don't need to be said. I don't ask questions, though. I figure if folks want to tell me their business, then they'll do it without me asking questions. She's been a good granddaughter to him . . . the old man. Comes along—regular as clockwork—once every couple of weeks, carrying a box of supplies for the old man. Not many young'uns these days are so generous with their time. Especially when it takes most of the day to get there and back."

"No, I imagine not," Thorne said gruffly. "Thanks again."

Rainey was aware of Sheppard watching them leave. And when they were out of hearing, she asked the question that had been bothering her. "Why didn't you tell him about Gustave?"

"Because he might tell Eulalie when she showed up and she would have no need to go to the house in the bayou. If our search proves fruitless, her visit to her grandfather may be our only way of finding her."

"But someone has to know about him," she protested.

"I'm aware of that. I'll go to the police station after I leave you at the hotel," he said. "And there's every possibility they may know something about Eulalie's whereabouts. It certainly won't hurt to inquire."

He left her alone then, and Rainey, restless for some reason, crossed to the window. The room overlooked a small courtyard, where there was a profusion of growing things. She recognized wisteria and hibiscus, could smell their fragrance, and suddenly she felt a yearning to see the mountains again, to race along the ridge with the wind in her hair. She imagined herself there, searching the sky for the small insect that flew in a straight line toward its hive. She'd enjoyed the pursuit enormously, but would she again. Now that she'd seen the wonders of another world? Would she be able to go back to the hills without regret, to a life where things would be so drastically changed?

The cabin that had been large enough for Grandpa and herself would be too small for five people. And George Watson would never consent to living elsewhere. Oh, God! She couldn't return to the cabin and share it with those god-awful boys of Sadie's. What would she do? Her place in life was gone now. She belonged nowhere.

Thorne went to the police station. The sergeant in charge—when presented with Thorne's credentials—was sufficiently impressed to take Thorne to his superior.

"Captain Brannigan, sir," the man said. "This is Thornton Lassiter from the Lassiter Shipping Lines. He's come to report a death."

The man behind the large desk cluttered with paperwork pointed to a chair. "Please be seated, Mr. Lassiter. I'm Captain Brannigan." He looked at the sergeant. "You can go."

He waited until the man left before he spoke again. "Now, what is this about a death?" he asked. "Who died?"

"His name was Gustave Larson," Thorne replied. "He lived in the bayou."

"I know of him," the captain said. "He's known as a hermit. Was it foul play?"

"No. The old man was bitten by a cottonmouth. He died shortly after I arrived."

The captain frowned. "If it wasn't foul play, why did you come here?"

"To report the death. I buried him beside his wife and daughter."

"He probably would've wanted that." The captain sighed heavily. "You were right to report his death. Someone would have wondered about him eventually." He shifted some papers around on his desk. It was obvious the man was harried, that he wanted to get back to work, but he would just have to wait, Thorne thought. "He had a granddaughter," Thorne said. "She happens to be my half sister and I would like to notify her myself."

"Quite right, too. But I fail to see what that has to do with the police."

Thorne frowned at him. "There's a problem with notifying her since I don't have the faintest notion where she is."

"You lost track of your sister?"

Thorne grimaced. "That seems impossible to you maybe, but the fact is, I have never met my sister." He settled himself more firmly in the chair and began the story that would hopefully lead to finding Eulalie.

The other man listened politely, then said, "What do you expect me to do about it?"

"I thought you might check on Eulalie's whereabouts," Thorne replied.

"Mr. Lassiter, this police department is drastically undermanned, and our funds are limited. If we pulled men off their beats to look for everyone's missing sisters, then trouble would break out over the entire city." He favored Thorne with a disgusted look. "Do you have the least idea how many men it requires to keep this city safe for decent citizens?"

"Not the least," Thorne admitted. "It's been years since I visited New Orleans and it's more than doubled in size since then."

The other man grunted. "My point exactly. The city has doubled in size but its police force has not. We have too small a force to contend with the murders, rapes, robberies and whatever else goes on in this fair city of ours. We most certainly do not have any time left over for finding lost sisters. Hell, she ain't in trouble anyway, from what the old man said. She's safe enough, working for one of the prominent families. But if you want to find her, the best way to go about it is to hire a detective."

"A detective," Thorne said musingly. "I never thought of that."

The captain grunted. "If you need me to recommend one, then we have the names of several good men on file."

"If you don't mind."

"Why in hell should I mind? It gets you outta here quicker." He went to the door and yanked it open. "Harvey!" he shouted. "Get a list of all the detectives we have on file and give it to Lassiter!" Leaving the door open, he returned to his chair and began shuffling the papers on his desk again, obviously meaning for Thorne to leave.

Thorne did.

It didn't take Thorne long to realize the list he'd been given was slightly out of date. The first name on the list, Sloan Brown, was no longer at the address listed, and none of his neighbors seemed to know anything about where he'd gone.

"He was there one day, and the next day he was gone," the clerk at the nearby grocery said. "He never was one for talkin' much, but you'd of thought he'd tell somebody where he was going. We get inquiries about him all the time. People lookin' to hire him. Guess he wasn't needin' work very bad, or he'd of left a new address behind."

The clerk was right, Thorne decided. The man must not need work very bad. And if that was the case, then he wasn't the man Thorne was looking for. He consulted the list again, went to the second address, and found the detective in his office.

A bleary-eyed man looked up from his desk as Thorne pushed open the door. "Whatcha want?" he asked sourly.

Thorne's nostrils twitched at the stale smell of liquor, even before he saw the bottle on the desk. "It appears I came to the wrong place," he replied.

"Shut the door on your way out," the man growled, hefting the bottle unsteadily.

Thorne closed the door behind him and crossed off the first two names and addresses. Moments later he was crossing off the name of Shooter Crawford, who'd been overeager to talk to a prospective client. There had been something about the man—a less than trustworthy look in his eyes—that had made Thorne keep silent about his reason for needing a detective.

He was mounting the steps at the fourth address, wondering if he should give up the whole idea of hiring a detective, when a big, burly, copper-haired man shoved rudely past him. He opened the door marked *Tyler Duncan, Private Detective,* entered the room, and slammed the door behind him.

Thorne's brows drew together in a heavy frown. If the new arrival was the detective, then Thorne had probably struck out again. His knuckles rapped against the door.

"Come in!" a voice barked from inside.

Pushing open the door, Thorne entered the room. The man who'd shoved so rudely past him was seated behind a large desk, pushing papers around as though searching for a particular one. He extracted a single sheet and perused it for a moment, then grunted and slid it into a drawer. Then he looked up at his visitor.

"Are you a prospective client or a salesman?" the man growled. "If you're a salesman, then you might as well know I'm not buying. That'll save us both time." The man's green eyes were piercing as they studied his visitor.

Thorne looked down at himself, then pointedly at the man again. "Do I look like a salesman?"

"Most salesmen around here take great care to wear the look of prosperity. You have that look. But if you're not a salesman, then you just might be what I'm setting here waiting for . . . a client."

"And if you're setting here waiting for a client, then you can't be a very good detective."

"You won't find any better than me," Tyler Duncan growled. "And that's no brag, just a fact." His heavy brows raised slightly. "If you're staying, then take that chair." He pointed at a heavy wooden chair, which looked decidedly uncomfortable. "And if you're leaving, there's the door."

Thorne's lips curled in an amused grin. "You appear not to care if I go or stay, but from the looks of this place—" He broke off and looked pointedly at the threadbare carpet on the floor. "—you can't be getting all that much business."

"I'll admit it's slow at the moment. But it will pick up later . . . I hope." The last words were barely distinguishable, having been uttered slightly above a whisper.

But Thorne had heard, and his grin widened into a smile. "I suppose I'm staying," he said. "You look big enough to handle most anything that gets in your way. How tall are you anyway?"

"Six foot five inches," Tyler replied. "And, before you ask, I weigh two hundred fifty pounds."

"Thought as much."

"About handling whatever gets in my way. . . . What did you have in mind?"

Thorne told his story to the detective, ending with his attempt to gain the help of the local police.

"The captain is right about not having time or manpower to search for your sister," Tyler said, reaching for a cigar box on his desk. The detective offered one to Thorne, who shook his head no, then bit off one end. A moment later he puffed on the lit cigar, then spoke around it. "It appears to be a simple enough job," he said. "Finding the girl might take a few days, though. New Orleans is a big place."

Thorne nodded abruptly. "That's why I'm hiring a detective. I don't want Eulalie going to her grandfather's house and finding his grave. It would be a hell of a way for her to find out he's dead."

"You think it's going to be easier if you tell her?"

"At least she'll know she's not alone in the world."

"She apparently knows that already, since she's blackmailing your father. She appears to be a greedy, little bitch, doesn't she? Wanting everything your father has worked so long to build up. I hardly think a woman like that would shed too many tears when she discovers her grandfather is dead."

Thorne studied the detective's face but could not read his expression. "I have a peculiar notion in my head," he said. "And I just can't let go of it. Why would she send her cousin to deal with my father? Why not go herself? She's supposed to be interested in the shipping lines. Wouldn't she want to inspect them, to see what she's bent on acquiring?"

"Perhaps she couldn't face your father."

"No. I don't think that's it. A woman who could do a thing like that would surely want to gloat. If I had been treated that way, then I'd want to face the son of a bitch and make him look me in the eye and admit what he's done."

"You think she might not know what her cousin is doing?"

"I don't know," Thorne admitted. "I'm just saying the whole thing is peculiar. Larson has been bleeding my old man for more than a year now. If Eulalie is getting any part of the money, then why is she still working as a maid cleaning somebody else's house?"

The other man grinned across at him. "I was wondering if you'd realized the discrepancy of that fact."

Thorne felt pleased with his choice of a detective. There was more to Tyler Duncan than what was apparent on the surface. "I suppose you suspected something fishy the moment I told you why I was searching for her."

"I did."

"Then, why did you say she was greedy?"

"I said she appeared to be greedy. There's a difference, you know. And I said it because I wanted to see your reaction."

Fury surged through Thorne. "The hell you say!" He glared at Tyler for a long moment, then the anger slowly faded and a smile slowly crept across his face. "You may be as dishonest as they come, Duncan. But I don't think so. There's something about you that inspires my trust."

"Then I guess we have a deal."

"We have a deal," Thorne agreed. "How soon will you start to work?"

"I started the minute you stepped through that door, Lassiter. Now tell me once again exactly what Gustave Larson told you."

Sixteen

Thorne returned to the hotel and was striding toward the wide staircase leading to the upper floors when he was hailed by the desk clerk.

"Telegram for you, Mr. Lassiter!"

Taking the telegram from the clerk, Thorne slit the envelope open. It was from his sister.

Have you found her? (stop) Please reply. (stop) Eloise.

"Will you be sending a reply, sir?" the desk clerk asked.

"Yes," Thorne said. "Do you have paper and pencil?"

The clerk handed it across the counter, and Thorne quickly penned his reply: *No word yet. (stop) Will write tomorrow and report progress. (stop) Thorne.*

Handing the paper to the clerk, he said, "Please send that to Eloise Lassiter, in care of the Lassiter Shipping Lines in St. Louis."

"Be glad to, sir," the clerk said, pocketing the money Thorne handed him. "And if I can be of further help, then please—"

"Perhaps you can be," Thorne interrupted. "I'm looking for a girl—a woman really—who is a maid for one of the prominent families in New Orleans. Trouble is, I don't know which family she's working for."

The clerk looked thoughtful. "I know some of the

servants around here. Not many, mind you. But perhaps . . . what's the girl's name?"

"Eulalie. Eulalie Lassiter. Or she might be going by
the name of Eulalie Larson."

The clerk shook his head. "The name has a familiar
ring, but that's not surprising. Eulalie is a common
name around these parts. You say she's working as a
maid?"

"So her grandfather told me," Thorne replied.

"Most of the wealthier families belong to a local club,
the Thespian Society. Someone there might be of help,
might even be her employers."

"Where is the Thespian Society located?" Thorne
asked.

The clerk told him, and Thorne, having already
turned toward the staircase again, altered his course
and headed for the front door. It wouldn't take him
long to make inquiries about his sister.

On the second floor of the hotel, Rainey lay abed,
staring up at the white ceiling. She'd been trying to
sleep for the past hour, but so far had been unable. She
was restless, disturbed by Thorne's continued absence.
But she was tired, too; her energy completely sapped,
as it had been since they'd arrived in New Orleans. Even
so, sleep continued to elude her.

Perhaps it was the queasy feeling in her stomach that
caused her unrest? She turned on her side to try to
alleviate that condition. When the queasy feeling only
worsened, she turned on her back again.

God, what was the matter with her? Had she eaten
something that had gone bad? It must have been the
fish. Fish was quick to spoil if not kept cold. And in this
heat . . . yes, it must have been the fish.

She looked at the door, wishing it would open and

Thorne would step inside the room. But it was a futile wish. The door remained firmly closed.

Rainey sighed and sat up on the bed, fighting a fresh wave of nausea. Pouring herself a glass of water from the pitcher left beside the bed, she drank it down quickly, then lay back down.

Her nausea deepened and she clamped a hand across her mouth. Oh, God, she was going to lose her dinner!

Throwing herself off the bed, she hurried toward the washbasin in the corner, barely arriving before she lost the contents of her stomach. She returned to the bed again and lay down, shivering and weak, damp with perspiration.

When she'd regained enough control of herself to stop shivering, Rainey became aware of the smell. Forcing herself off the bed, she pulled the bell cord to summon the maid. The elderly woman who came took in the situation quickly.

"Oh, you poor thing," she said. "I'll just take this away and bring you a clean one." She picked up the soiled bowl and towels. "Do you need a doctor?"

"No," Rainey said. "I think I ate some spoiled fish."

"Not here," the woman said sternly. "The cook's real careful about the food." She looked uncertain. "Are you sure you don't want me to call the doctor?"

"I'm sure," Rainey replied. "I just need to rest."

"Of course you do. You go to sleep. I'll be real quiet when I bring another bowl and more towels. You won't even know I've been here."

And Rainey didn't know. When she spread herself on the bed again, the sleep she'd been courting finally arrived. She woke more than an hour later, feeling rested and refreshed, every sign of nausea having completely disappeared.

Rainey rose and went into the sitting room, hoping

to see Thorne there, but he was still conspicuously absent. She seated herself on the settee, leaned back and closed her eyes, remembering the night she'd spent in his arms. That marvelous, fantastic night would live in her memory forever. Oh, God, it had been wonderful. Even though she'd been unfulfilled when it was over, the leading up to the culmination had been glorious. But it was an experience that would never be repeated, she knew, even though Thorne had told her if there were any consequences, he would—

Consequences!

A baby!

Rainey sat bolt upright, perspiration beading her brow as a sudden thought struck her. Could she be carrying Thorne's child? Was it possible? After just the one night together?

Oh, God, if it were only true!

And it might be. It would certainly account for the queasiness that she'd been feeling, for the sleeplessness that she'd been enduring. She counted back and discovered that her body functions, which had always been regular in the past, were late.

Was that the reason? she wondered. Was she going to have a baby? Thorne's baby? All the signs pointed to it.

Just the thought of having Thorne's child excited her more than she'd like to admit. Yet, if it were so, then she must keep the news from him because he'd made it clear from the beginning that he would marry her if the need should arise.

And she didn't want him like that! If Thorne were forced to marry her because he thought she was having his child, the marriage would never work. She'd already decided that, before she realized such a thing might actually come about.

Oh, God! What could she do?

Finding herself unable to sit still, Rainey rose to her feet and began to pace the floor. She felt more impatient than ever that Thorne hadn't returned. Yet, if he returned at that moment, astute as he was, he'd be sure to know something was amiss.

More than an hour later Rainey became aware that she was hungry. Since Thorne had not yet returned, she left the suite to find herself something to eat. As she descended the stairway, her gaze scoured the lobby for some sign of Thorne. The desk clerk stood behind the counter, speaking to a familiar-looking man. Rainey's gaze narrowed slightly as she realized the man was Cage Larson.

What was he doing in New Orleans? she wondered.

His presence struck her as undeniably peculiar. His turning up in the very hotel where they were staying could not be a coincidence. She was suddenly sure of that. Was he following them for some reason?

She slipped behind a huge potted tree and waited until he'd left the hotel, then she crossed the lobby to the counter. "What did that man want?" she asked. "The one you were just talking to."

The clerk smiled at her. "He was looking for Mr. Lassiter. I told him he was out. Should I have sent him to you?"

"No. You did right to send him away," she assured the man.

Now, what could Cage want with Thorne? she wondered.

Thorne was admitted to the Thespian Society by a decidedly reluctant butler dressed in somber black. "The club is closed to nonmembers," he said.

"I realize that," Thorne said pleasantly. "But I've

been thinking of joining and I thought it wouldn't be out of order for me to look around first."

"Our club members are the cream of society," the butler said, tilting his head back so he could look down his long nose at Thorne. "Its members are carefully selected. None but the best families are allowed to join."

"So I heard," Thorne said, somehow managing to keep his dislike of the imperious butler from tinging his voice. "That's exactly why I came to this club first. The heir of Lassiter Shipping Lines deserves only the best." He threw back his head and took on a haughty look that put the butler's to shame.

"The heir to Lassiter Shipping Lines?" The butler barely controlled a gulp of surprise. "Excuse me, sir. Of course you are welcome here."

"Of course," Thorne murmured dryly. "Now, if you will be so kind as to show me to the bar . . ."

"Of course. This way, sir. Right this way." He led Thorne down a long hall to a large room filled with gaming tables. On one side of the room was a well-stocked mahogany bar, behind which a bartender was kept busy filling glasses.

"Would you like me to introduce you around?" the butler asked.

"No," Thorne replied. "I don't want the others to know why I'm here right now. That way, if I decide against joining the club, there will be no hard feelings."

"But they know you're not a member," the butler protested.

"Are members allowed to bring guests?"

"Of course."

"Then, if anyone inquires, just say I am here at the invitation of a member." He took the butler's hand

and squeezed it, leaving behind a good-sized tip. The butler dipped his head in agreement, then made a quick departure.

Thorne joined the men at the bar and there made a few discreet inquiries. None of the men knew anything about Eulalie. He was on the verge of leaving when a man about his father's age approached him.

"I hear you've been making inquiries about Grace Larson's daughter." His dark eyes were keen as they took in Thorne's expertly tailored suit. "Do you mind telling me what business you have with her?"

Thorne studied the other man briefly, then decided he looked trustworthy enough. His question was most certainly one a man of conscience would ask. "I have only recently learned of Eulalie's existence," he said. "Or I would have come sooner." He wanted the man to understand why he was only now coming forward. "Eulalie is my half sister, the daughter of my father, Eugene Lassiter."

"Eugene Lassiter." The man's eyes darkened. "I knew him. But that was years ago." He stuck out his hand and Thorne shook it abruptly. "I'm Sam Cross. And you are . . ."

"Thornton O'Brien Lassiter."

"Good to meet you," Sam said gruffly. "So you're looking for Grace Larson's daughter. She loved him, you know. Never could see what Grace saw in Eugene. I suppose he loved her . . . as much as a man like that could love anyone other than himself. He left before Grace had her baby, though. And that surprised the hell out of me. Far as I know, he never came back to New Orleans. Not even to see Grace buried."

Thorne didn't want to talk about his father's short-comings, but he needed to know something and realized his father would never reveal the information. "Do you know why he left Grace?"

"You got it all wrong, son. Eugene didn't leave her. She left him. She joined a convent."

"Joined a convent?" Thorne echoed. Nothing the man could have said would have surprised him more. "She became a nun?"

"Not a nun. A novice. She died before she could take her vows."

"Is that when my father left town?"

"Yes. Eugene left when Grace entered the convent." Sam Cross's gaze narrowed suddenly. "I'm not even sure he knew there would be a baby."

"No. He didn't. Not until recently." Thorne was silent for a long moment, wondering about the girl whose mother had chosen to become a nun. "What happened to Grace? How did she die?"

"In childbirth."

"And the girl?" he queried. "She was sent to live with her grandfather, Gustave?"

"Yes," the man replied. "She grew up in the bayou. I didn't know she'd left until recently. It's too bad that you didn't come sooner."

"Why? She's not dead?"

"No. But she might be better off if she were."

"What do you mean?"

"Last I heard, she was working at Joy Wang's whorehouse."

The words struck Thorne deeply. *A whore.* He looked away from the other man and stuck his hands deep into the pockets of his breeches. She must have been desperate for work. *Must have been.* He couldn't believe she'd have taken the work otherwise, even if he didn't know her. Perhaps he was wrong, though. She might enjoy such work. That would account for the reason she was still working there when she didn't have to . . .

since she had thousands of dollars that had been taken from his father's pockets.

He returned to the hotel, depressed at what he'd learned.

Rainey, who had returned to her room, was seated beside the window staring down into the courtyard when Thorne pushed open the door to the sitting room. "You look exhausted," she exclaimed, hurrying to him.

"I feel terrible," he replied glumly.

"I didn't expect you to be gone so long," she said. "I have been worrying for the past two hours."

"I'm sorry about that." He unfastened his tie and slumped down on the settee. "I hired a detective while I was gone, then went to a club—where all the prominent citizens gather—to look for information." He patted the spot next to him. "Come sit beside me."

She dropped down beside him and he slid an arm around her shoulders and pulled her closer. "If you hired a detective, then why'd you go looking for information? I thought that was what a detective was for. To gather information for you."

"It is. But when the desk clerk told me about the club I was so sure that news of my sister's whereabouts was close at hand. I couldn't wait a moment longer." He sighed deeply. "I was a fool to be so eager."

"You didn't find out anything?"

"I found out too much."

"I don't understand."

"I know where she is, Rainey."

"Did you see her?" she asked eagerly.

"No." He sighed again. "And I don't really wish to do so."

"Why not?"

"Her grandfather said she worked in a big house. And she does just that. But not as a maid, Rainey. My sister is a whore."

"Who said she was?" she snapped, jerking upright.

"The man who told me was Samuel Cross, one of New Orleans's leading citizens."

"What does he lead?" she asked grimly. "A group of gossipmongers?"

"He wasn't trying to slander Eulalie," Thorne said. "It was obvious he felt sorry about her circumstances." He sighed deeply and raked distraught fingers through his dark hair. "To think a sister of mine is working in a place like that." He sighed again.

"It ain't—isn't—right you should take somebody else's word for a thing like that," Rainey said. "You go find your sister, Thorne. Ask her straight out if she's doing those things."

"I intend to do just that," he admitted. "I went back to Tyler Duncan's office—he's the detective I hired— but he'd already left for the day. Since I have no idea where he lives, notifying him will have to wait for tomorrow." He pressed his fingers against his right temple and groaned. "God! I wish I could get rid of this headache."

She straightened immediately. "I can help you," she said. "Just take off your shirt and stretch out on the floor. No! Maybe the bed would be better. You just stretch out on the bed and I'll massage your muscles like I do Grandpa's when he's feeling poorly."

"It probably wouldn't be a good idea for both of us to be on your bed, Rainey," he said gruffly. "We'd better use the floor."

She blushed at the implication of his words. He stood up and stripped away his shirt, exposing chest and arm muscles, which rippled with each movement of his body.

Feeling utterly fascinated by his naked upper body,

Rainey tried to hide her interest by appearing casual. She pretended he meant nothing to her as she straddled his torso and kneaded the neck muscles, which were knotted tight with strain. And when they began to relax, she moved lower, kneading his shoulders in a circular, pressing motion.

Thorne groaned with appreciation as she worked, and Rainey was barely able to control her smile of satisfaction as he groaned again and again, each sound punctuated by a definite relaxing of his body.

She wasn't sure when his breathing began to change, only knew that each breath became quicker, more rapid than the last one.

When she realized it was her hands that were responsible for the change in his breathing, Rainey smiled inwardly. It was an impulse that made her lean over and press her lips against the nape of his neck.

He rolled over quickly then, his hands catching the back of her head and shoulders, and he pulled her across him until her face hovered only inches above his own. "Do you know what you do to me?" he whispered huskily.

"I feel it," she said. And she did. The hardening of his lower body was unmistakable.

"And you don't mind?"

"I don't mind at all."

"Come here," he growled. And then he was covering her lips roughly, his teeth grating against her soft flesh as though trying to devour her mouth.

Thorne's hands were hard, his grip tight and rough, as he worked his way into the moist depths of her mouth.

Rainey felt the shock of his possession. His hands went to her thighs to draw her closer against his male strength, and she caught her breath and moaned. His grip tightened even more, and she realized he was as hungry for more as she was.

When his mouth left hers, and he stared deeply into her eyes, she whispered, "Kiss me again, Thorne. Again and again. Don't ever stop."

"In a minute," he said, "but first, I want to see you." He unfastened her clothing while she lay before him, trembling with desire. When her bodice was open, he peeled away the fabric and studied her breasts with masculine appreciation.

"Do you like what you see?" she asked huskily.

"I like," he muttered. He touched her breasts with slow, tender hands, and her body reveled in his touch. Her knees were weak, and she knew, had she been standing, they would have buckled beneath her weight. She closed her eyes, and his lips brushed across her eyelids with infinite tenderness.

Then, feeling him draw away from her, she opened her eyes to find him unfastening his breeches. She watched avidly as he stripped away his garments, kicking aside his pants, before peeling down his underwear. And when his throbbing masculinity was finally exposed, her face flushed with hot color, but she could not look away. He was magnificent . . . purely and utterly male.

He peeled away the rest of her clothing then and came to her. And when he covered her body with his own, she felt as though she'd been reunited with a part of her that had been absent until then.

Thorne loved her then, kissing every part of her body—even the heels of her feet—and when he was done he started over again, licking his way from her cheek to her lips, then down her neck and across her shoulders until he reached her right breast.

Rainey was jerking and twitching and moaning so loudly that she was afraid someone would hear and come to investigate the sounds. But she couldn't seem to help herself, couldn't stop herself from erupting. Finally, she was bucking wildly beneath him, pushing against the bulge at his groin, desperately needing his complete possession.

Thorne continued to deny her that complete union. Instead, he suckled at her breast like an infant, driving her so wild that she was on the point of screaming by the time he left her breast and returned to her mouth again.

"Take me," she begged. "Please, Thorne, don't make me wait, please hurry, hurry, hurry."

She knew she was babbling. She also knew she must have him soon, or die with the agony of wanting.

And then he was poised over her, hovering at the apex of her thighs.

"Do it," she groaned. "Please, Thorne, do it now."

As though he'd only been waiting for that moment, Thorne plunged downward, filling her with his manhood. And then he took her to heights she'd never before imagined. And this time she wasn't left hovering, waiting, wanting. This time he brought her to fulfillment, and as she reached that ultimate moment in time, Rainey screamed out his name.

"Thorne, Thorne, Thorne!" She wailed his name over and over again, her voice rising in pitch until it became a never-ending wail.

Seventeen

The auburn-haired girl knelt on the kitchen floor and scrubbed at a greasy spot that marred the polished wood. The kitchen was the only room in the brothel that wasn't carpeted, and Lolly thanked the Lord for that small favor, since cleaning the floors was one of her own seemingly never-ending chores.

Lolly grimaced wryly and scrubbed harder at the spot. Three years of backbreaking work in this place lay ahead of her, and she had her cousin to thank for that. And the ungrateful wretch had taken himself off, the moment Lolly had offered Joy Wang her services in exchange for his gambling debt.

If only she'd been able to stay with Joy. But she hadn't. Some kind of deal had been worked between the two madams. And it was a deal where Lolly came out the loser.

Lolly told herself that it didn't really matter which woman she worked for—a house of prostitution would be the same whatever its name—but she couldn't quite convince herself of that fact. Especially when it was obvious that Madam Louise entertained thoughts of Lolly becoming one of her *girls*. But Lolly knew how foolish the madam's hopes were. She'd die before she'd service even one of the men that arrived on schedule each night when the doors were opened for the evening. Circumstances might force her to work for Madam Louise, but she refused to take the ultimate step that would plunge her into the depths of depravity.

"Lolly!" The shout came from the front parlor. It was Helen Bannister.

Giving the floor a final swipe with her mop rag, Lolly pushed herself to her feet and arched her tired back muscles. God, she was exhausted. But there would be no rest for hours to come. The evening callers would be arriving soon, and there was still much to prepare before that time.

A pox on her cousin, Cage, for getting her into this mess and then disappearing without even a thank-you for your trouble.

"Lolly! Where the hell are you?"

Lolly hurried toward the parlor. "I'm here, Helen," she said, sending her voice ahead of her. "What do you need?"

She saw Helen then, and the woman's quick smile warmed Lolly's heart as it usually did. There were so few whores who worked in Madam Louise's bordello who were so warmhearted.

"Honey," Helen said quickly, "I hate to add to your workload but Madam Louise has just informed me there's a distinguished gentleman coming to visit me within the hour. Since he's not one of my usual customers and probably fastidious as hell, I need you to change my bedsheets. My last client smelled like he'd been rooting with the hogs."

"Complaining about my choice of customers?" an acid voice nearby asked.

Lolly and Helen both turned to see Madam Louise watching them intently. Helen's lips twitched at the corners as she summoned up a faint smile. "No, Madam. Of course not."

As Madam Louise continued on her way, Helen muttered beneath her breath. "Old warthog! This is supposed to be a high-class place. But I swear! That woman is money hungry. She'll probably sell us for two bits a night if business ever slows down." The outer door opened and she uttered a startled oath. "Dammit! There's my customer now. He's early, but the old bag will make me go with him anyway." Her expression took on a look of panic. "The bed's not changed yet, Lolly!"

"Don't worry," Lolly muttered. "It won't take long to change it. If you can stall him for five minutes, your room will be fresh as a daisy."

"Consider it done," Helen said.

As Helen swaggered toward the newcomer, swinging her hips back and forth, Eulalie Lassiter hurried up the stairs to clean Helen's room.

Thorne rose early next morning and, although he wanted nothing more than to linger in the large bed with Rainey, he forced himself to forgo that pleasure so he could perform some necessary chores. After he'd gathered together his clothing, his gaze lingered on the woman in his bed for a long moment. *Later, my love,* he silently promised. Then he tiptoed quietly from the room.

Barely half an hour later he knocked on the door of Tyler Duncan's office.

"Come in!" a voice barked.

Thorne pushed open the door and entered the office.

"I'm glad I found you here," he told the detective, who was seated behind a paper-covered desk.

"I didn't expect to see you until I had something to report," Tyler said.

"You can forget about the job. I've already found her."

"That right?" Tyler's eyebrows lifted. "Quick work. You had more luck than I did then. Do you mind if I ask where you found her?"

"Suffice it to say, I'm not pleased with my findings. Her employment is not what one would call reputable."

Tyler's bushy brows lifted higher. "Are you saying she's still at Joy Wang's whorehouse?"

"She's there," Thorne muttered.

"Dammit, that woman lied to me!"

"What woman? Joy Wang?"

"Yes," Tyler said grimly.

"You spoke to her?"

"Damn straight I did. But she told me she had no notion where the girl was. Said she left her employ real sudden only last month. And that, as far as she knows, Eulalie took a slow boat to China."

"Then she's not there," Thorne muttered, slumping into a chair. He felt as though he'd had the wind knocked out of his sails.

"She's not there?" Tyler inquired. "If she's not at Joy's, then where in hell is she?"

"How the hell should I know?"

Tyler sighed deeply. "Didn't you just walk in here and say you knew where she was?"

"Yeah. But I thought she was at Joy Wang's whorehouse."

"Then you hadn't been there?"

"No. Not yet. I came to see you first."

"Then we're back to square one." He was silent for a long moment, then he asked, "Do you want me to go on with the job?"

"Yes. I need to find her, wherever she is. I am not going to let her have the Lassiter Shipping Lines, and I intend to tell her that."

"Thought you were looking for her to help her."

"Well, damn it! I was. But the fact that she's a prostitute puts an entirely different slant on things. Surely you can see that."

"Maybe she doesn't like being a prostitute. You ever think about that?"

"No. I guess I didn't. But if she's not where she wants to be, the whole thing makes no sense."

"Why?"

"She has funds. Ample funds. She certainly took plenty from my father. And she'll get her share of the inheritance when the time comes. But no more than that."

"Interesting."

"What is?"

"Your attitude. Now me . . . I wouldn't believe anything about her until I heard the facts from her own lips."

"Why not?"

"Because I have a gut feeling about this. Had it since you walked through that door. And I usually trust that feeling. The whole thing sounded fishy to me from the beginning. You said your father never spoke to her, nor heard from her, except through that cousin of hers. Have you ever considered that maybe she doesn't know what he's doing."

"That's unlikely."

Tyler shrugged his shoulders. "It might be worth checking out, though. Anyway, if you want me to go ahead with the search, then you'd better leave me to it."

"Yes," Thorne said thoughtfully. "Go ahead with it."

"Do you have any idea what she looks like?" Tyler asked.

"No. We've never met."

"Guess then. What color hair would she have? And her eyes and build?"

"I assume she'd be dark haired, and probably has

brown eyes. Her mother was Cajun and my father's hair used to be black when he was younger, and his eyes are gray."

"We'll assume her hair is dark," Tyler said, scribbling in a small notebook. "And her eyes will either be gray or brown." He closed the notebook. "That's not much to work with, but I guess it will have to do."

Thorne left him sitting at his desk, staring thoughtfully out the window, hopefully working on his client's problem.

Rainey was seated at the writing desk in the sitting room composing a letter to her grandfather, but her attention wasn't on what she was doing.

She couldn't put last night out of her mind.

It had been glorious, that feeling she'd shared with Thorne. She'd never believed loving could be so wonderful. If only he loved her in return. But it was obvious that he did not.

Did he still believe she wanted Robert for a husband? If he did, then he was a fool. But she could not tell him different. Didn't want him to pity her for falling in love with him.

Even though she knew their relationship would one day end, she would not think about that; she would live only for the moment and take comfort from his presence. She was making memories that would have to last her a lifetime, and she intended to make as many as she possibly could.

It was time for the noonday meal when Thorne returned to the hotel. They went to the restaurant and ordered steak and potatoes, and while they were eating, Rainey remembered she hadn't told him about Cage Larson.

"Why would Cage Larson be looking for you?" she asked.

"Cage Larson?" He frowned heavily. "He was looking for me? Are you certain of that?"

It was her turn to frown now. "I saw him in the lobby. He was talking to the desk clerk. After he left I went down and asked the clerk what he wanted, and the man said he was looking for you."

"When did this happen, Rainey?"

"Yesterday."

"Why in hell didn't you tell me then?"

The hard tone of his voice flustered her. "You were tired when you came back, and then . . . and then . . . I forgot. Does it really matter?"

"You're damn right it does!" he said grimly. "I would've thought you'd have known that, too. Anything that scoundrel does is of extreme interest to me."

"Scoundrel?" She was confused. "Why do you call him that?"

"What else would you call him? He *is* a scoundrel. A damned blackguard."

"You sure did take a dislike to him, didn't you? And what for anyway? Just because the two of you had words don't—doesn't—mean he's a—"

"Had words?" His lips thinned. "What in hell are you talking about, Rainey? I never met Cage Larson."

"Never met him?" Now she was getting angry. "You damned sure did!" Her voice had risen and she was vaguely aware of heads turning in their direction. "You threatened to beat him to a pulp at the dance." She knew her words were an exaggeration but her anger was such that she didn't really care. Anyway, he *had* been angry.

"Dance? What in hell are you talking about anyway? I don't remember meeting Cage Larson at any dance. I never attend da—" He broke off suddenly and stared at her with sudden comprehension. "In Lizard Lick? He was the man you danced with and—Holy hell! I had completely forgotten about that."

"If you forgot about it, then why did you call him a scoundrel?"

"He's the man that's been extorting money from my father . . . Eulalie's cousin."

"Cage Larson is—"

"My sister's cousin. And for some reason he came to the mountains looking for me. Now I wonder why?"

"He was in St. Louis, too."

"You saw him there?" At her quick nod, he asked, "Where?"

"In the hotel. The morning I brought you breakfast in bed and we—" She broke off, blushing wildly.

"And we made love," he finished softly, studying her rosy cheeks with his keen eyes.

"Yes. We certainly did that."

He covered her hand with his own. "Don't look like that, Rainey, or I'll be forced to take you back upstairs and repeat the process."

She shyly lowered her eyelids to hide her expression. She couldn't allow him to see how very much she wanted just that. "What do you think Cage Larson is up to?" she asked in a carefully controlled voice.

"I'm not sure," he replied, his voice becoming hard again. "But I damn sure intend to find out."

They fell silent then and attended to their meal. When they had finished eating, Thorne offered to show her the city. Rainey eagerly agreed.

They hired a carriage, which took them through the French Quarter, down Chartres and Royal Street, and past the French Opera House. "One day I'll take you there," Thorne said, nodding toward the opera house.

"Really?" she asked, wide-eyed.

"Yes," he said gruffly, brushing his palm lightly over her cheek. "Really."

They left the carriage and strolled past fine restaurants with exquisite grillwork, past carriage entrances mellow with age leading to sunny courtyards, past narrow, musty tunnelways opening into flowered patios, flagstoned alleys, and countless shops that displayed their wares in large paned windows.

Suddenly Rainey saw a monkey and an organ-grinder.

"He's so cute," she said, kneeling beside the small creature that was dressed in a red hat and shirt. "Look! He's holding out his hand to me."

"He's begging for money," Thorne explained with a laugh.

"Really?" she asked, avidly watching the cute creature. "I wish I had some to give him."

"How thoughtless of me, Rainey. I should have considered your lack of funds before. Here." He handed her some coins and she gave the monkey one of them. The monkey hurried to the cup beside the organ-grinder and dropped the coin in, and then came to her again with its hand out.

"No," Rainey said. "One was enough, you greedy, little thing."

The creature turned away from her then, as though it had understood her every word, and ran to a nearby woman who'd stopped to exclaim over him. The process was repeated, until the money was in the cup, and the monkey turned to look for another benefactor.

"I guess he isn't interested in us if we're not giving him money," she said, feeling somewhat disappointed.

"You can give him some more if you'd like," he said, laughing indulgently.

"No, Thorne!" she exclaimed. "I wouldn't waste your money that way."

"You're a thrifty, little thing, aren't you?" he said.

"You'll make some man an excellent wife one of these days."

Some man. Not him, but some man. The words struck her like a hammer blow, and she chided herself for feeling that way. He had never said he wanted her for a wife. She'd always known that. But to speak so easily of her having another man for a husband hurt badly.

She turned away and blinked quickly, drying the tears that had moistened her eyes. And when she turned back to him again, there was no sign of them having been there, nothing to show him her frame of mind.

Forcing a quick laugh, Rainey said, "I guess I've seen enough here. Let's go to the park. It's beautiful over there with that lake in the middle of it."

"Yes, it is," he agreed. He directed his gaze to the passersby, and she noticed that he avoided her eyes.

Was he thinking about Robert and feeling guilty that he'd taken her innocence instead of saving it for her husband? She didn't know, but she suspected he was. And she couldn't reassure him without some embarrassment to them both, so she decided to hold her silence.

Even so, Rainey knew in her heart that, no matter what happened in the future between Thorne and herself, she would never marry Robert Golden. She'd been a fool to think herself in love with him.

But no more.

It was Thorne she loved, and if she couldn't have him, then she didn't want anyone.

Eighteen

"Now come on, Joy," Tyler said, keenly staring at the small Asian woman. "You and I both know you're lying about the girl. And we also know that I won't leave you alone until you tell me the truth."

She sighed heavily. "I don't have time for this, Tyler. I have work to do, schedules to arrange, and little time left to do it."

"Then stop wasting time, Joy. We both have more important things to do. And the sooner you tell me where she is, the sooner you'll see the back of me."

She reluctantly gave in. "The girl is with Madam Louise." She put a hand on Tyler's arm. "Please don't say who told you where to find her. Louise would never forgive me if she finds out. And she'd sure enough do something hateful out of spite. She might even lure my girls away, might ruin my business."

Tyler's gaze narrowed. "What reason does she have for keeping the girl's presence there a secret?"

"I won't say any more, Tyler," the Asian woman said. "You got what you came for, now you must leave here." She rose to her feet. "And please use the back door. I'd rather nobody saw you leave. It would give the house a bad name."

He laughed abruptly. "The house already has a bad name, Joy. There's little I could do to make it worse."

"You lie!" she hissed. "The house of Joy Wang is the best brothel in New Orleans. My clientele is carefully selected. Only men of great import are allowed to visit my girls."

"The cream of society," he said sarcastically. "I suppose your girls are of the best quality, too."

"Of course," she said. "I make certain of that fact before I allow them to come here."

"Then what about Eulalie Lassiter? How do you account for her presence here? The girl is a swindler, out for everything she can get, yet she lived here until recently."

"A swindler!" she gasped, her eyes becoming round with disbelief. "That is not true. There is no way you can make me believe such a thing of that girl."

"It's true," he said gruffly. "And whether or not you believe me is not important."

Tyler left her then, deliberately striding toward the front parlor. Although Joy muttered a protest, he paid no heed, just continued on until his long strides carried him to the door, then through it and down the wide steps to the paved walk.

He wondered why Joy was so certain that Eulalie couldn't be a swindler. Wondered, too, why Madam Louise wanted to keep the girl's presence in her whorehouse secret. Whatever the reason, he decided, he wouldn't allow himself to be swayed from his goal. He would find the girl, make certain of her whereabouts, then take the information back to his client. What Thorne Lassiter did with that information was entirely up to him. Once the information had been passed along, Tyler would collect his money and be done with the whole affair.

* * *

It was late afternoon when Rainey and Thorne returned to their suite at the hotel. The door had barely closed behind them when Thorne apprised her of his intention to leave again. "I'll come with you," she said quickly.

"No, Rainey." He smoothed her cheek with his palm. "You can't come where I'm going."

"Why not?" she pouted.

"Because I'm going back to the gentlemen's club. And ladies are not allowed there."

"Why not?" she asked again.

He smiled at her. "Because it's a man's club, Rainey. A place set aside for men only."

"What are the men doing there that they don't want their women to know about?"

"Nothing devious, I assure you."

"Assure me all you want to, Thorne, but I ain't gonna believe you." He laughed lightly and his eyes glittered with amusement, making her realize she'd reverted to her former speech pattern. She threw her head back and chose each word carefully before she spoke. "If the men of New Orleans need a club where they can go without the ladies, then there is probably something devious going on there. Something they don't want their womenfolk to know about." She arched a dark brow. "They might even have those fallen women—the ladies of the night—there." The thought of such women brought her next words out quickly. "You watch yourself, Thornton Lassiter. Them loose lollies that sell themselves for two bits a night ain't to be trusted. And I won't be so quick to jump in bed with nobody that's been with one of 'em."

He pulled her swiftly into his arms and gave her a quick hug. "A loose lolly would never be able to satisfy me since I've bedded the likes of you, Rainey Watson. I'm afraid you've spoiled me for other women."

"Really?" She blinked up at him, trying to dry the moisture that suddenly dimmed her vision.

"Really," he whispered.

Then he kissed her, and it was like the first time their lips had touched. The world exploded around her, taking her with it. She felt as though she'd shattered into a thousand pieces, and only Thorne's embrace could make her come together again. She wondered if he could hear the sound of her heartbeat, which thudded frantically beneath her rib cage like a trapped bird trying to escape the confines of its cage.

When his head lifted, she muttered a word of protest and tightened her arms around his neck. "No, Thorne," she whispered. "Don't go now. Not while this hunger is in me."

"I have to go now," he muttered, pulling her arms away from him and setting her aside. "If I don't, then I won't leave you until tomorrow."

"Would that be so bad?"

"Don't tempt me, Rainey," he growled. "We have to find Eulalie and get that business settled before we can think of our own future."

He left her then, striding swiftly across the room and hurrying out the door. Rainey stared at the closed door for a moment, her body shivering with the memory of his touch. It had been so easy for him to leave her, she thought. Even though his breath had quickened at their kiss, he had set her aside to go about his business. Why couldn't she do the same? Why was she left trembling with hunger, desperately longing for him to return, to take her in his arms and carry her to his bed?

Oh, God, why did love have to be such a desperate, one-sided thing?

Rainey paced the floor, trying to control her quivering nerves, but she could not. There were too many memories in the room of Thorne and the way he'd touched her and loved her.

Crossing the floor to the window, she stared down into the small courtyard. The green foliage reminded her of the mountains, of the peace and quiet that she found among the pines and evergreens. Perhaps if she entered that courtyard, she would find the peace she searched for.

Rainey left her suite and went downstairs. She was crossing the lobby when the desk clerk called out, "Miz Lassiter, ma'am!" He hurried around the counter and joined her. "That man was here again," he said.

"What man?"

"The one that was inquiring after Mr. Lassiter," he explained. "I thought you looked a mite worried when I told you he'd been asking after Mr. Lassiter, so I thought you'd want to know he'd been by again."

She frowned at him, realizing he must be referring to Cage Larson. "What did you tell him?"

"Only that Mr. Lassiter had gone out again and didn't say where he was going," the clerk replied. "I hope it was all right for me to tell him that."

"It couldn't hurt anything," she said quickly.

"Good. There's something about that man that's not quite trustworthy," the clerk said. "And I sure wouldn't want to cause you folks any trouble."

She smiled to reassure him. "You haven't." She continued on her way, turning the clerk's words over in her mind. "Why is Cage so concerned about Thorne's whereabouts?" she muttered, unaware that she'd spoken aloud until a gentleman who'd been passing by stopped and spoke.

"I beg your pardon?"

The man was so obviously speaking to her that she halted abruptly and stared at him, confused. "What?"

"You spoke to me?" he inquired.

"Oh, no! I was thinking out loud, I guess. . . ." Her voice trailed away as the gentleman grunted and strode away quickly.

Controlling the urge to laugh, Rainey made her way to Canal Street. On the corner of Canal and Chartres a large five-story building was located. The ground floor housed the Godchaux Clothing Store, and the upper floors were used for business offices. According to Thorne, the building was constructed only two years before by Leon Godchaux, Sr., a merchant and plantation owner who specialized in the growing of sugarcane.

Rainey entered the store and browsed through the merchandise displayed on racks and shelves and glass cases. She was enchanted by the array of colors and fabrics that had been used to make the gowns and hats, which sported birds and flowers and feathers. Even though she coveted the merchandise, she was aware of the enormous price tag on each garment and refrained from spending the funds Thorne had provided her with.

She left the store and continued on her way, stopping occasionally to look closer at some item that had caught her eye in a display window, but never entering a store to buy.

But that changed when she was passing a specialty shop and saw the tiny gown displayed in the window. She stared at the delicate pink garment that had obviously been designed for a newborn, and her heartbeat quickened.

Her feet seemed to move independently, and she found herself inside the store. The tiny garment beckoned. It seemed to have been placed in the window just for that particular moment when she'd be passing by. She fingered the delicate fabric, marveling at the soft, silky feel of it. If her suspicions were true, and she was expecting a baby, what would it be? she wondered. A girl would need a pink gown. Soft like this one, with fabric so silky it wouldn't scratch the delicate flesh of a newborn.

Should she purchase it?

"May I help you?"

Rainey had been so taken by the tiny infant gown that she'd failed to see the salesclerk approaching. The woman was middle-aged, graying slightly at the temples. Her lips were lifted in a gentle smile. "It is a beautiful garment, isn't it?"

"Yes," Rainey agreed, smoothing her finger across the delicate gown. "The stitches are so tiny, they are hard to make out. Do you know who made it?"

"It's the work of Marie DuBois. Her work is quite unique. And easily identifiable since she has no equal. Old Marie specializes in infant clothing."

"Old Marie?"

"Yes. she is quite elderly. I imagine she's nearing her ninetieth year . . . a great age for a woman of our time."

"Yes," Rainey agreed. "Most of the womenfolk in the Ozarks get worn out fast. The men seem to go through several wives during their lifetime. But I've known some women who've lasted near ninety years. Not many, but a few." She'd guarantee a better life for her own child, she decided suddenly. She wouldn't allow her daughter to marry a man who'd work her to death without the least bit of thought, then marry the next available woman to continue the chores.

"When are you due, dear?" the saleswoman asked suddenly.

"Due?" Rainey echoed.

"Your baby. When are you expecting it?" The woman's pleasant blue eyes studied her intently. "You *are* expecting a child, aren't you?"

"I-I'm not real sure," Rainey replied. "I think I might be, but—"

"Oh, I'm sure you are, dear," the woman replied. "You have that glow about you that women get when they are waiting for a special little package to pop from the warming oven."

Rainey uttered a laugh. "That's a nice way of putting it," she said. "A warming oven." She slid her hand over her stomach. "Do you really think I have one of those special packages in here?"

"I'm almost certain of it. And so are you, or we wouldn't be having this conversation."

"You're right." Rainey smiled at the woman. "I'm almost certain there's a baby inside me." She lowered her voice so it wouldn't carry beyond the two of them. "My woman-time is late, and yesterday I upchucked. That's something I haven't done in years." She felt odd talking about such things with a stranger, but there was no one else with whom she could share her secret. "Is there any way of being certain about such things?"

"None that I know of," the saleswoman said dryly. "Not until more time has passed. Then a doctor will know."

"I wish there was a way I could know for sure," Rainey said wistfully. "I don't think we'll be here much longer, and I sure would like that pretty pink gown for my baby . . . if there is a baby and it turns out to be a girl."

"You should buy it while you have the chance," the saleswoman advised, pushing for the sale. "It's one of a kind, which means you'll never find another one like it. Marie has been failing steadily this past year, and I'm afraid her days of sewing are past."

Rainey fingered the garment again, feeling saddened that anyone who could make such magic with her fingers should have to die. "She makes such beautiful things," she murmured. "Do you know if she has a family?"

"Oh, yes," the saleswoman replied. "I know Marie

well. She is a dear friend, has been for many long years. And she does have a family, a very large one, in fact. She will be mourned by more than a hundred souls when she is gone, but she is not saddened at the thought of death, dear child. She told me just last week that her Henry—her late husband, you know—is waiting for her . . . just beyond the rainbow."

There had been a catch in the woman's voice when she'd added the last four words, and sympathetic tears momentarily blurred Rainey's vision. For some reason she was reminded of Gustave Larson, who lay beside his wife in the little glade deep in the swamp. Had he felt that same way toward death? Did he welcome it, knowing he would be seeing his beloved wife again when he passed through the gates of oblivion?

"Maybe somebody else might copy your friend's design and make some more of these beautiful gowns," Rainey said, fingering the tatting on the tiny garment.

"They might try," the other woman said. "But no other woman has ever been able to equal Marie's skill when it comes to tatting. No." She sighed deeply. "I'm afraid there will never be another like Marie." She took the garment from Rainey, holding it carefully as though fearing she would damage it. "This design is special, so delicate that no other has ever succeeded in her attempt to match it. Nobody else could ever create such delicate tatting. I very nearly didn't put the gown on sale for that very reason." Her voice was soft, remembering. "Marie is part of New Orleans's history, my dear. A woman whose memory will survive long after her frail body leaves this earth."

The look on the woman's face told Rainey she was in danger of losing the infant gown, and she couldn't allow that to happen. Not now; not after learning something about the old woman who made it. She must have it for her baby . . . it would be a legend to hand down from generation to generation.

"May I have the gown?" she asked softly. And when the saleswoman reluctantly handed it over, Rainey clutched the tiny garment against her breast. "How much do you want for it?" she asked, needing to close the deal before the woman changed her mind about selling it.

"Too little," the woman said. "Not near what it's worth." She named a figure that seemed enormous to Rainey, but Thorne had given her money and she gladly handed it over. She watched anxiously while the woman wrapped the gown in soft white paper, then inserted it in a paper bag with the name of the store printed on it.

Moments later Rainey closed the door behind her and hurried down the street toward the hotel.

She didn't know why she looked across the street. Perhaps it was an almost imperceptible movement that caught her attention. Whatever the reason, her gaze slid sideways and she halted abruptly. A man strode along the sidewalk opposite her, deliberately matching her stride for stride.

Realizing that she'd seen him, he ducked furtively inside the nearest store, leaving her staring in consternation and fear.

For his swift departure had been too late.

During that one fleeting moment when she'd caught sight of him, Rainey had quickly realized his identity. The man had been none other than Cage Larson, the pseudosalesman. Once again he'd surfaced, and this time he appeared to be following her.

Her heartbeat quickened in fear at the thought. She looked around quickly for some means of escape. When she realized she'd only gone a short way from the specialty store, she hurried back again, seeking shelter with the woman who had been so kind to her.

"Did you need something else, dear?" the helpful saleswoman asked.

"Uh . . . yes," Rainey said, trying to think of an excuse for returning, while keeping a sharp eye out for the man who'd set her heart to racing with fear. "Do you have a . . . have a . . ." She glanced around frantically, saw a bonnet displayed on a rack, and said, "A bonnet! I need a bonnet to go with the gown."

"Of course," the woman said. "Allow me to show you what we have."

By the time Rainey made her selection she was chiding herself for being a foolish coward. So what if Cage was following her! He couldn't do her any harm. Not in a city the size of New Orleans.

"Is there anything else I can help you with?" the saleswoman asked, handing the package to Rainey.

"No. Wait! Yes. Maybe you could tell me where to find a restaurant."

"Just go down the street to the first crosswalk and turn left. You'll find it a few doors down."

"Thank you." Rainey's body was tense as she continued on her way, but there was no sign of Cage Larson, a fact that made her heave a sigh of relief.

Her footsteps were slow as she continued on her way. She was unaware of danger until she heard a sound in the alleyway she was passing. By then, it was too late.

A shadowy movement turned her head, just before hard fingers wrapped around her arm and dragged her inside the dark alley. Then a hand covered her mouth, stifling her breath while stopping her scream before it was born.

The hand holding her mouth shifted slightly to allow his arm to hold her against him, while he dragged her deeper into the alley. And then his free hand was on her white throat, squeezing, squeezing.

"Where is Thorne Lassiter?" he whispered huskily, his fingers loosening just enough so she could draw a quick breath. "What is he doing in New Orleans?"

She tried to free her arms, but that was impossible. His grip was much too tight. Her heartbeat was erratic, her fear overwhelming. Spots danced before her eyes. "D-don't," she whispered. "Let me go!"

His hard fingers were brutal, his expression without the least bit of compassion. "Talk, bitch! Tell me what Thorne Lassiter is doing here?"

"His sister," she whispered. "He wants to find her."

He swore softly. "Just as I thought. And he's the kind that won't stop looking until he's found her!" His fingers had loosened enough so that she could suck in more air, and she felt the faintness fading away, felt her legs becoming stronger. If he'd only allow her one moment, she could dart away from him, could scream for help.

"The two of you should've stayed in the mountains," he snarled. "But you had to interfere with my plans, didn't you?"

She shook her head, denying the fact that she had done anything, but his grip around her neck tightened.

Realizing that if she didn't break free quickly she would surely die—along with the new life that she was carrying—Rainey summoned every ounce of strength she possessed and yanked her right arm free from his grip. She lashed out quickly, raking his face with her fingernails.

As beads of blood bubbled out of his injured cheek, he released her, muttering a loud oath as he covered his bleeding flesh with one hand.

Rainey jerked free and spun away from him. She darted toward the light at the end of the alley, where she knew there would be people and, hopefully, protection from the man who sought to end her life.

He dashed after her, too late though, because she was already in the street.

Gathering up her long skirt, Rainey raced down the street, running as fast as her legs would carry her across the cobblestones, past courtyards and alleys, past people who had gathered to watch her flight. And never once did she consider appealing to anyone for protection. Her fear was too great, too overpowering to allow her to stop.

Death was behind her, and safety from that eternal darkness lay in the hotel. In the rooms where she had found love.

Then she saw it . . . the hotel. Only a block distant. Her heart lifted at the sight. She would be safe now. In only moments she would reach that haven of safety ahead. And the madman chasing her would have no recourse except to leave her alone.

But the fury driving him appeared to be all consuming. He continued to race along behind her, his heavy footsteps thudding against the cobblestones with the rapidity of bullets fired from a repeating rifle.

Reaching the hotel only moments ahead of her pursuer, Rainey ran through the door that a guest had just pushed open. She had one glimpse of the startled desk clerk as she ran past him, dashing toward the stairs that led to the upper floor.

Her heart beat like a trapped butterfly caught in a spiderweb as she hurled herself up the staircase.

Oh, God, she cried inwardly, racing up the stairs to the first landing. *Let me make it, let me make it, let me make it—*

Her silent litany was interrupted when she was suddenly brought to an abrupt halt by a hand that wound tightly through her long hair. A quick jerk caused her to become unbalanced, and then, as she flailed out for balance, another jerk sent her careening down the stairs.

Rainey's terrified scream sounded through the hotel as she bumped against each step on the long descent, which carried her to the bottom of the staircase.

She felt a hard blow against her temple, which sent pain streaking through her head and set her senses reeling. Stars danced before her eyes. And, although she fought against the darkness that closed in around her, it was a useless fight. The last thought she had before darkness claimed her was about her unborn child.

Nineteen

Thorne, finding himself unable to bide his time while the detective he'd hired conducted his investigation, made his way to the French Quarter, where Joy Wang's house of pleasure was located.

There was nothing to set the house apart from the buildings on either side of it. No way for a stranger to know its purpose, unless he'd been told of its existence. It rose three stories above street level, with decorative iron grillwork that bore the look of heavy black lace.

Striding quickly up the wide steps, Thorne picked up the heavy iron doorknocker, which bore a remarkable resemblance to a lion's head, and let it drop against the thick wooden door. It made a satisfying thud, which quickly routed a servant somewhere inside the building. The door was pulled open abruptly by a dark-skinned maid wearing a long black dress covered by a white apron. When Thorne requested an audience with Joy Wang, the maid ushered him into a large room, where heavy red draperies covered the windows, blocking out the light from the afternoon sun.

Thick carpet of a crimson color covered the floor, muffling their footsteps as they crossed the room and entered a long hallway. Moments later Thorne found himself in a smaller room, decorated much as the larger one had been, waiting for the mysterious madam to appear.

The walls were hung with gilt-edged mirrors and paintings of amply endowed women in various stages of undress, and the room was furnished with heavy mahogany sofas and high-backed chairs, which were covered with the same fabric that adorned the windows.

Thorne was wondering who had chosen the colors for the bordello when his question was suddenly answered by a young, girlish voice, coming from behind him. "She happens to *like* red."

Spinning around, Thorne frowned at the girl who had spoken. He judged her age to be somewhere between ten and twelve years old. Her stature was small, not more than five feet in height, and she was rail thin, completely undeveloped.

"What are you doing here?" he asked gruffly.

"I live here," she answered calmly. Her dark eyes were slanted, definitely Asian, and yet, young as she appeared, those eyes held a world of knowledge. "My name is Lynn Wang."

"This is no place for a young girl," Thorne said grimly. "You should be with your parents."

"I have only one parent," the girl said, something flickering in her dark eyes. "A mother. And since this is her home, it is also mine."

"Joy Wang is your mother?"

"Of course." She dropped onto a sofa and curled her legs beneath her. "She doesn't like me to tell her guests, though." Lynn Wang looked curiously at him. "You have come too early, you know. Joy doesn't make her girls work until dusk. It's a long time before then."

"I haven't come looking for a woman," he explained stiffly. He didn't like explaining his presence there to the girl, yet perhaps he could gather information from her about his sister. "I came looking for information, Lynn."

"We're not allowed to give information to anyone," she said solemnly. "Loose talk could close us down."

"The information I'm after couldn't hurt anyone," he told her.

She thought about that for a minute. "Joy told us to keep our mouth shut around strangers."

If this young girl had been so instructed, then Joy Wang herself would most certainly be uncommunicative, he realized. He seated himself across from her so he wouldn't appear as formidable to the youngster. "If I introduce myself, then we won't be strangers," he said. "My name is Thorne Lassiter."

"Lassiter?" She frowned heavily. "I know a Lassiter. She—"

"Is my sister Eulalie. And I'm looking for her, Lynn. That is why I came here. To find my sister."

"But she's not here," she said quickly. "Didn't you know?"

"No."

A door slammed somewhere in the house, then a voice called out, "Lynn! Where are you, Lynn?"

"Uh-oh," she said, sliding quickly off the sofa. "That's my mother. She's come back! Don't tell her I was here!"

She hurried across the room toward a small alcove and pushed aside the heavy crimson drapes. It was then Thorne saw the doorway that was secreted there.

"Wait, Lynn," he exclaimed. "Where is my sister?"

"Joy traded her to Madam Louise." The reply was only a whisper, then the room was empty, save for Thorne himself.

But not for long. A woman entered the room. Her appearance was so much like Lynn's that Thorne knew this must be the mother, Joy Wang. The Asian woman's gaze slid quickly around the room, then returned to rest on him. "It is too early for guests," she said evenly. But there was something in her expression that told Thorne she knew he'd not come for the usual purpose.

"I haven't come to be entertained," he said abruptly. "I'm looking for information."

"We have no information here," she informed him coldly.

"How can you know that, when I have not yet asked my questions?" he asked.

"We mind our own business in this house and expect others to do the same," she said.

"Eulalie *is* my business," he said, cocking a dark brow at her. "Eulalie Lassiter. She is my sister."

"I do not know of such a person," she said calmly. "Now if you don't mind, you may leave the house the way you came. By the front door."

"Perhaps you would prefer to speak to the police," he said.

The threat had no effect on her. Her expression remained unchanging. "The authorities have no problem with the house of Joy Wang," she said. "I run a clean house and they respect that. And," she added, invoking a threat in her own voice, "they come whenever they are needed to eject unwanted guests." She cocked a dark brow at him. "Will they be needed this time, Mr. Lassiter?"

Disgusted with himself for his failure to learn more, Thorne left the house of pleasure and hired a carriage to take him back to the hotel. Halfway there, he changed his mind. "Do you know of a place called Madam Louise's?" he asked the driver.

The driver nodded. "It is a house of pleasure," he said. "Do you wish to go there?"

Thorne pulled out his pocket watch and studied the face. It was barely five minutes past four o'clock. Too

early for the girls to be receiving guests. But Madam
Louise should be available. That knowledge did nothing to encourage him, though. He'd received no information from Joy Wang and guessed that Madam Louise
would be as tough a nut to crack. The girls who worked
there, the prostitutes, were the answer. They would be
his best source of information. But, since they would
be in seclusion until the evening hours, he would return
to the hotel and wait there with Rainey.

The thought of her brought forth the memory of
how she'd looked with her legs wrapped around him,
and her face flushed with passion. Oh, God, how he
loved that woman!

Even the thought of the pleasure that could be found
in the soft folds of her body affected him. His lower
body throbbed with tension, hardened with desire. It
was for that reason that he instructed the driver to take
him to a well-known gaming club instead of the hotel.
If he returned to his room he would be sure to lose
track of time. And he must not do so. Eulalie must be
found as quickly as possible. He'd already spent too
much time away from his farm.

It was almost dusk when Lolly received word that
Madam Louise wished to see her in her office. "Whatever she wants could surely have waited until I had my
chores done," Lolly grumbled to herself as she hurried
down the stairway toward the large room that nobody
was allowed to enter unless they were especially invited
there. "She expects me to make certain everyone is
ready for the night but allows me no time to do it!"

"What did you say?" a voice asked suddenly.

Lolly looked up and saw Sandy Cowan, who had obviously been on her way upstairs, studying her with a
puzzled expression.

"I was just grumbling," Lolly explained. "Madam Louise sent for me and I really don't have any time to spare." She gestured to the bottle of whiskey she carried in her right hand, and the chemise and gown she carried over her left arm. "Rose is waiting for her clothing. She said her first customer is overdue already. But Madam is insistent about me going to her office."

"I could take that stuff to Rose," Sandy said, her voice almost sympathetic.

"Thank you, but no. You know Madam," Lolly said quickly. "She told me to do it . . . before she sent word that I come to her office immediately. Perhaps if she sees me with these things she'll get the idea that she's pushing me too hard."

"She'll never get that idea," Sandy said grimly. "Everyone here knows what she's about, Lolly. She wants you to entertain her customers. But you'll never do that, will you? No matter how much work she loads on you." There was a touch of bitterness in her voice. "Women like you—so high and mighty—would rather break than resort to prostitution." Every trace of sympathy had disappeared from her voice. "Well, goody for you! But we can't all be like that, can we?" she asked nastily. "Some of us are made of stronger stuff. We do whatever it takes to survive!" Without another word, she lifted her chin haughtily, then continued on her way up the stairs.

Lolly stared after the girl, feeling shamed for some reason. She knew there was no reason to feel that way, though. It was just that she'd never known the other women viewed her in that manner—as a woman who was proud of the fact that she'd never stoop to their level. Sandy had been wrong in her estimation of Lolly's character, though. Lolly was a survivor, too. She would do whatever she needed to survive. And had she found herself in the same circumstances as Sandy—whatever those circumstances had been—she might be in the same boat as the other woman, servicing the customers that arrived in droves to Madam Louise's house of pleasure.

The interview with Madam proved to be a short one. They'd had the same conversation many times before. Many times. And Lolly never wavered in her decision. "No, Madam," she said calmly. "I will not become one of your prostitutes. Not now, nor will I ever do so."

"You owe me, Eulalie!" Madam Louise said coldly. "I bought your services from Joy Wang and I paid a high price for them, too."

"You are being paid, too, Madam," Lolly replied. "I am working here in the same capacity that I worked for Madam Wang. I am bound in servitude for three years. And I perform my duties without question, until it comes to prostitution. That was never part of my duties. Nor will I agree to any such arrangement."

The madam's lips thinned. "If you would consider the circumstances, Eulalie, you might change your mind. One month working here as a prostitute or three years working here in the lowliest position . . . with more backbreaking work piled on you than one woman can possibly accomplish."

Although the last words were a threat, Lolly chose to ignore that fact. "I will not work as a prostitute," she said again. "Now, if there is nothing else, Rose is waiting for these things."

"Go on then!" the madam said, surprising Lolly by her sudden acceptance of the girl's refusal.

Lolly hurried out the door and headed toward the wide stairway leading to the upper floor. She knew Rose would need the liquor to help her get through the long night ahead.

That thought had barely occurred when a shout from upstairs caught her attention. "Lolly!" Rose yelled, leaning over the banister railing and looking down below. "Hurry up with that gown. And pour me a glass of that whiskey. I got a customer coming real soon."

"I'm coming, Rose!" Lolly shouted. She snatched a glass off a nearby tray and quickly poured it full of the amber liquid she carried. Rose would need the hard liquor in her belly to fortify her for the night.

"Hurry the hell up, Lolly!" Rose shouted again.

Lolly hurried toward the staircase, her gaze on the amber liquid that swirled as she moved. She'd have to hold it away from the garments she carried, lest it spill and soil them. She was so intent on her chore that she didn't see the tall, burly man coming until she collided with him. She gasped with horror as the whiskey glass upended, spilling its contents across him.

"Oh, my God!" she cried, staring wide-eyed at the somber, auburn-haired man whose shirt dripped with whiskey.

Although he had reacted instantly, reaching out quickly to steady her, he spoke not a word, just stared at her with a curious, green-eyed gaze.

"I'm s-sorry," she stuttered. "T-terribly sorry! But, you see, Rose needed the wh-whiskey that—that—"

"I'm wearing on my shirt," he finished calmly.

She nodded her head quickly. "Yes. She—her customer—Oh, God! I'm doing this badly. It's just that—that—"

"You're feeling flustered at ruining my shirt," he said, again completing her sentence for her.

"Yes," she gasped. "That's it! Flustered! I didn't mean to—I mean—you see. I was in such a hurry that I didn't—didn't—" His eyes were doing strange things to her. And she could hardly think with him towering over her. He appeared to be counting the freckles sprinkled across her nose. "R-Rose is in such a hurry, you see. Not that I'm laying the blame on her," she said quickly. "But this has been such a hectic day and the

customers are due to arrive any minute now and—"
Her green eyes widened and she clapped a hand across
her mouth. "Oh, botheration! You must be one of
them! A customer, I mean! And I'm keeping you standing here and—and . . ." Her voice trailed away and she
blushed wildly, reaching out to brush at the whiskey
stain covering his formerly white shirt.

"Never mind," he said brusquely. "It will wash out."
Tyler Duncan had been drawn to the woman with
auburn hair the moment he'd laid eyes on her. And
those green eyes, so like his own in color, were so like
the sea that he could almost drown in them. And the
pink bow mouth looked as though it had been made
for the express purpose of kissing.

"Lolly!" Rose shouted furiously. "Where the hell are
you? I need that gown!"

"I'm coming," Eulalie called. She lowered her voice
to a whisper. "I have to go. Rose needs her gown. If
you'll take the shirt off while you're being pleasured—
uh—serviced—Oh, dear! If you'll leave your shirt outside the door, then I'll wash the stain out for you. That
is, if you're g-going to b-be up there very l-long."

She didn't know why she was stuttering so badly. He
wasn't handsome, not with that imposing nose and
brooding brow. But his mouth wasn't bad. For a man,
it was really quite nice.

"I really must be going," she stammered. "Like I said,
Rose is waiting for me. H-have a nice time . . . that is . . .
uh . . . goodbye!" She hurried up the stairs, then
turned around again. "Don't forget to leave the shirt
in the hallway. I'll see that it's washed by the time
you're—uh, finished."

Lolly left him then, almost running up the stairs
where the dark-haired prostitute waited. "Who were
you talking to?" Rose asked curiously.

"Some man," Lolly replied. "A customer. At least I supposed he was."

"Who else comes here except customers?" Rose asked, taking her clothing from Eulalie. She frowned at the liquor bottle. "I thought you poured me a glass."

"I did," Lolly said quickly. "But it wound up on that man's shirt. That's why I was so long in coming."

"Oh, my God!" Rose exclaimed. "Do you think he'll complain to Madam?"

"He seemed nice enough," Lolly replied. "I don't think he'll say anything. I offered to wash his shirt while he was being serviced."

A grin played along Rose's lips. "Did you really? And what did he say to that?"

"He didn't say anything. But I suppose he'll leave the shirt outside like I suggested."

The two women parted then. Rose entered her room to don her garments and fortify herself for the long evening that lay ahead, while Lolly continued down the hall to check each room in turn so Madam would have no reason to complain about the work she was doing.

Tyler Duncan had been captivated by the young woman who had tossed liquor on his shirt. She had blushed easily, and that fact alone made him believe that the only services she performed in the house were those of a maid. He hoped he was right, that she performed no other services there, but refused to contemplate why it should matter to him one way or another. He quickly dismissed thoughts of the woman, though, knowing he must not allow the needs of his body to clutter up his mind. He would need all his wits about him to secure answers to his questions without arousing suspicion. His lips curled in a sardonic smile as he remembered his plans. His body would soon be satisfied, and, if he had his way, his questions answered to his satisfaction. And all without raising the least suspicion of his real reason for coming to Madam Louise's house of pleasure.

He continued across the room to the parlor, where several scantily clad girls lounged. And after speaking for a while with each woman, he made his choice known, then followed the dark-haired woman from the room. He was mounting the stairs behind her when he heard a heavy knock on the door. Having no interest in Madam Louise's customers, he continued on his way. Had he looked down, he would have seen Thorne Lassiter enter the bordello, bent on conducting his own investigation.

Lolly had completed her chores and was coming out of a room at the end of the corridor when she heard the front door open below. A quick peek over the bannister told her the man who entered had been there many times before. His face had become a familiar one this past week, even to Lolly, who usually managed to keep herself hidden from the customers who entered the house each night.

It was Madam Louise who had introduced her to Julian Hamstead, owner of a huge plantation that was located a few miles out of New Orleans.

Lolly had been surprised that Madam Louise had felt it necessary to introduce them, until she'd seen the possessive glint in Julian Hamstead's eyes. He made no bones about the fact that he desired Lolly, and that desire was obvious to any who witnessed when he looked up and saw her standing on the landing above him.

Stepping back quickly to avoid his gaze, Lolly hurried about her duties, finishing them as quickly as she could so she could retire to her room and lock the door, as was her usual practice each night until the last male guest had left the premises.

But that wasn't to be allowed, she discovered, when not more than an hour later, Madam Louise knocked on her door. "Unlock this door, Lolly. Rose needs your help!"

Lolly carefully eased the door open and peeked out at the older woman. "I thought Rose was working."

"She finished with her customer, but her gown is torn. You'll have to sew it up before her next customer comes." She gripped Lolly's arm with talonlike fingers and tugged hard at the girl.

Lolly resisted. "Wait," she said. "I'll need a needle and thread." She hurried to her sewing box and found a needle and thread, then returned to where the madam waited impatiently.

"Go along with you now," she said harshly. "And don't dawdle along the way."

Lolly hurried up the stairs and down the long hall that led to Rose's room. And as she did, she looked for the auburn-haired man's shirt but it was nowhere in sight. Perhaps he hadn't stayed, she thought, and for some odd reason, hoped it was so.

Upon reaching Rose's room, Lolly knocked softly, then turned the doorknob and stepped inside the shadowy interior. "Rose," she called out. "Why do you have it so dark in here? Light the lamp so I can see what I'm doing."

Silence.

"Rose? Are you there?"

Suddenly the door that she'd left open was shut behind her. Iron grated against iron, followed by a loud click. She whirled around and grasped the doorknob, trying to turn it but it appeared stuck. Fear washed over her as she realized she'd been locked inside the room.

She whirled around again and searched the shadows

with narrowed eyes. "Who's doing this?" she cried. "Rose? Are you there?"

"Nobody is here except the two of us," a hard, masculine voice said from across the room. A light flared suddenly and a match was put to wick, and Lolly stared in horror at the man who was seated on the bed, illuminated by the circle of lamplight. "Come here, my little wren," he commanded.

Terrified, Lolly backed against the door. "I thought R-Rose was in here," she stuttered. "Madam said she n-needed me to help her."

"Now, wasn't that naughty of her to lie," he replied. "Madam sold you to me for the night, and the cost was high, my dear. But for a virgin such as yourself I do not argue. You are worth the price. Come here and take those rough garments off." He patted the side of the bed, then pointed to his groin that stood out beneath the fabric of his breeches. "Harry is eager and ready for you."

She flushed hotly and looked away from him. She couldn't believe this was happening, that she was locked inside the room with the evil, little man. Her gaze flickered back to him, and to her consternation and fright, he had stripped away his clothing and stood up, his manhood extended to a dreadful size. She gulped and darted toward the door that connected with the next room, praying silently that it wasn't locked against her.

But, as though he were able to read her thoughts, Julian Hamstead reacted quickly, reaching the door at the same instant that she did, obviously intent on keeping her from leaving the room.

Oh, God, she silently cried. *Don't let this happen!*

As Julian reached for her, Lolly grasped the doorknob and gave it a hard jerk. To her utter amazement and relief, the door popped open. Without a second thought she raced through the door . . . then stopped short at the sight of the naked couple who lay on the bed, their limbs entangled together like vines on a tree.

Julian circled her wrist with clawlike fingers and jerked her toward him. "Come on, Lolly," he said angrily. "You can't escape me!" He pulled her toward the door again, intent on dragging her into the other room.

"No!" she cried, her heart jerking with fear. "Stop! Helen! Help me!"

She was vaguely aware of a woman's head jerking past her companion's shoulder. Dark eyes stared at her with shock. "Lolly! What's the matter?"

Before Lolly could reply, Julian Hamstead, having become tired of her resistance, struck her a hard blow on the chin. When she collapsed, he scooped her into his arms and carried her toward the other room.

"No! Don't!" Lolly screamed.

"Move, Tyler," Helen cried out, then with a furious glare at Julian, she clambered off the bed. "You let her go!" she cried. "She ain't no whore!"

She launched herself toward Julian, who knocked her aside swiftly and continued into the other room. Before Helen could recover, the door was kicked shut in her face.

Julian threw Lolly on the bed, then turned to lock the door but he was too late. It was shoved open abruptly and the large figure of a man filled the entrance.

"Stay out of this!" Julian Hamstead shouted, spreading his legs in a furious stance. "I paid for this girl and nobody's going to stop me from having her!"

The huge man, who proved to be the one she'd spilled whiskey on, reacted with a swiftness that surprised Lolly, as well as her attacker. His fingers curled around Hamstead's neck and he lifted the smaller man off the floor. The expression on his face was enough to put the fear of God into a much larger and braver man. "She *said* she's not a whore!" The big man shook Julian

Hamstead hard. "And any man who'd take a virgin against her will is lower than a polecat!" He bared his teeth and shook the man again, appearing to take pleasure from the head that bobbed back and forth before him. "And I never did like polecats."

Lolly lay on the bed, tears rolling down her cheeks while laughter shook her small frame. Alternately amused and embarrassed, but she was no longer afraid. How could she be afraid when the huge man had obviously appointed himself her protector? And the situation was so absurd, with everyone naked except for herself. Oh, God, what could be more amusing? Everyone naked, but the men showed no sign of arousal. There was Helen, glaring so furiously at Julian Hamstead, whose head bobbed back and forth as the huge man shook him as furiously as a dog would shake a rabbit in his mouth.

Then suddenly, as though the situation were not absurd enough, the hall door was shoved open and a stranger burst into the room. He stopped short, his gaze narrowing visibly as he took in the scene before him.

There was Lolly, sprawled across the bed, her clothing ripped and torn, tears glistening on her cheeks, shaking as though with extreme fear. And there was Helen, naked as the day she was born, standing erect and glaring at Julian, who hung at least two feet above the floor, held there by the large man, who had paused in his punishment of Hamstead long enough to direct his attention toward the newcomer.

Lolly could hardly believe it when the large man began to smile. "Thorne." The words rumbled out of his chest. "You're too late. I already found her."

The newcomer, the one the large man had addressed as Thorne, looked at Lolly again and said, "I hope to hell your name is Eulalie."

Twenty

Rainey regained her senses slowly. She became aware of sound, of voices that seemed to be coming from a long distance, but she couldn't make sense of the word. "Wake up," the voice said. "Come on, Mrs. Lassiter. It's time to wake up." The voice belonged to a man, and although it was gruff, she sensed the kindness beneath the tone.

"Wake up," he said again. "Come on, Mrs. Lassiter, open your eyes and look at me." The words were accompanied by a light slap on her right cheek, making her realize the man must be speaking to her. But why did he call her Mrs. Lassiter? she wondered. That wasn't her name.

She opened her mouth to tell him that, but instead of words she heard only a moan.

"That's good," the voice said. "Come on now. Open your eyes. Look at me, Mrs. Lassiter. I need to have you awake so I can finish examining you."

She blinked eyelids that seemed as heavy as a chunk of iron, then managed to keep them open long enough to see a heavyset man with silver-colored hair leaning over her. In the instant before her eyes closed again, she realized he held a stethoscope in his hand.

A doctor. He must be a doctor. In that instant she recalled her last memory, just before Cage Larson shoved her down the stairs. "My baby?" she asked huskily, forcing her eyes to open again.

"You lost it," the kindly gentleman said. "I'm sorry, my dear, but there's no reason why you can't have other children. You're a young woman and you have no internal damage."

"No," she moaned, turning her head aside to shut out his face. "No more children."

"Nonsense! I know you're feeling a terrible loss right now. But you weren't very far along, my dear. Be thankful for that. At least you hadn't developed a real attachment to the baby. And you've plenty of time for more children."

She swallowed hard around the knot, which suddenly formed in her throat, and tears leaked from her eyes. How could he know how attached she was to her baby? How could he possibly know?

He turned her head back toward him. "Open your eyes," he said gruffly. "Let me see them."

She allowed him to lift her eyelids and peer into her eyes. "How is your vision?" he asked. "Do you see me all right?"

She nodded her head and groaned from the pain the movement caused.

"You might have a concussion," he said. "Wouldn't be the least bit surprised the way you struck your head against the floor." He parted her hair and examined the wound there, then grunted with satisfaction. "You have a cut on your head but it isn't very deep. There're a few knots on that head of yours, too, but otherwise, even though you've lost your baby, there was no permanent damage."

She could have told him that losing her child was just about as permanent as it could get, but instead, she chose to remain silent, unwilling to speak at all.

He turned away from her and fiddled in his bag. A

moment later he held a small bottle of pills toward her. "That headache will bother you for a while," he said gruffly. "When it does, take two of these pills, but not more than six of them each day."

"I don't need your pills," she choked. "They won't bring my baby back."

"Nothing can do that," he admitted. "But the pills will help the headache, and I have a powder that will help the depression over losing the baby."

His words were the catalyst that broke the dam holding back her tears. They rained down her face as she curled herself into a ball and sobbed out her sorrow.

There would be no baby now. No part of Thorne to keep with her on the lonely nights that would come. Oh, God, how could she bear it. The years stretched out before her, barren, lifeless, without joy. She might as well be dead as to face those years alone.

She didn't know she was voicing that thought until she felt a hand sliding behind her shoulders to lift her up. Her eyes flashed open and she saw the doctor holding a glass to her mouth.

"Drink this," he said gently. "It will make you feel better."

She drank the bitter liquid, even though she knew it wouldn't make her feel better. Nothing would.

Confusion swept through Eulalie as she studied the angry man who had spoken to her.

"My name *is* Eulalie," she said, wondering who he was. "But how could you know that?" She looked past his shoulder and saw Vivian hovering there, as though afraid of entering the room where everyone had taken leave of their senses.

"I didn't know," he replied. "Only hoped it was so. I'm your brother, Thorne. And I believe, as such, that

I am due an explanation of what you are doing in a room where every other occupant is naked as a jaybird."

Very few of his words registered in Lolly's mind after he'd laid claim to being her brother. Her brother! She didn't have a brother! Her green eyes were round as she studied his grim features. "You must be crazy," she finally said. "I don't have a brother. Furthermore, sir, you are a complete stranger to me."

She was unaware of the man who'd appointed himself her protector until he dropped his squirming, red-faced captive and directed his attention toward her. "Are you certain he's not related to you, miss?" he growled.

"Quite certain," she replied firmly.

"What do you have to say about that, Lassiter?" the man asked the newcomer.

"Lassiter?" she echoed in a faint voice. "Your name is Lassiter?"

"Yes," he replied. "Thornton O'Brien Lassiter. My father is Eugene Lassiter." He held her gaze calmly, waiting for his words to sink in.

"Then perhaps . . . perhaps we are related," she said, her gaze flickering between the two men. "But how did . . . how did you find me?"

"It wasn't easy," the man who claimed to be her brother replied.

Eulalie thought about the irony of the situation. She had a brother and now, finding her this way, he was likely to deny her existence. She cleared her throat. "I'm afraid my circumstances might have led you to believe something that is not true."

"No," he replied. "Vivian has told me the truth of the matter," Thorne said. "How you come to be in this situation." His gaze flickered to the naked men, and his lips tightened grimly. "For God's sake, Duncan, take yourself and that piece of trash you dropped out of here, and put some clothes on."

The big stranger, whose name was obviously Duncan, frowned as he looked down at himself, then his gaze swept to Eulalie again. "Ma'am, are you comfortable enough with the situation for me to leave long enough to dress myself?"

"Uh, yes . . . I imagine I will be fine while you are gone," she said, lowering her eyes from his perfectly formed masculine body.

"Then I'll go," he said. "And I'll take this polecat along with me." He slung the other man over his shoulder like a bag of grain and strode from the room, the bare cheeks of his buttocks gleaming whitely as he went.

Eulalie turned her attention to the man who claimed to be her brother. "You said your name was Thornton Lassiter?" she inquired. "Why have I never heard about you before?"

"I suppose for the same reason I never heard of you," Thorne replied.

At that moment Madam Louise arrived on the scene. "What in hell is going on here?" she asked coldly. "Vivian! Who is this man? And what is he doing here?" Without waiting for the prostitute to reply, her gaze swept across the room, passing Lolly, then returning again. "Where is Julian?" Her voice rose to an hysterical pitch. "You haven't done anything to him, have you? Do you realize how important the Hamsteads are, young woman? If you've set him against me, then you'll live to regret this day."

The tall form of Duncan appeared in the doorway. He looked across at Madam Louise and said, "Shut up, Louise! Or you'll be the one who'll regret this day!"

She sucked in a sharp breath and turned toward him. As her gaze found him, her face drained of color. "Tyler Duncan! Who let you in?"

"Someone who didn't recognize me," Duncan said, his voice as grim as his expression. "If you don't want me to persuade my client to press charges against you, then you'll close your mouth and leave while you have the chance."

"Charges?" Her gaze narrowed. "What charges could possibly be lodged against me, Tyler? The girl is here of her own free will . . . and what did you mean when you made that claim about a client? Exactly, who is your client?"

"She is," Duncan said. "Isn't that right, Miss Lassiter?"

"Uh . . . of course," she agreed quickly. "Like he said, I'm his client." She tightened her lips. "So I suggest you shut up and leave." Lolly had no idea what the woman was being threatened with, but she would agree to anything Tyler Duncan had to say. Every semblance of fear had fled the moment he'd become her champion.

"You're bluffing about bringing charges," Madam Louise said harshly. "I've done nothing wrong."

"Except conduct a little white slavery."

The words made her face lose what little color it had managed to retain. "You wouldn't dare," she said, but her uncertainty was evident in her voice.

"Try me."

"I have no interest in trying you . . . nor in ever laying eyes on you again." She strode stiffly out of the room then, without a backward glance.

Lolly looked at Vivian and Helen, and the three women smiled at each other. It had been good to see the woman get her comeuppance, no matter what the reason. And that reason had not yet been made clear to any of them. But it was obvious Tyler Duncan knew something about the woman that she would rather not have revealed.

At Tyler's direction, Lolly packed her few belongings, and left Madam Louise's house of pleasure. Although she had no idea what lay ahead in the future, she knew it couldn't be worse than what she was leaving behind.

The cool night air blew softly against her face as she walked between her brother and Tyler Duncan. As they spoke together she began to realize how they had met. She realized, as well, that Tyler's presence in the bordello had not been accidental, that he had been in Helen's room for the explicit purpose of gathering information that would help in his investigation.

It had been fate that he had chosen Helen, instead of one of the other prostitutes. Because, although Helen would have done her best for Lolly when she burst into her room seeking help, her efforts would not have been enough.

A cold chill swept over Lolly and she shuddered when she thought about what would have happened if Tyler had not been there to help.

"Are you cold, Lolly?" Tyler asked.

She'd thought he had forgotten her presence until he spoke. "No," she replied quickly. "I was just thinking about what could've happened if you hadn't been in Helen's room."

"Don't think about it," he ordered brusquely. "I was there. And I'm grateful for that fact."

They fell silent then, all three busy with their own thoughts. Then, Thorne asked a question that had obviously been bothering him for some time. "What made you decide to make my father pay for what he'd done to you, Eulalie?"

"Make him pay?" she asked, her gaze flickering uncertainly to him as her footsteps faltered. "I don't understand, Thorne. I have never met your—our—father. It was obvious he didn't want any contact with me, so I've respected his wishes and left him alone."

"Until recently, you mean."

"I have *never* tried to contact him."

"Not personally," he said gruffly. "But indirectly you have."

"No," she insisted, stopping short to stare at him. "Not even indirectly."

"Then what about your cousin, Cage?"

Her gaze narrowed with sudden suspicion. "Cage?" she asked. "Cage Larson?"

"Yes," he said dryly. "That is the one."

"Cage is my cousin. He's the reason I was in that mess. His gambling debt and those men threatening to tear him limb from limb. And they would've done it, too. Cage was certain of that. He was trembling when he told me, absolutely terrified, fearful of his life and the torture they would inflict before they killed him. That was the only reason I went to Joy Wang. She loaned me the funds to give him. And it really wasn't so bad at her house, but when she traded me to Madam Louise—" She broke off suddenly and her gaze flickered between the two men who had become silent and watchful. Then Tyler began to curse.

"That damned scoundrel! He's got more than one black mark against him! And when I get my hands on him, he's going to wish he'd never been born."

"You didn't know?" Her gaze left Tyler and found Thorne. "And neither did you. But you said he—that you—What were you talking about before?"

"Our father has been giving large sums of money to your cousin for the past few years. Cage told Father that he was your agent, that he was acting on your behalf, at your request."

Lolly gasped with horror. "And your father believed him?"

"He had no reason not to do so, Lolly."

"Is that why you are here then?" she asked, feeling a terrible weight of disappointment. "Because he got tired of making payments to my cousin?"

"No," Thorne replied.

He went on to explain the way he'd gotten involved in the whole thing. And when he was finished, Lolly realized how little she had really known her cousin.

"I should have known Cage was up to something when he asked so many questions of my grandfather," she said angrily. "I never knew anything about this, Thorne. I would never have condoned such a plan."

"I know that now."

Tyler patted her hand. "Nobody is blaming you, Lolly. But I'm afraid that isn't all that we have to tell you."

"There's more?" She heaved a deep sigh. "You might as well tell me the rest of it. What else has he been up to?"

"It's not Cage this time. It's your grandfather."

"My grandfather?" She frowned at them. "What do you know of my grandfather?"

Tyler put his arm around her shoulder and leaned closer. "He . . . your grandfather passed away a few days ago, Lolly. Thorne was with him and he—"

"Grandpère!" she cried. She could feel the color leaving her cheeks. "You cannot mean it! It is not true. *Grandpère* is all I have . . . all that is dear to me. No, no! He could not be gone! He is a young man yet. There should be many years left to him."

Tyler pulled her against him and smoothed his hand down her hair. "He did not suffer, little one," he said gently. "And his last thought was for you."

"Where is he?" she asked, tilting her head to look into his face. "Where did they take him? I have to see him."

"That is not possible, Eulalie," Thorne said. "He is at rest now. We put him beside your grandmother. We thought he would want that."

"Yes," she murmured, wiping her eyes. "Yes. Thank you, Thorne, for doing that. He wanted to be there when the time came. But . . . what happened? Why did he die?"

He explained to her what had happened, and by the time he'd finished speaking they were at the hotel. "I'll get another room," Thorne told them. "Why don't you wait over there?" He pointed toward the settee.

Lolly was grateful for the suggestion. Her knees were weakened from the news she'd received. Her dear, beloved grandfather, her *grandpère*, was gone. Now there was nobody left for her in the whole world. Nobody who really cared for her, anyhow.

Her cousin, Cage Larson, most certainly didn't care. He'd proved that many times over. And her father . . . he had tried his best to keep her existence hidden from the world. There was Thorne, though . . . her brother, obviously a good man, but he was a stranger. And there was the detective who hovered over her as though she were the most precious gem in the world.

Tyler. She looked at him through a mist of tears, and what she saw in his eyes made her realize there was a whole lifetime ahead of her.

Thorne crossed the lobby swiftly. The desk clerk leaned against the long counter, studying the ledger.

"Do you have a room adjoining my suite?" Thorne inquired brusquely.

"Mr. Lassiter!" the other man exclaimed. "I didn't expect to see you here. How is your wife doing?"

Thorne frowned at the man. "Very well, I suppose. I haven't seen her since earlier today, though." His words were meant to convey humor, but the look on the desk clerk's face made him uneasy. "Why do you ask?"

For a moment the man looked confused, then his eyes widened. "I—I—it's just that your wife is—was—so delicate and all. And for such a thing to happen, sir!

And in our hotel, too." He looked around and lowered his voice, which took on a funeral tone. "Have they caught the man who did it?"

A cold chill settled around Thorne and he could feel the blood draining from his face. "What in hell are you talking about?" he demanded. "Caught what man? Has something happened to Rainey?"

As though he suspected Thorne would do him physical harm, the clerk backed away, putting more distance between himself and the angry man who faced him. "I'm sorry, Mr. Lassiter," he said. "I thought you knew."

"Knew what? Dammit, man! What happened to Rainey?"

"Why, she had an accident, sir! A man . . . an animal, really, chased her into the hotel and pushed her down the stairs. I wasn't here when it happened. Jimmy Crawford was standing in for me, but he said it was horrible. That she just lay there, all crumpled up like a doll that had been thrown in the trash."

"Oh, God!" Thorne whispered.

"I'm sorry, Mr. Lassiter, sir," the clerk said. "I wouldn't have told you if I'd known you didn't know. Jimmy said it was the most terrible thing that he'd ever seen, with her laying there like that . . . at the bottom of the stairway . . . with all that blood pouring out of her head and soaking into the carpet. The maid couldn't get the blood out, either. She said the stain will never come out and—"

"Where is she?" Thorne asked, his gaze boring into the clerk. "Dammit, man! Where the hell is she?" In his mind's eye he could see her, crumpled and broken, her lifeless eyes gazing endlessly at nothing. "Where did they take her?" he demanded harshly.

"Upstairs!" the clerk said, his voice quivering with fear. "Back to your suite. The doctor went in there awhile back, but as far as I know, he never come out again."

Uttering an anguished cry, Thorne dashed toward

the staircase. He was unaware of the startled looks of those he passed in his flight. He knew nothing, save the need to reach his suite as quickly as possible.

When he opened the door to the sitting room, he was immediately aware of the silence. It roared out its presence, curled the hair at the nape of his neck. Was he too late? Had he lost her completely, to a place far removed from him?

Oh, God, what would he do without her?

He couldn't lose her! He could not live without her!

"Rainey!" he shouted, making a dash toward her room. He yanked open the door and his gaze swept the room, took in the man seated beside the bed, where a huddle of quilts seemed to mock its empty state.

"Rainey," he cried, his voice almost breaking as his heart had already done.

"Be quiet, man!" The words were issued in a hard voice. "Do you want to wake her?"

"She's not dea—how bad is she?" Thorne's voice was hushed. He had been afraid to speak of death, lest the spoken word made it so.

"Bad enough," the doctor replied. As Thorne covered the distance between himself and the woman he loved, the other man studied him from beneath beetled brows. "I suppose you're the husband."

Thorne didn't bother to deny it. In his heart he had been Rainey's husband since they'd first made love. "Will she recover?" he asked, his gaze settling on her pale features.

"Her injuries, although painful, are not life threatening," the doctor replied. "She regained consciousness once. But only for a short while. When she learned she'd lost the baby she took it hard. I thought it best to give her some sleep powders."

"The baby?" Thorne asked, his heart jerking with surprise. "There was a baby?"

"Yes. I take it you didn't know."

"No," Thorne said softly. "And I don't think she did, either."

"You're wrong," the doctor said gruffly. "She knew." He reached for a package that had been placed on a nearby table and handed it to Thorne. "It appears she had been out shopping when she was attacked. She dropped her package on the sidewalk. We wouldn't have known about it if the lady who made the sale hadn't found the package on her way home. She brought it to the hotel and left it with the desk clerk."

Thorne opened the package, and a knot of pain coiled around his heart as he pulled out a tiny pink garment.

Twenty-one

Rainey was drowning, sinking in the dark-black sea of death that had already claimed her child. She'd tried to save it, had tried so hard. But she had been unable to reach the babe in time. It had been too far away, yet she'd been able to see it clearly through that shadowy world beneath the water. She'd fought so hard to reach the babe, but her efforts had been useless. It had sunk down, down, toward the cold grave below, and all the while its eyes were wide open, begging her, pleading with her to save it.

But she could not. And now there was nothing for her, nothing left in life except this dreadful pain in her heart. Oh, God, how could she stand it?

She watched the flowing vines that grew in the watery depths wrap around her babe, and she swam toward it, wanting to touch it, needing to hold it in her arms. But the vines twisted and curled, blocking her way, refusing to allow her near the babe.

"No, no," she cried, thrashing wildly to gain release. But her efforts were in vain. She could not free herself, and the vines were moving her farther away, twisting, twining around her, seeming intent on taking her life, as well.

Rainey looked upward and saw a narrow beam of sun-light far above her head. That tiny, narrow beam meant air; it meant escape from this suffocating darkness that trapped her within its clammy reaches. *Oh, God*, she cried, but no sound escaped her lips. *Let me get away! Let me escape from this watery existence.*

The light blinked out suddenly, leaving her in a darkness that was so absolute that she screamed out her terror. *"Eeeeeaaaaaaaa!"*

The shrieking sound jerked her upright. And as she sucked in sharp, raspy breaths of air, she blinked rapidly, trying to clear her fuzzy mind, as well as her sleep-drugged eyes.

The sound of running feet ended when the door to her bedroom was suddenly flung open. "Rainey!" Thorne cried, striding across the room quickly. "Are you all right?" He knelt beside the bed and pulled her into his embrace.

"I had—had a nightmare," she whispered shakily, leaning against him. "I dreamed there was a baby and it was drowning and I couldn't save it no matter how hard I tried and I—" She broke off, remembering suddenly. "Oh, God!" she cried, pulling away from him. "There was a baby. But it died. He killed it when he threw me down the stairs."

She began to cry then, hard, convulsive sobs that shook her whole body. And all the while Thorne held her. Finally, when sobs no longer shook her body, she pulled away and looked up . . . into a face that was white and drawn, into eyes that glittered with hate.

Rainey jerked away from him then, scrambling across the bed as quickly as her weakened condition would allow. "Go away!" she cried, her body shuddering with fear. "Leave me alone!" Her gaze skittered back and forth, stopped on the doctor who had entered the room. "Make him leave!" she cried hysterically. "Get him out of here!"

But the doctor didn't have to do anything. Without a sound, Thorne turned and left the room.

Thorne shook with silent rage as he joined Tyler and his sister in the sitting room. Eulalie's expression was sympathetic. She'd obviously heard everything. "She didn't mean it, Thorne. She's grieving so much that she doesn't know what she's saying."

"She knows," Thorne said grimly. "And she hates me for what happened to her." He looked at Tyler. "Did you find out who did this to her?"

"Yes." Tyler's gaze shifted to Eulalie, then returned to meet Thorne's again. "We could talk downstairs."

"Don't try to spare my feelings," Eulalie said. "It was Cage, wasn't it?"

"Yes. I'm afraid it was."

Thorne's hands tightened into fists. "Does anyone know why?"

"No. He didn't hang around to give any reasons. They wouldn't have known his name if the desk clerk hadn't become suspicious of him a few days ago."

"Days ago?"

"Yes. He had been hanging around, asking questions about you. The desk clerk became suspicious and made him show some identification. Anyway, Cage took one look at her lying on the floor in a pool of blood, and he took off like a scalded cat. He stopped at the livery stable long enough to hire a horse—guess he didn't have one of his own—and then he rode out of town, taking a northeasterly direction."

Thorne could see why Tyler Duncan had an impeccable reputation around town. He had not waited for direction from Thorne, and had begun an immediate investigation into the circumstances surrounding Rainey's fall.

"What time did he leave?" Thorne asked quietly.

"An hour after he pushed her," Tyler replied. "You're going after him, aren't you?"

"Yes. I'm going."

Tyler sighed. "Then I guess you'll have a traveling companion."

"You don't have to come."

"Yes, I do," Tyler said grimly. "Not for your sake, but for Lolly's."

Thorne and Tyler crossed the river at daybreak, stumbling upon a natural fording place, where the current had thrust a sandspit halfway across the dark and sluggishly twirling stream. The woods grew thickly to the river's edge in a matted tangle and they had to dismount, leading the horses and working their way foot by foot through small natural avenues. Now and then Thorne was forced to take a sharp-bladed knife out and hack additional yards to link a corridor before they could proceed.

"He's headed for the old man's cabin," Thorne remarked as he turned back and edged out of an impassable lane to try again at a more favorable spot. "It would have been simpler if we had known that. We could have taken the pirogue."

"But we didn't know it," Tyler replied. "And neither did he when he began his journey. Or else he would have gone by boat instead of taking this damnable route. But since he went through here, there must be an easier trail, a passage that we haven't come across yet."

"I'm sure you're right," Thorne said grimly. "But we could spend the rest of the day looking for it, and we don't have the time to waste."

They came upon the sandbar suddenly. It stretched

in a high, golden triangle out from the dense willows. Around its tip the current raced with bubbling eagerness, forming small, spinning whirls that sucked at floating leaves and branches, pulling them beneath the mahogany-colored surface and releasing them several yards distant downstream.

"We're going to get wet," Tyler said, eyeing the water skeptically.

"It won't be the first time," Thorne replied.

They made the crossing, clinging to the bridles of the horses. They held their guns above their heads, with the saddlebags secured high on the backs of the animals, out of reach of the lapping water. When they finally stood on the opposite bank, dripping but triumphant, the two men smiled at each other, sharing a sense of achievement.

Looking back over his shoulder, Tyler surveyed the stream. "It doesn't look like much now," he said, "but I was afraid we'd never make it across."

"I never thought we wouldn't," Thorne said. "There's no way I'm going to let Cage Larson get away from me. I would have crossed the damned river, if I'd had to swim all the way by myself."

"You wouldn't have made the distance without the horses," Tyler told him.

They rode steadily throughout the morning, following the meandering stream, traversing the same route that he had traveled before, except now he was on horseback. They followed the stream as best they could on ground that was so marshy that at times it had to be detoured around. There were times when the woods broke away completely, leaving great cleared patches in which grass rose waist high, and every few yards the horses kicked out coveys of quail that beat a drumming flight to safety. Turkey, deer, rabbit, and plump doves crowded the bushes, but Thorne was ever aware that the wildlife was not their prey. Occasionally there were signs that Cage Larson had come before them. The unmistakable print of a shod horse; the butt of a half-smoked cigarillo. But there was never any sign of the man himself.

Nevertheless, Thorne knew he would find him. There was no way the man could escape him, even if he fled to the ends of the earth.

Thorne didn't know they were so close to their destination until he came upon the small clearing, dappled in sunlight, where two headstones and one wooden cross marked the graves of the old man and his wife and daughter. He dismounted and fastened the reins of his horse to a nearby tree.

"The house is only a short way from here," he muttered. "We'll have to be quiet from now on."

Tyler nodded his head, and the two men slipped down the path leading to the house. It appeared deserted. But Thorne was unwilling to accept that he'd lost his quarry. He slid his gun out of its holster and moved closer.

His heartbeat quickened. He was eager to see the man who'd caused the death of his child, and made the woman Thorne loved turn against him. With his hand on the doorknob, he called, "Come on out, Cage! You're surrounded. There's no way out except through this door."

There was the sound of muffled curses from within, followed by a mad dash across the floor. Realizing Cage was trying to escape through one of the windows, Thorne rushed around the corner, just in time to see his quarry roll through the open window and strike the ground hard.

Thorne was on him immediately.

He struck Cage a hard blow on the nose and felt the gristle crunch beneath his fist. Larson's eyes watered from the pain. Before he could recover, Thorne wound one hand in his opponent's coarse hair and hit him in the face again. The blow landed with a heavy thump and Cage went down as though he'd been poleaxed.

Cage lay on the ground, stunned. Then, uttering a loud bellow of rage, he sprung to his feet and made a flying leap for Thorne's throat. Thorne grinned savagely and stepped aside, quickly kicking out with his right foot, catching Larson in the pit of his stomach. Cage pitched forward, bent over with agony.

"That's enough, Thorne," Tyler said.

Thorne ignored the detective. He stood, with clenched fists, watching Larson flounder onto his hands and knees. He continued to wait, grim and silent, until Larson regained his footing, then kicked him savagely in the ribs.

"Stop it, Thorne!" Tyler growled. "He's had enough."

Larson's breathing was labored, he was sweating profusely, but he managed to stagger to his feet once again.

For all the good it did him, though. Thorne closed in, striking Larson with a thudding impact, knocking him against the trunk of a large magnolia tree.

Thorne went after him then, grabbed him up and hit him in the face with a loud smack. He continued to pound the man about the head and shoulders, gratified by the sounds of flesh against flesh and the pain-filled grunts that punctuated each thud of his fist.

"That's enough, Thorne," Tyler said, grasping Thorne's arms and pulling him away from the heaving mass of flesh on the ground. "You've already had your revenge. There's no sense in killing the man."

"Why not!" Thorne demanded harshly. "He killed everything that I held dear. Scum like him don't deserve to live."

"You can't play God, Thorne. It isn't up to you to decide who has the right to live or die."

"If you don't have the stomach to watch him die, then you can go on ahead," Thorne said viciously. "He isn't fit to live among civilized beings."

"Perhaps not. But he has a right to a fair trial."

"Hell, man!" Thorne exploded. "He won't even go to jail! They don't hang you for killing unborn babies. He'll go free and I won't stand for that."

"You can't decide his fate," Tyler said, stooping to pick up the unconscious man. "Anyway, you should consider Eulalie. How would she feel to know that her brother—whom she has only just found—has killed her cousin?"

"Damn proud if she's any kind of woman!" Thorne snapped.

"Watch your mouth, buddy," Tyler said shortly. "Lolly is a gentle, caring woman. You know that as well as I do. And I won't let you do anything to hurt her."

Thorne gave a snort of disgust. "If the shoe were on the other foot—if it were Lolly who had been pushed down the stairs and *your* baby had died—then you would feel different about the whole thing."

"I imagine I would," Tyler admitted. "But it wasn't Lolly and I'm trying to act in her best interests. And that doesn't include having her brother hanged for killing her cousin."

Reluctantly, Thorne gave in.

Twenty-two

Rainey woke abruptly, her hair wet with perspiration. She'd been dreaming again, having that same old nightmare that had plagued her for the past two weeks—since Cage Larson had pushed her down the stairs.

How long would she be plagued by that dream? How many more times would she find herself floating in that same dark sea, watching her baby drown, while its eyes pleaded for help that she was unable to give?

She swallowed around the tightness in her throat. She felt hollow inside, felt an emptiness that went much deeper than mere hunger. *Oh, God, would this pain never end?*

Realizing she had begun to wallow in self-pity, Rainey wiped the moisture from her eyes and tried to control her runaway emotions. She tried to convince herself that things had happened for the best, that Thorne would have felt bound to marry her when he learned she was expecting his child. But no matter how hard she tried to convince herself of that fact, she could not do so.

She loved Thorne desperately. And she had loved their child, even though it was barely more than a thought when she lost it.

How had Thorne felt when he discovered their loving had resulted in new life? He did know, she was certain of that! And yet the few times they were together, the subject had been carefully avoided.

Oh, Thorne, she silently cried. *Things could have been so different. If you'd only loved me.*

But he had not, did not! And she felt so empty inside.

It was then that the full force of what she felt for Thorne burst inside her. She'd always known that she cared for him, but hadn't really known just how much. Not until now. For years, without her knowledge, he had been her whole world, her very reason for existence. And to have his baby would have been the ultimate joy.

But it was not to be.

So intent was she on her thoughts that she didn't hear the door open, never knew she was no longer alone until she heard a quiet voice inquire: "Are you all right?"

Rainey turned her head to see Thorne watching her from the doorway. He came to her quickly and knelt beside the bed. "What's wrong, Rainey?" he asked gently. "Are you in pain?"

Yes. She was in pain. But it was a pain of the heart, not of the body. A pain that stabbed deep, that could not be remedied, because it was a sickness of the soul.

She looked into his eyes and saw the fear in them. What had put it there? she wondered. Was he afraid of the future, that she would expect more from him than he was willing to give?

Her pride found that completely unacceptable, so she hurried to correct that notion. "It's past time I went home, Thorne. Would you make the arrangements for me?"

"You want to go home?" It was obvious he was puzzled by her request. "Why, Rainey?" he asked. "You aren't well enough to travel yet."

She could not dispute the words since she always felt

weak as a kitten whenever she left the bed for even short periods of time. "I will be soon, though," she told him. "And I want to leave the moment the doctor says I'm well enough to travel."

"All right," he agreed. "But we must detour by St. Louis first. I have some unfinished business there . . . with my father. Eugene Lassiter has some fences to mend and I need to make sure he doesn't shirk that duty. He must be made to provide for Lolly's future."

"You like her, don't you." It was more a statement than a question.

"Yes. I do. Even though they have different mothers, she is very much like Eloise. And no matter the place where she worked, it is obvious to me that she is of very good character."

"I am sure of it even though I've never met her." She looked around him, toward the door. "Is she in there, Thorne? In the sitting room?"

"No. She went out with Tyler. She expressed a wish to visit her grandfather's grave, so he rented a boat to take them to the bayou."

"Tyler? He's the detective you hired?"

"Yes." Thorne grimaced ruefully. "Tyler Duncan seems to have appropriated my sister. A bystander would take him for her brother instead of me."

"Do I detect a note of jealousy there?"

"Perhaps. But only a little. A new brother would expect to receive some attention . . . at least a passing interest, but Tyler Duncan is always around. From the moment she wakes in the morning until she goes to bed at night. He's even neglecting his business, and the Lord only knows if he can afford to."

"Things sound serious between them." She looked down and fingered the coverlet. "Do you expect them to marry?"

"I'm afraid that's what Tyler has in mind," he said

grimly. "And I intend to speak to that young man soon about his intentions."

"Why do you sound so grim?" she asked. "Would marriage to Tyler be so bad for your sister?"

"It's not just marriage to Tyler," he explained. "I would find her marriage to anyone just as objectionable."

"Most women want to marry," she said softly.

"And they are usually so eager to attain that state that they marry the first man who comes along," he said gruffly. "But I do not intend for that to happen. Eulalie deserves to be happy. And I intend to see that nobody, however likable he is, takes advantage of my sister while she is so vulnerable." Thorne rose to his feet and crossed to the window, staring down into the courtyard below. When he returned to her, his face was set in determined lines. "Rainey," he said gruffly. "We haven't yet talked about what happened."

"You know what happened," she said. "Cage Larson pushed me down the stairs."

"I know what he did, and he's paying for that," he said abruptly. "But that's not what I was talking about. It's the baby, Rainey. Why didn't you tell me there was to be a child?"

"I didn't—"

"You *did* know," Thorne interrupted. "The woman who sold you the infant gown brought it to the hotel."

Then the gown hadn't been lost after all. She was glad of that. It was the only thing left of her child . . . except its memory. "I wasn't sure about it," she said. "I guessed, thought it might be true, but it was too soon to be certain."

"You bought the gown," he said again.

"It was just that . . . it looked so pretty in the store window . . . and I thought . . . there was a chance there was a baby, and I wanted that dress for it to wear," she finished in a rush.

"And you were happy about it?"

Tears moistened her eyes and spilled over. "Yes," she replied. "I was happy about it."

"There could be other children, Rainey," he said, kneeling beside the bed and cupping her face between his palms, and wiping the tears away with his large thumb. "We could have many children . . . if you'd marry me."

For a moment Rainey couldn't speak. She wanted to marry him. God, how she wanted it. But he was only proposing because he thought he had to. Thorne had always taken care of her. From the moment he'd arrived on Thunder Mountain, he'd made that his primary duty.

And he was still doing it.

She couldn't allow him to ruin his life by making that ultimate sacrifice, even though he seemed bent on doing just that. And when Thorne made a decision, there was no swaying him. But she had to, just had to make him see what he was doing to both of them. She loved him desperately, but if she married him without his love, then their marriage was doomed before it even began.

"I can't," she said softly, even though it was like tearing out her heart to say the words. She sought a way to sway him, to make him see it would not work. "I really ought to say yes, though," she told him. "It would serve you right if I did."

"Serve me right?" He studied her intently. "What do you mean, Rainey? Why can't you marry me?"

"You ought to know why, Thorne," she said sharply. "Marriage is for people who love each other in a certain way. If one of them only loves the other—like a brother loves a sister—then the marriage would never work."

She swallowed around her pain, and felt a tear roll slowly down her cheek.

He wiped it away gently, and the grim look slowly left his face. "You're right," he said sadly. "A marriage like that would never work. We would wind up hating each other, and I don't want that, Rainey. I couldn't stand the thought of you ever hating me."

"I won't ever do that, Thorne," she said, leaning her cheek against his, taking comfort from his nearness. "No matter what happens I won't ever hate you."

He sighed and rose to his feet. His gaze never left her face. "Rainey. Is it Robert Golden? Is that why you can't . . . love me?"

"Robert Golden?" For a moment Rainey had trouble remembering who Robert Golden was. Then suddenly it came to her. He was the teacher she had been so fascinated with. She opened her mouth to deny any feeling for the man, then realized she'd been given an out. Thorne would believe she was in love with Robert Golden, and they would both have their pride left to them. "Yes," she said, dropping her eyes to evade his probing gaze. "It's h-him."

"I see." He straightened abruptly, lifting his head at a sharp angle. "I should've known, I guess. But somehow, I thought you'd forgotten him."

I did, her heart cried. *I had forgotten, Thorne. My heart remembered no one but you, dear heart.* But she couldn't say the words aloud. She dared not do so.

Thorne must never, never know how she felt.

Twenty-three

"Look, Lolly!" Rainey exclaimed, leaning forward in the carriage and pointing toward the Lassiter house. "That house up ahead . . . the big one, is where your father and your sister live."

Lolly frowned and studied the large house they were approaching. She'd known her father had money but had had no idea just how wealthy he was. The house was larger even than Madam Louise's house of pleasure. She leaned closer to Tyler and he covered her hand with his own. She couldn't help but notice that Thorne had seen the gesture and that it was most likely what caused the frown on his face. For some reason he objected to Tyler's attention to her.

All too soon they were at the front door. It was opened abruptly, even before they could knock, making it apparent someone had been watching for them. The young woman who faced them was so like Thorne in appearance that it was obvious they were related, even before she spoke.

"Eulalie." The woman spoke with a smile. "Come inside and let me look at you."

Eloise was everything Lolly had dreamed of. She welcomed her long-lost sister so enthusiastically that it made up for Eugene Lassiter's cool reception. It was obvious from the first time they met that he'd rather keep her identity hidden from St. Louis society.

But Thorne would not allow that. Eloise and Lolly and Rainey went on a shopping spree to end all shopping sprees. Each one of them tried on so many gowns that they were totally exhausted by the time they returned home. But they enjoyed those trips of theirs, each woman having taken to the other instantly as though they'd known one another all their lives.

And when they'd decided enough clothing had been purchased to launch both Eulalie and Rainey into society, Thorne and Tyler escorted them to the opera.

They'd only barely arrived at the opera house when they bumped into Mary Burton, an elderly matron who was considered the head of St. Louis society. The woman was wearing a pale-rose gown made of heavy velvet. It was obvious the woman was suffering from the heat, because she fanned herself continually while they spoke together.

"Gossip has it that you brought a long-lost sister home with you," Mary Burton said, her gaze flitting between Rainey and Eulalie. "I suspect one of these young women is that same sister?"

"Your suspicions are right, as usual," Thorne said, clasping his fingers around Eulalie's arm and pulling her forward slightly. "Allow me to introduce my sister Eulalie Lassiter. Lolly, this outrageous lady is Mary Burton."

"Outrageous am I?" Mary smiled widely and, closing her fan with a snap, she slapped Thorne's wrist smartly. "This brother of yours was always a teaser." She looked across at Tyler. "I don't know this young man. But it's obvious that he's in love with your sister. Is there a wedding in the offing? If there is, it's too bad." Tyler scowled at her. "Yes, young man. Too bad. The young woman has only just met her family and now you plan on taking her away again. Shame on you."

Lolly blushed rosily. "No, ma'am," she said quickly. "We've made no plans for such an event."

"You'd best get to it soon, young man," she said. Then, to Rainey's extreme discomfort, she became the object of Mary Burton's attention. "Who is this young woman, Thorne? And why is she standing here gaping at me?"

"My name is Rainey Watson, ma'am," Rainey said quickly, revealing her own identity, lest the woman say something outrageous about her association with Thorne. "And I didn't mean to gape."

"I'm sure you didn't, but—"

Thorne's fingers curled around Rainey's forearm. "I'm sorry, Mary, but you must excuse us. We have to find our seats while there's still time."

They left her then, and when Rainey chanced a quick, backward look, she saw that Mary Burton had already turned her attention to another couple.

"I swear," Eloise muttered. "That woman's tongue is constantly wagging. Don't pay her any mind, Lolly. She really doesn't mean any harm. But she does have a knack for asking the most embarrassing questions."

"Yes," Lolly muttered, her face still warm with color. "She does, doesn't she."

Rainey enjoyed the opera immensely. But her pleasure was dimmed by the knowledge that she must leave soon. To stay longer would surely invite heartache.

That night, long after the others had retired, Rainey tossed restlessly on her bed, wondering if she was making a mistake in leaving so soon. It was a decision, though, that could be put off no longer.

Sorely troubled, and knowing that she'd never fall asleep while in such a restless state, she donned her robe. The garment had been a gift from Eloise, a soft, silky, blue thing that clung to her curves in a way that she found slightly embarrassing. But it was late enough that the others should have retired for the night. Or so she thought until she entered the library.

Thorne lounged beside the fireplace, a glass of amber liquid in his hand.

"I didn't expect to find anyone here." She pulled at the robe, where it gapped between her breasts. The action only served to draw his gaze. "Is something wrong?"

His cheeks were flushed and she realized he must have been drinking to excess, something that she'd never known him to do before.

"What could possibly be wrong?" he inquired, shifting his gaze to his glass. "I just felt like a drink."

"Several drinks," she corrected.

"Whatever," he said indifferently. "Why are you here?"

"I couldn't sleep. I came for a book."

"Help yourself." He waved toward the wide bookcases that lined the wall. "I don't suppose you would like a drink?"

"No, thank you." She crossed the room to study the spines of the books. "I'll just get my book."

"Couldn't sleep?"

"No."

He quickly downed the contents of his glass and went to pour another one. "What's your excuse?"

She studied him for a long moment, noticing a vulnerability about him that she hadn't seen before. She was reluctant to tell him of her decision to leave, yet knew there would be no better time than the present to do so.

"Thorne, I've been meaning to talk to you about going home."

"Where is home, Rainey?"

Wherever you are, her heart cried, but she spoke no

words, just held his gaze over the distance that separated them.

Appearing to be unaffected by her decision to leave, he reached for a handful of peanuts, which were kept on a nearby table. Then, darting her a quick look, he said, "It's past time I went home, too. I have a good foreman but he's been handling things alone for some time now. Too long. Lolly is settled in, so there is nothing else to keep me here."

"You don't have to come with me," she said.

"Yes, I do." His voice was gruff. "When do you want to leave?"

"Tomorrow." It had been easy after all. So easy that she could have cried. He seemed to care nothing that when they returned to Thunder Mountain they would go separate ways. He, to his farm; she to her grandfather's cabin.

Did he care nothing at all? She studied the glass in his hand. Carefully averting her eyes from him, she whispered, "Why do you feel a need for spirits, Thorne?"

His voice was husky, jerking her gaze back to his. "Because I can't stop thinking of those nights we shared."

"Neither can I." Her voice was a shaky whisper, and she could feel the hot color flushing her cheeks, but she refused to look away.

"What are we going to do about it?" He watched her intently. "We can't just pretend those nights never happened. Can we?"

His gaze shifted to the fullness of her breasts, and her color deepened, yet she remained silent. After all, what was there to say? She was afraid if she uttered a sound, it would be to beg him to come to her room.

Would that really be so wrong? a silent voice asked. *Why shouldn't I take what he offers? Why can't I be happy for just a little longer?*

She was aware of him watching her silently from

across the room, the glass in his hand completely forgotten.

"I want to be with you desperately, Rainey," he said
huskily. "Let me come to your room."

She looked up apprehensively, helpless in the pull of
his silvery eyes. "We can't, Thorne," she whispered.

Suddenly he was across the room in three long
strides, his nearness unsettling as he pulled her into
his arms. Bending his head, he brushed his lips over
her eyelids, her eyebrows, in a silent caress that made
her tingle with incredible sensations. The featherlight
touch of his mouth against her flesh made her knees
weak, and they seemed to be made of nothing more
substantial than wet noodles.

"Why?" he asked softly, drawing back to watch the
play of emotions cross her face. "Why can't we?"

She gazed at him, mesmerized, her eyes darkened
with slumberous passion.

Thorne's breath rasped harshly as he met her look
with one of hunger. Desire burned in his eyes as his
hands caressed her face tenderly, his thumbs outlining
her lips, seeming to sense her surrender. "You want it
as much as I do," he said huskily, persuasively.

It was true. She wanted the feel of his naked flesh
against hers again, its hard strength that took her
breath; the touch of his hands on her breast, stroking,
caressing.

His mouth closed over hers again, tenderly, so sweetly,
that she caught her breath at the exquisite sensation.

Easing up on her tiptoes, her fingers entwined in his
dark hair, she held him closer, ever closer. "Thorne,"
she whispered pleadingly, achingly.

"Yes, Rainey," he exulted, lifting her into his arms.
"Yes, darling, yes."

He carried her up the stairs, into her bedroom, and
laid her down on the bed, joining her swiftly. A tender

smile curved Rainey's mouth as she gazed up at him. She didn't care anymore. Tonight she would take what he offered. Tonight she would lie in his arms again.

Thorne's hand moved to smooth back her hair, his fingers curving gently around her chin. He lifted it to allow his lips access to hers. His tongue and lips tantalized the corner of her mouth, gently stealing her breath away from her.

Sliding his hand around her waist, Thorne pulled her closer against his hard, lean frame. Her body melted against him then, her silky legs sliding intimately between his, while her fingers moved up his chest, curving into his shoulders.

Her mouth savored the slow exploration of his lips and tongue, and with firm pressure, she responded naturally and easily with her own.

His heart pounded in erratic unison with her own as he dealt quickly with their clothing, and despite the weakness that assailed her, her senses were sharp and alert.

Rainey felt his hands slide down to curve possessively over her buttocks as he pulled her tightly against his hardened thighs. Desire mounted, and her breath came in short gasps. His body proved to be so well acquainted with hers that he knew the instant she was ready to receive him. He plunged into her, deeper, fuller, so certain of his right to take her.

Every part of him concentrated on that mysterious haven that was the very essence of Rainey. She felt fully alive for the first time since she'd lost the baby, and she reached heights of loving that went far beyond the physical union.

The next morning Rainey packed her valise, preparing for the long trip ahead. She'd told Eloise and Lolly of her decision to leave. Although they had protested her decision, they realized they could not sway her, so they accepted the fact that she'd be leaving them.

"But we'll expect a visit from you sometime soon," Eloise had said.

Rainey hadn't seen Thorne all day. When she woke at dawn, she had found a note on her pillow. It had simply said, *see you later.*

She could have cried with disappointment. She remembered last night and the way she had felt with Thorne holding her closely against him. How could he just leave like that after all they had shared together? Hadn't it meant anything to him at all?

She sighed heavily. She had known from the beginning that he didn't care for her. Now she must learn to live with that fact. Last night hadn't changed anything at all as far as Thorne was concerned, but Rainey's own emotions were like coals. Once stirred, they flared to life, threatening to consume her in their flames.

Perhaps it would be wiser to keep away from him in the future, she decided. There was less chance of getting hurt that way.

That decision stayed with her on the long journey home. Rainey deliberately sought the company of Sarah Warner, an elderly lady whose mouth moved almost as fast as the train as she spoke continually of the loved ones that she was going to see.

"There's little Janie," Sarah said. "She's just turning four, you know. And the biggest, bluest eyes that you have ever seen." She smiled at the memory. "One time she went to sleep beneath the shade of a bush and had the whole town out looking for her. Everyone was sure some wild Indians had left the reservation and come and stolen her away." She laughed softly. "Janie got her bottom smacked for that little prank. Not that I approved, of course. I think there are better ways of punishing a

child than to strike them. But who am I to say?" Her
voice was sad, mournful. "After all, I'm only the grandmother." Her eyes filled with tears of remembrance.
"She didn't mean any harm, you know. She just—"

Rainey smiled and nodded her head and met Thorne's
eyes from across the aisle. He grimaced and motioned
to the empty seat beside him. She shook her head and
pretended politeness kept her beside the woman, when
all the while she was afraid to be near him, afraid her
foolish heart would betray her.

They reached Lizard Lick at dusk. Thorne left Rainey
at the station while he went for the horses. Most of the
luggage had to be left since Rainey had acquired so
much during her trip, but the stationmaster promised
to have it brought to her later.

The cabin appeared the same. It stood in the clearing, a beacon of light that beamed through the darkness, seeming to welcome the weary traveler home.

Suddenly the door opened and Grandpa stood in the
opening. He looked out at them. "Rainey? Is that you,
child?"

Rainey flung herself off the horse and ran to him,
hugging him close against her. He was so dear, so familiar. She was home again, home again, and that fact
made her want to bawl like a baby.

She was unaware of Thorne leaving. Only knew that
when she looked up he was gone. Gone, just like that.
Without oven telling her goodbye.

Three weeks had passed since Rainey returned to the
mountains, and during that time she'd not even had a
glimpse of Thorne. But she would see him tonight, she
vowed, as she prepared herself for Robert Golden's
birthday party.

Rainey dressed in a silk dress that clung lovingly in

all the right places, displaying her curves to advantage. It had a narrow black belt that accentuated the full curve of her breasts, and the color was a deep shade of green that left her arms bare and flattered her tan.

She brushed her newly washed hair until it fell like silken waves about her shoulders, gleaming with blue highlights. She carefully applied powder, not daring to question her reason for wanting to look as glamorous as possible.

Rainey had chosen Sadie's oldest son for an escort, knowing that he wouldn't dare give her trouble on the way, something she couldn't say about Zeke or Willis.

When they arrived at the party, they found it in full swing. Her pulse quickened at the sight of Thorne's horse, reins looped around the hitching post. As the door opened, lamplight spilled out, and Rainey wiped nervous hands down the sides of her gown as she exchanged greetings with Robert. It was only nerves, she told herself uneasily . . . but maybe she shouldn't have come.

"Hi, Rainey." Willis waved as he danced by with a petite blonde in a soft, pink dress. "I was beginning to think you weren't going to make it. Save a dance for me." Rainey felt a glass pushed into her hand and turned to thank someone, but she saw nothing except a broad back and head carrying a tray, already halfway across the room making sure that everyone had something to drink.

Sniffing suspiciously at the glass, she took a cautious sip. It seemed innocuous enough, but she'd heard the other women talking about the drinks served at parties. It was better to be cautious now, than sorry later.

Rainey's eyes searched the crowded room until they found him. He looked distinguished in a black evening suit and snowy-white shirt. He looked even more attractive than she remembered.

Her gaze slid over the tall, willowy brunette wearing a black dress that clung to her rounded bosom like a second skin. She was a stranger to Rainey, who took an instant dislike to the woman.

Rainey felt a chill go down her spine at the sight of them together, and her hands tightened convulsively on her glass. She had a sudden impulse to confront them and claw the woman's eyes out.

Taking a controlling breath, Rainey managed, some- how, to stifle the urge.

Morosely, she watched Thorne and the dark-haired beauty. He appeared to be making quite an impression on her. Rainey reminded herself that she had no right to feel possessive about him. He certainly hadn't given her any reason to feel that way.

Taking another sip of the punch, she frowned as the brunette clung tightly to Thorne's arm. "If she gets any closer, she'll melt all over him," she remarked aloud. Angrily, she finished her drink in one swallow.

Rainey found herself a shadowy corner, where she could watch them while remaining unobserved. Thorne smiled at his partner often, encouraging the brunette to cling even tighter.

Agonizing over the situation, Rainey wondered if she'd made a mistake by attending the party. She was only making herself miserable by watching them so av- idly. And did he even care?

No. He did not.

But she cared. She loved him . . . loved every line of his face; loved the way his dark hair curled around his ears, the way his shirt stretched across his wide shoul- ders. She had become used to having him around on a daily basis. He was so big a part of her life that she could no longer bear the thought of being apart from him.

Her eyes dulled with pain as she thought of how she

missed him. *Oh, God, how will I stand a lifetime without him?*

He looked up and saw her across the room. And she knew by the expression on his face that he'd caught a glimpse of the sadness that must still linger on hers. She felt her body tremble and her legs threatened to buckle at the knees. She wanted him, ached for him, and she was afraid he could read it in her eyes.

Suddenly he was coming toward her, his partner seeming to be forgotten. His eyes were fierce with a blatant hunger that matched her own.

"Rainey." Willis's voice came from behind her, shattering the intimacy of the moment. She made a visible effort to control her emotions and turned to face him. "That Mr. Golden, he sent me after you. Said you was to come to the library. Said he wants to talk private-like to you."

"Thank you, Willis."

Disappointment flooded through her. Thorne's progress had been stopped by seeing them together.

"I ain't seen much of you lately," Willis complained. "How'd you like St. Louis?"

"It was an enjoyable trip. But it's good to be home."

"Enjoyable, you say? You come home talkin' like one of them educated dudes, Rainey. You go to school whilst you was away?"

"Something like that." She smiled at him. It wasn't his fault that Thorne had turned away and become engaged in conversation elsewhere. "Thorne hired me a tutor."

"What's that?"

"A teacher." She turned away. "I'd better see what our teacher wants with me." Moments later she was closing the wide double doors behind her, and the discontinuance of noise was blissful. She sighed with relief as she hurried along the wide hall until she reached the study.

"You've changed the room," she said, as she saw him standing near the window. "The last teacher had yellow curtains on the window."

He gave a delicate shudder. "They were horrible things. Do you like the change?" he asked, motioning her toward the black settee made of leather, which occupied one side of the room. A wide desk took up the other, its cleared surface showing the man's liking for uncluttered things.

She wondered again what reason he had for sending for her. He looked distinctly uncomfortable while she waited quietly for him to explain.

Clearing his throat, he began, "Rainey, I guess you're wondering why I sent for you?"

"Yes, I was wondering that."

"Well, it's just that . . . I have a problem." He stopped suddenly, averting his eyes from her.

"A problem you think I can help with?" she prompted.

"Rainey, I know you have no reason to help me, but it's a fact that I've come to you for just that."

"I'm afraid I don't understand."

"This job . . . this position . . . is not what I expected it to be, and yet I see no way to get out of it."

She slumped down on the couch. "You don't want to teach here any longer?"

"That's right." He raked a hand through his golden hair. "I come to the conclusion that I am not right for the position of teacher."

"I'm not sure what you want me to do," Rainey said, her voice revealing her confusion.

"I signed a contract, Rainey. And the board is likely to hold me to it, unless someone can speak on my behalf and make them understand."

"Me?" she squeaked. "You want me to talk to the school board? Why me?"

"Because your stepgrandmother, Sadie, is the head of the school board. If you get her to listen to reason, then the others will follow suit. Of course I'll finish out the school year."

"Of course," she said dryly. "Especially since it's just about over."

"Yes. I know it's not much notice. But things have drastically changed since you were here. I'm afraid I've become involved with a young lady and . . . I've been thinking about taking a wife, and Rainey—"

They were abruptly interrupted as the library door was suddenly flung open. Thorne stood there, his gaze hard, his hands clenched into fists. Rainey sensed a leashed energy about him, a turbulence that reminded her of a caged animal. She felt a momentary fear of the man who continued to watch them with gray eyes that appeared frozen.

Twenty-four

The fine hairs at the nape of Rainey's neck stood on end, and color slowly left her cheeks as she forced herself to meet the cold fury in Thorne's gray eyes.

His gaze slid down her body, taking in every detail of the way she looked, and she blushed hotly. Had her dancing partners left her disheveled for him to look at her with such contempt?

As he noticed her blush, his expression hardened. Then his eyes turned to Robert, who stood watching him with a puzzled expression.

"Something I can do for you?" Robert asked.

Thorne moved then, covering the space between them with frightening speed. And, before either of them could react, Rainey felt herself lifted off her feet and set down several feet away from the men.

Then, while Rainey was still trying to catch her breath, Thorne drew back his fist and struck Robert Golden squarely on his dimpled chin. It happened so fast that Rainey could hardly take it in. One minute they had been staring at each other, then the next thing she knew, Robert was knocked across the room, where he landed heavily against the far wall.

Suddenly, Ginny Lou was there. "What're you doing?" she shrieked at Thorne. "Have you gone crazy?"

She flung herself toward Robert, cradling his head in her lap. "Are you hurt?" she asked.

"Of course I'm hurt," he muttered. "My head hit the damn wall."

"How could you, Thorne?" Rainey's eyes were round with surprise and fury as she berated him. "What did that poor man ever do to you?"

"That poor man seems to be getting plenty of female sympathy without your support, Rainey. Look at him! Surely you can see what's been going on while you were gone."

She gave him a hard glare. "I fail to see why anything he does should concern you." She looked at Robert, who was wiping at the blood that seeped from his split lip. "I'm sorry, Robert."

"You have no need to apologize to him, Rainey. Just open your eyes and look at him. Look at *them*. That scoundrel was on the point of asking you to marry him, and it's obvious from the way Ginny Lou is acting what he's been up to while you were gone."

"You *are* crazy," she said. "He was doing no such thing." She started toward Robert but found her wrist caught in a grip of steel.

"Stay away from him," Thorne said through tight lips. His voice was low and dangerous, and his grip tightened as he pulled her to his side.

"Thorne, he's bleeding," she said anxiously, eyeing the blood running from Robert's cut lip. "I'm so sorry, Robert," she apologized again. She twisted her wrist, trying to free herself, but Thorne refused to loosen his hold on her.

"You'll be a damn sight sorrier and he'll be bleeding a whole lot more if you don't keep away from him," Thorne told her savagely.

She struggled furiously with him, kicking out at him. And when her foot connected with a shinbone, she heard him swear profusely, but he refused to turn her loose.

She watched helplessly as Robert rose to his feet, his white linen handkerchief pressing against his cut lip. "You can turn her loose, Lassiter," he said calmly. "I'm not going to touch her."

"She's fine where she is," Thorne said, his face still suffused with anger.

"I don't see what your objection is, Thorne," Robert's voice was reasonable. "After all, Rainey's not wearing your brand. Or did I miss something somewhere along the way?"

Rainey gasped at Robert's words. Why was he saying such things? There was nothing between them. Why make Thorne believe there was? It didn't make sense. None at all.

Thorne was silent, seeming to be at a loss for words. He was white and breathing harshly. Unconsciously, Rainey held her breath until she felt his muscles begin to relax, then his hand reluctantly fell away from her.

He stood there a moment, his hands clenching and unclenching at his sides. Slowly he seemed to take in Ginny Lou, clutching Robert's arm, staring at him as though he had gone mad.

"Hell!" he said savagely, swinging around and striding to the door. He went out and slammed the door shut behind him.

Rainey stared wordlessly at the closed door, then turned to spy a grin on Robert's face; a grin that was quickly suppressed. She looked at him quietly for a long moment, then asked, "Are you all right?"

"Sure," he said cheerfully. "As right as can be expected after being knocked down by a sledgehammer."

"What are you so happy about, Robert?" Ginny Lou asked. "You just got knocked flat on your face by Thornton Lassiter."

"That's what I find so funny," Robert said. "The un-flappable Thornton Lassiter losing his temper over a woman. I never would have believed it if I hadn't seen . . . and felt it . . . with my own eyes and flesh."

"I really don't know what got into him, Robert," Rainey said. "I've never known him to be so angry with anyone." Then it began to dawn on her. Thorne had acted like he was jealous. Of Robert?

She looked up to see Robert watching her intently.

"I'm afraid he thought . . ." Rainey couldn't finish the sentence. It was too ridiculous to even put into words.

"Yes, he did, didn't he?" Robert observed with a smile. "And I must confess I feel flattered by his suspi-cions."

"Robert, would you please tell me what's going on?" Ginny Lou said plaintively. "What was Thorne so angry about?"

"I'll tell you later, love," Robert said, patting her hand.

It was obvious to Rainey just who Robert had chosen to be his wife.

"But, Robert," Ginny Lou persisted. "Why—"

"Later, love," he repeated firmly, and Ginny quickly grew silent.

"I think I'll go home now," Rainey said dispiritedly. The life had gone out of the party for her when Thorne had walked out the door. "I had a nice time, Robert," she said politely, like a little girl suddenly remembering her manners. "Thank you for inviting me."

Robert burst out laughing. "Rainey, you really take the cake. After all that's happened here, you can still stand there and tell me you had a nice time?"

"Well, at least the first part of it was nice," she said defensively. "And the part that wasn't nice most cer-tainly wasn't any fault of yours."

"I'm just teasing," he said, patting her shoulder gently.

Rainey left the house and unfastened the reins of her mount from the hitching post. Thorne's horse was nowhere in sight. It was obvious he'd left before her. It was easy to find the trail leading to her cabin, for the bright moonlight came from a full moon. She'd only gone a short way down the trail when she reined her horse around and took the path leading to Thorne's farm.

Half an hour later she saw his light in the distance. Her mount's hooves made only a soft thudding sound as she rode into his yard and dismounted.

After tying the reins to the porch rail, Rainey turned to see a figure separating itself from the shadows. Her pulse leaped with fear, and her muscles tensed as she prepared to take flight.

"Rainey." Thorne's voice was hesitant, as if he weren't sure of his reception. "I didn't expect to see you here."

"I didn't intend to come," she said.

"Well, why did you?" he asked.

She despised herself for the way her pulse leaped as she followed him inside. "I wanted an explanation for your actions," she said grimly.

"I have no explanation that would satisfy you," he said gruffly. "But I won't apologize for my actions, Rainey. I'd do the same thing over again under the same set of circumstances."

"Why?" she asked angrily. "Robert has done nothing to offend you. You had no call to attack him that way."

He seemed at a loss for words and turned away from her to move restlessly around the room, picking things up at random and putting them down again.

"Thorne?" she demanded, unable to take the silence any longer, "what is wrong with you?"

He turned, the lamplight catching the shine of his

dark hair above wide shoulders. "Nothing is wrong with me, Rainey. Not anything that you could fix."

Her stomach muscles tightened. She had to know if her suspicions were true. "Are you jealous of Robert? Is that why you struck him?"

He moved behind her and she felt the warmth of his body against her, felt his breath, warm and moist on her ear.

His fingers lightly touched a wispy curl, tucking it behind an ear, and she stiffened involuntarily. "Rainey . . ." he sighed heavily. "You don't know how hard I've tried to stay away from you but it's impossible. I can't." His arms slid around her waist and pulled her closely against his large frame. "Stay here with me, Rainey. Don't go."

She froze against his body. *Stay with him.*

The words sang in her heart. *Stay with him.* If he only knew how much she wanted to. She wanted to turn and throw her arms around his neck, but something held her back. She asked cautiously, "What do you mean?"

"Do I have to spell it out?" he rasped, and the words seemed forced from him. "I want you to come live with me. I want you to marry me."

Marry him! Had she heard right? Were her ears playing tricks on her? The words echoed, reverberating in her mind. Slowly she turned around, taking a deep controlling breath, looking into his shadowed eyes. "Why, Thorne?" she whispered, forcing the words from between stiff lips.

He looked down at her for several long seconds, a pulse beating wildly in his jaw. "Hell! Isn't it obvious?" he ground out. "Do I have to say the words?"

Rainey stood there in the circle of his arms, her eyes as wide and unblinking as a startled fawn's as she waited for his answer.

"Because I love you, Rainey," he said, his voice suddenly like dark velvet. His face was taut with barely concealed emotion as his gaze held hers.

"You love me?" Her body began to tremble violently as her mind struggled to accept what she had heard.

"Yes," he grated, waiting for her reaction. His silvery eyes held a vulnerability that she had never expected to see there.

"Don't say that if you don't mean it, Thorne," she whispered, still unconvinced. Could she really believe him, or was this just his way of trying to get her to stay with him?

"Of course I mean it," he said harshly, his eyes never leaving her face. "I've been fighting this thing from the first moment I saw you. You were so young then. Only a child. But I told myself that I could wait. That I'd wait forever if it took that long." He kissed her ear. "Don't you know how much I care for you, Rainey? Couldn't you guess? You're in my bloodstream, under my skin. Without you, I think I'd even stop breathing. I know I'd go on loving you even if I never saw you again."

Rainey listened to him, her whole attention focused on what he was saying, forced into believing it by the desperation revealed in his voice. She had never known Thorne to speak so seriously.

"I fell in love with a young girl," he continued. "I felt so foolish. I didn't know what hit me. There you stood, your hair so wild and tangled, and there I was, struck like a ton of bricks. I made myself responsible for you that day, Rainey. Not because of any ideals, but because I knew even then that my future lay with you."

Rainey could hardly believe what she was hearing. She held her breath, fearful she would wake up and discover that she had only been dreaming.

Thorne watched her emotions play across her face, then he looked away from her, clenching his hands as though he were on the point of violence. "I was even jealous of Robert! What a laugh! A man like that," he grated. "I had heard he was engaged to another woman, but when I saw you together, then I thought . . . well, you know what I thought." His mouth twisted in self-derision. "You've got me twisted up in knots, Rainey. I hurt, and it's a pain that's hard to bear. It never stops."

His gaze moved back to her face. He watched silently for a moment, then said, "Are you going to put me out of my misery, Rainey?"

"Could I do that?"

"Yes. You could. If you wanted to. Stay with me, Rainey. Let me love you. Give me a chance to make you love me."

"But I already do," she whispered softly in his ear. "Didn't you know that?"

"Why didn't you tell me?" he groaned, pulling her roughly against him. He cupped her face in his hands and bent to kiss her gently, reverently, on the lips. "I love you, Rainey," he whispered huskily. "You'll never know just how much I love you, but I'll take a lifetime showing you."

She returned his kisses, feverishly, unreservedly. "A lifetime suits me just fine," she said.

Laughing, he swooped her into his arms and headed for the bedroom door. Pausing just inside the room, he hesitated with a foot lifted to kick the door shut, then as if changing his mind, he laid her gently on the bed and returned to close the door softly. At her puzzled look, he explained, "I don't want to take any chances that the door slamming would bring you to your senses."

She laughed, rejoicing in his love as she pulled his head down to meet hers.

ROMANCE FROM FERN MICHAELS

DEAR EMILY   (0-8217-4952-8, $5.99)

WISH LIST   (0-8217-5228-6, $6.99)

AND IN HARDCOVER:

VEGAS RICH   (1-57566-057-1, $25.00)

TALES OF LOVE FROM MEAGAN MCKINNEY

GENTLE FROM THE NIGHT*   (0-8217-5803-$5.99/$7.50)
In late nineteenth century England, destitute after her father's
death, Alexandra Benjamin takes John Damien Newell up on his
offer and becomes governess of his castle. She soon discovers she
has entered a haunted house. Alexandra struggles to dispel the
dark secrets of the castle and of the heart of her master.
    *Also available in hardcover (1-577566-136-5, $21.95/$27.95)

A MAN TO SLAY DRAGONS   (0-8217-5345-2, $5.99/$6.99)
Manhattan attorney Claire Green goes to New Orleans bent on
avenging her twin sister's death and to clear her name. FBI agent
Liam Jameson enters Claire's world by duty, but is soon bound
by desire. In the midst of the Mardi Gras festivities, they unravel
dark and deadly secrets surrounding the horrifying truth.

MY WICKED ENCHANTRESS   (0-8217-5661-3, $5.99/$7.50)
Kayleigh Mhor lived happily with her sister at their Scottish estate, Mhor Castle, until her sister was murdered and Kayleigh had
to run for her life. It is 1746, a year later, and she is re-established
in New Orleans as Kestrel. When her path crosses the mysterious
St. Bride Ferringer, she finds her salvation. Or is he really the
enemy haunting her?

AND IN HARDCOVER . . .
THE FORTUNE HUNTER   (1-57566-262-0, $23.00/$29.00)
In 1881 New York spiritual séances were commonplace. The mysterious Countess Lovaenya was the favored spiritualist in Manhattan.
When she agrees to enter the world of Edward Stuyvesant-French,
she is lead into an obscure realm, where wicked spirits interfere with
his life. Reminiscent of the painful past when she was an orphan
named Lavinia Murphy, she sees a life filled with animosity that
longs for acceptance and love. The bond that they share finally leads
them to a life filled with happiness.

*Available wherever paperbacks are sold, or order direct from the
Publisher. Send cover price plus 50¢ per copy for mailing and
handling to Kensington Publishing Corp., Consumer Orders,
or call (toll free) 888-345-BOOK, to place your order using
Mastercard or Visa. Residents of New York and Tennessee
must include sales tax. DO NOT SEND CASH.*